A LANDEN ACRES NOVEL

NATALIE JESS

To my family.

Copyright © 2024 by Greenstone Publishing

All rights reserved.

No portion of this book may be reproduced in any form without written permission from the publisher or author, except as permitted by U.S. copyright law. Without in any way limiting the author's and publisher's exclusive rights under copyright, any use of this publication to "train" generative artificial intelligence (AI) technologies to generate text is expressly prohibited.

The story, all names, characters, and incidents portrayed in this production are fictitious. No identification with actual persons (living or deceased), places, buildings, and products is intended or should be inferred.

No generative artificial intelligence (AI) was used in the writing of this work.

Dust Jacket by Storyville Designs

Hardcase Art by Winda Chu

Hardcase Format by Luna Blooms PA

Interior Format by Luna Blooms PA

Edits by My Notes in the Margins and A. Martin

Contents

Notes from For Avery	1
Prologue: Tommy	3
Chapter 1: Sam	9
Chapter 2: Tommy	17
Chapter 3: Sam	23
Chapter 4: Tommy	29
Chapter 5: Sam	35
Chapter 6: Tommy	41
Chapter 7: Sam	47
Chapter 8: Tommy	53
Chapter 9: Sam	59
Chapter 10: Tommy	65
Chapter 11: Sam	69
Chapter 12: Tommy	75
Chapter 13: Sam	81
Chapter 14: Tommy	87

Chapter 15: Sam	93
Chapter 16: Tommy	97
Chapter 17: Sam	103
Chapter 18: Tommy	109
Chapter 19: Sam	115
Chapter 20: Tommy	121
Chapter 21: Sam	125
Chapter 22: Tommy	129
Chapter 23: Sam	135
Chapter 24: Tommy	141
Chapter 25: Sam	147
Chapter 26: Tommy	153
Chapter 27: Sam	159
Chapter 28: Tommy	165
Chapter 29: Sam	171
Chapter 30: Tommy	177
Chapter 31: Sam	183
Chapter 32: Tommy	189
Chapter 33: Sam	193
Chapter 34: Tommy	199
Chapter 35: Sam	205

Chapter 36: Tommy	211
Chapter 37: Sam	215
Chapter 38: Tommy	221
Chapter 39: Sam	227
Chapter 40: Tommy	233
Chapter 41: Sam	239
Chapter 42: Tommy	245
Chapter 43: Sam	251
Chapter 44: Tommy	257
Chapter 45: Sam	263
Chapter 46: Tommy	269
Chapter 47: Sam	275
Chapter 48: Tommy	281
Chapter 49: Sam	287
Chapter 50: Tommy	293
Chapter 51: Sam	299
Chapter 52: Tommy	305
Chapter 53: Sam	311
Chapter 54: Tommy	317
Chapter 55: Sam	323
Chapter 56: Tommy	329

Chapter 57: Sam	335
Chapter 58: Tommy	341
Chapter 59: Sam	347
Chapter 60: Tommy	353
Chapter 61: Sam	359
Chapter 62: Tommy	365
Chapter 63: Sam	371
Chapter 64: Tommy	377
Acknowledgements	383
About the Author	385

Notes from *For Avery*

A few things happen on the page in *For Avery* that are helpful to know about before reading *For Sam*. If you haven't read *For Avery* and don't like spoilers, I highly recommend starting your Landen Acres journey with that story.

Sam is new in town and meets Jackson, Tommy's oldest brother, at a town meeting that Tommy would have normally attended. She's terrible with names and Jackson hates crowds, so they paired up where he introduced (and reintroduced) Samantha to everyone and then she took over the conversation allowing Jackson to disengage. This also kept those who had slept with Jackson from coming back for more when they appeared to be together.

Avery, one of Tommy's two best friends, returns home to bid on Jackson at a charity date auction and finally comes clean with her feelings towards him. At the auction, Jackson tells Tommy that he never dated Sam, they just let people make their own assumptions. Both Tommy and Courtney, Tommy and Avery's other best friend, know about Jackson and Avery secretly dating because Avery's brother Chase is Jackson's best friend who is against the match because of Jackson's dating history. Tommy talks with both Jackson and Avery to make sure they're both on the same page before they really dive in because he can't stand to see either of them hurt.

Prologue
Tommy

Six Months Earlier

Golden oldies play through the speakers of my brother's SUV as we drive past neighboring farm fields. Jax taps his thumb in time with the tune and I look out over the familiar terrain of my best friend's family acreage. God, at least Avery can *date* someone. I let out a sigh at how pathetic I feel.

"Did I miss something?" Jax asks from across the cab.

I shake my head, smiling. "Nah, just prepping for the meeting."

He grunts in return. It's not like me to have to prep on the way to a city meeting. I'm the one usually on top of everything. At least I was before Maisy Jones turned my world upside down.

Damn it. Half a year has gone by since I started questioning everything and everyone. No matter how much I try to analyze it, I still can't figure out how I missed the fucking signs. The times she came home and went right to the shower... Did she smell like his cologne and I even missed that? My head gets dizzy simply trying to revisit each detail for the thousandth time. No. I'm not letting my mind go back down that road. There's nothing but pain and confusion in Maisy Jones' wake.

Fuck, I can't even look out the window without my stomach twisting up in knots from all of this shit.

"Hey, you okay?" Jax's voice pulls me out of my mini-spiral.

I nod and force a smile, knowing he's not one to talk about feelings. Why the hell can't I get my mind back on track and just focus on what's in front of me so he doesn't worry about me? Again. "All good, must've looked down during the last turn."

Jax's gaze locks onto mine for a moment. "You never get carsick."

I shrug, my dizziness slows, and my stomach relaxes as I ground myself in this moment. "First time for everything. It was either that or momentary indigestion from Bryant's mountain of beef."

To drive the point home, I pat my stomach. "I'm pretty sure he slapped an entire pound on my sandwich. He must be trying to fatten me up."

Jax chuckles. "He must feel lonely being the beefiest Landen brother by far."

"I don't know, I think his muscles keep him company," I say, managing to attempt a joke.

"Maybe that's why he's so cranky around people. He spends his energy talking to his pecs," Jax says, his charm coming through.

An image pops into my head of our huge, burly, and a little surly, brother talking to his massive chest and I bark out a laugh. Jax sneaks a glance my way and can't hide a little smile. My heart squeezes for a different reason now. He always seems to know when my mind goes to what she did, the signs I *missed*, and when the pain comes back. It doesn't hit very often, I mean, I've had six months to get over her. And I am. I don't love her anymore. I don't want her back. I don't even want her in the same state as me. Only now, instead of dating again, I see people with the potential to fuck me over. Because knowing how it ended? How long had it really been over for her and I didn't have a clue? It still sneaks up on me. Especially the feeling that slammed into me when she was packed up, thinking she'd be able to move out before I returned... God, I'm the nerdy Landen brother, the one who loves math, the one who sees patterns for fuck's sake. But I had no idea.

Why can't I be more like Jax? He just has to wink at someone and they'll leave with him for short-term, no-strings sex. He seems happy enough with that. Except, I've seen the way Jax looks at Avery when he thinks no one is looking. All these people over the years have been distractions. As much fun as a distraction might be, I'm not the kind of person who can do that without an emotional connection. But everyone in this small town has a dozen red flags because I'm so paranoid.

And now I'm right back at the starting line of why I've been an unfocused, unreliable guy lately.

Jax pulls up to the very same apartment building, throws his SUV in park, and shoots off a text. At least I'm back in the present moment. "Should I move to the back seat?"

"Why?"

"So he can sit in front?"

Jax looks over at me with a frown. "She."

"Sam's a *she*?"

"Yeah," he says absentmindedly, reading the response that just came through. I definitely haven't been paying attention like I should be… She's the new hire for the city of Greenstone. I'm the Landen brother who's on committees, for crying out loud. How does Jax know more than me? "She knows you're coming and it's a short drive so don't change seats. Plus, she'll feel guilty if she sees you moved for her. She's already coming out the door."

I look out the window and blink a few times to make sure what I'm seeing is real.

Holy shit.

Sam is without a doubt the most beautiful human being I've laid eyes on. Her blonde hair is in loose waves down her back that look silky smooth. She's wearing what I would describe as no-nonsense pants: perfectly tailored blue slacks that flare over her heels and have a crease running down the front and back. Her almost-white top is sleeveless with a loose tie and it shows off her toned arms and that creamy, slightly freckled skin all the way to her shoulders. Gold bracelets dangle on her wrists and a series of matching necklaces.

Her face has a look of pure concentration as she momentarily stares down at a folder tucked into her grip with two different color pens in her free hand. Before she walks down the steps, she looks up and gives us a friendly wave and a smile.

Jesus, I already know I'd sell my right kidney to see that smile every day, and I'm pretty sure that there's so much more that can be unlocked to make it truly shine.

Reality crashes down around me like a ton of bricks.

Jax is picking her up. He doesn't bring people to things. He doesn't date. But he's picking someone up so they will show up together and I just so happened to come last minute.

She walks at a clipped pace towards us.

"When did this start?" I ask.

"What?"

"You two—"

I'm cut off by the sound of Sam opening the door.

"Hey, Jacksy," she says, getting a grin out of my oldest brother. "And you must be Tommy, or do you prefer Thomas?"

It takes me a minute to respond, but my head bobs, so that's something. She sets her clipboard in her lap, holding her hand out to shake mine. It's an awkward maneuver since she reaches out her right hand and I have to twist all the way around, but it gives me a legitimate excuse to turn around.

"Just Tommy," I manage, finding my voice.

"I'm Samantha Davies, but everyone calls me Sam."

Her hand is soft and smooth, and she seems a little nervous but like she's trying to hide it.

"Do you prefer something else?" I ask.

She looks confused. "Pardon?"

I don't think I've heard anyone under the age of seventy say that.

"You said that everyone calls you Sam, but do you have a different preference for what name people use?"

"Oh," she says, still holding my hand, and I fight the urge to run my thumb back and forth across her knuckles. "I guess I haven't really known anything different."

"Okay, Sam it'll be, unless you let me know it should be something else."

Samantha Davies looks at me like I just gave her a riddle to solve.

As Jax drives, I remind myself that he's going to tonight's event with this blonde bombshell. He doesn't take people to any sort of event, not unless they're his date.

And why on earth would someone like Samantha Davies want to settle for the dorky, overlooked, younger brother of the guy who has been with pretty much anyone he's ever looked at?

Chapter 1
Sam

Present Day

A deep sigh of relief washes over me. Less than one month after the night of my first big event for the city of Greenstone I have all the data entered, the equipment ordered for Rebecca, our new vet in the area, and just finished the final thank you note. They're all hand-written, well, hand-calligraphed and there was no script so every single one is unique and tailored to the donor of the item or the highest bidder. Everyone in attendance that I was able to note has their more simple thank you as well.

Oh dear, I hope I didn't miss anyone.

All of the cards stick halfway out of their envelopes so I can triple check they're going to the right home. It's easier for me to mark them as complete on my list. Or lists. Actually, list of lists.

I resist the urge to check everything a fourth time. Good grief, Sam, this isn't fifth grade when you accidentally gave Brady Johnston the Valentine you wrote for your best friend, Terry, at the time. I groan, remembering the look of betrayal on her face when he showed the entire class what I had written on the card. "I love you the most!" was supposed to go to her while Terry's was one of the generic ones from a pack. My body flushes with shame but I force myself to loosen my tensed up shoulders and take the final sip of my iced coffee with a splash of oat milk.

I might as well relax because these can't be sent until the post office opens tomorrow morning. It's just one more night before I'll have my kitchen table back. Normally, my home office is more than big enough for the work-overflow from my office at city hall, but this project called for more surface space than usual.

My phone and watch vibrate, helping refocus my thoughts more efficiently than any technique I've tried in the past twenty years.

Tommy: Did you remember to drink water today?

Butterflies fill my stomach.

Tommy Landen's checking in on me again. Who does that? My ex of two years didn't even notice when I dyed my hair fire-engine red that one week. I could have drank nothing but cherry cola for a year and he would have been none the wiser. But that's Tommy, always looking out for people.

Sam: Five full bottles. And that's not counting when I refilled the bottle when it was only halfway empty.

Ever since the auction cleanup day in May, he sends me reminders to drink water because I was clearly dehydrated after that huge night. It's sweet that he thinks to check in.

Not that he's checking in on me for any reason other than just being a nice guy. An easy-going guy would never settle for someone so neurotic like me.

Not that he's thinking about being with me. Even though I've been thinking about him for months.

Stop.

I take a deep breath and remind myself that I am worthy of love. Love from someone other than my parents. Real love. Not love that tries to keep you in a mold, but love that frees you to live as your true self.

Another vibration.

Tommy: Even better than yesterday! You'll need a bigger bottle for the council meeting tonight, maybe fill it with caffeine.

Another vibration.

Tommy: Or booze.

I feel like I'm walking right into his plan by asking, but I take the bait.

Sam: And why is that?

Three dots appear immediately, so I watch and wait, letting my nerves twist themselves in knots.

Tommy: Because there's a fire safety course coming up. We don't need to practice anything and we already do the required drills, but each year we have someone who wants to do something with a crazy amount of candles, or something like that, so we get to learn about what we've all been tested on annually.

I can almost hear the tone of his voice, the way it animates even something that could be mundane to someone else. He adds life to everything he touches.

Sam: I'll be sure to take good notes and might even bring hot tea along with my water. Can't take any chances.

My thumb hovers over the message, ready to unsend it, but he's already read it.

Tommy: I wouldn't expect anything less from the town's PR expert.

My cheeks burn.

Sam: Hardly an expert, as we've already established.

Those three dots are immediate once again.

Tommy: I'm pretty sure that we've established you're so much more than an expert at this point.

My stomach flips at his praise as my thumbs automatically move to type out something self-deprecating. Before I even type one word, I lift them off the screen with a grimace. It wouldn't do any good to contradict Tommy about how I do my job because he always has a new reason for why I'm good at what I do. And maybe, for once, I can accept a compliment with grace. Or at least use the distance of texting to appear to take that compliment with said grace.

Oh. He's typing again.

I wait.

And wait.

What on earth could he be talking about? Did he remember something I messed up? My brain starts to sift through details of the past few days and I'm about to mentally go through everything from the fundraiser when my phone's vibrations help me refocus.

Tommy: I know that it can be hard, especially in a town that still might feel new to you, to feel like you're really in your groove. But what you did for the auction fundraiser really was special. Not only was there a great line-up of bachelors ;) but half of the town showed up. That's no small feat. We've had so many community functions that have truly been flops, but you've already found ways to get people excited and come together. Plus, that night raised record numbers of funds for something that the community desperately needed. So, chin up, take credit where credit's undoubtedly due, and I'll see ya tonight.

How the heck am I supposed to reply to that? I'm surely not going to tell him that my eyes are welling up with tears. Instead, I lamely like the message. Hank raved about my performance, even though all I saw were the ways it fell short. But seeing this from Tommy versus my boss? It hits differently. It's not the first time he's told me that I did something great, but it's like he knows what my brain needs to shut off the doubts that always creep in.

I walk into the kitchen to refill my water bottle that has three stickers stuck to the metal. The first that I put on was one I got the day I started working for this small town: a holographic Greenstone sticker. Avery, who I'm guessing will officially be Tommy's sister-in-law before the end of the year, gave me a tour of Barnett Farms and afterwards, I placed an order for one of their stickers that has a bundle of veggies with BF in the corner. The tour felt like an official turning point for us and we've been becoming friends after a semi-rocky start. And then Tommy, not Jackson, who was my fake-dating-buddy when I first arrived, which was the likely reason for Avery's initial frostiness towards me, brought me a black-and-white Landen Acres sticker saying that my water bottle needed to be "better aesthetically balanced" since the first two stickers were too close together.

All three have made me feel more and more welcome here. I'll always be a "transplant" as newcomers are called, but I really have been treated with more kindness here than any other city, and I mean big city, I've lived in. Which only means I feel a whole new type of pressure to do well. I've never wanted to belong to a place as badly as Greenstone. There's something that calls to me here and it's not just because it's a small community. This is a place where everyone truly knows each other and supports everyone. I've always wanted to be part of something that changes lives for the better and be seen for exactly who I am.

Another vibration gets my attention.

Tommy: A few of us are getting drinks after the meeting tonight, so this is a multi-part question, I hope you're ready for it! Part I - Would you like to come out with us? Part II - Would you be okay if I drove you? Part III - Would you like me to pick you up from your place to go to the meeting and drinks? (I won't have more than one beer and won't have any if you're at all uncomfortable with me driving. We usually hang out for about two hours and get apps and I'll eat and drink a ton of water either way.)

Oh my.

Did he just ask me out?

No, this is a group thing.

Hank mentioned it earlier this week in passing. Can't be a date.

But he wants to pick me up so we can go together?

No, he's not asking me out. He just wants me to be comfortable with being able to have a drink myself.

Yes, that's what he's offering.

I need to stop reading into things that aren't there.

Chapter 2
Tommy

Chewing the inside of my cheek, I wait for Sam's brain to stop running scenario after scenario. I'm still really intentional with my word choice ever since we started texting regularly. She can stress over what seems like the simplest detail and I want tonight to feel fun.

I'll ask her out on a proper date, eventually, but I want her to feel completely comfortable around me. Something inside me says that her past relationships have been centered around what her boyfriend wanted. She drops little hints about her past when her guard is down and she doesn't feel like she has to be perfect for everyone. I honestly think she doesn't realize she's let something slip when it happens.

Samantha Davies is incredible, plain and simple. She's smart, caring, thoughtful, organized, gorgeous, and funny. I just hope that she can see it one day.

Well, I hope that I get to be there with her when she realizes it.

Three dots appear on my screen.

Then disappear.

Then reappear.

My mind tries to look for something that I might be missing about why she hasn't responded, yet, but I remind myself that she's an over-thinker who always needs to work through her words.

Sam: That sounds like fun and it would be nice to not drive myself home after dark, so thank you. Is there a dress code?

Smiling, I type my reply while telling off that little voice in my head looking for trouble.

Tommy: Whatever you're wearing now will be plenty dressed up, I promise. It's a bar with great apps, including buffalo chicken wings. So don't wear white.

Tommy: I'll pick you up at 5:45?

She likes the first text and is quick to respond that she'll be ready.

"Tommy! Can you remember to get more pepper flakes from Mark at the meeting tonight?" Matt calls from the kitchen, immediately pulling me out of the fantasy to reply telling her it's a date. I'm not taking her out on a date that's linked to a work function. It would feel like a cheapened experience after all the time I've taken to get to know her. And I want her to feel seen and special. Tacking a date to one of the most boring meetings this town has ever known would be the opposite of making her feel special.

The smell of garlic, tomatoes, and fresh basil draws me to the kitchen where Matt is cooking a massive pot of marinara. I dip a clean spoon in, spinning away from him as he tries to swat me out of the way.

"You had to yell instead of walking the ten steps through an open doorway to the office?" I ask, blowing across the spoon.

"I can't leave this unattended with Chuck roaming around the house," Matt says, waving a hand over the steaming pot. "I'm splitting it up for a few houses and I'll have to start over with his constant double-dipping."

I can't argue with that. Matt gives me an expectant look and I taste the sauce, flavor exploding in my mouth.

"Damn, that's good."

His face splits into a grin that could charm the boots right off a cowboy. None of us know how he got so good at cooking, but our baby brother keeps us well-fed. He likes to make extras for a few families whose ranches and farms are facing tighter times. I reach over to muss his hair, which he promptly dodges, and resumes his ever-vigilant watch over the pot.

"You want me to start some pasta? I can get you something before you have to leave."

"Nah, there's leftover rice, I'll put the sauce on that," I reply. He gives me an affronted look.

"That's not—"

"I like it and I don't do it when we're all eating together, so let me have my weird food quirk."

His eyes narrow at me and he points the spoon in my direction. "Just this once."

My hands raise in surrender. "Just this once."

We both know I'm lying, but he doesn't fuss as I scoop the leftovers into a dish and put it in the microwave. I could live off rice, which is why there are leftovers in the first place. Matt's our main cook, but the rest of us rotate in regularly. Whenever it's my turn, it's either kebabs with rice, stir fry with rice, or pineapple fried rice. Everyone stopped complaining a few years ago, just like we don't complain when Bryant walks in with a comical pile of beef on his nights.

The microwave dings and I grab my dish, alternating hands to avoid getting burnt.

"Do you want chicken? I haven't shredded it, yet, but it's good." And by good, he means melt-in-your-mouth-perfection.

"You know I do."

He nods and grabs the tongs to pull out a chicken breast that's falling apart. My mouth waters. When he finishes ladling sauce over my chicken and rice, he gives me a look of pure judgment.

"Just this once," I whisper, grabbing my feast and tiptoeing backwards out of the kitchen to the office. I set my food aside and open up the calendar. It didn't take me long to realize that my brothers are terrible at sharing calendars online. They're not Neanderthals, but you'd think I was asking them to take the LSATs instead of checking one calendar at the start of every week.

Apparently, they're too damn stubborn to do that, so I track their schedules on a weekly, bound calendar that's color-coded. Bryant comes by and checks the calendar every Wednesday, like he thinks it might have changed, but otherwise, I'm the only one touching it.

Footsteps approach and I turn around to find Matt holding out a full glass of milk.

"You need more vitamin D. You're inside too much."

I snort out a laugh. "Thanks, Matt."

He grunts, taking after Bryant and Jax, and turns on his heel.

Within seconds I hear a scuffle in the kitchen.

"God damn it, Chuck! I leave for two seconds and you're already in the sauce!"

Chuck lets out a *whoop* right before Matt likely has him in a headlock because a moment later he's straining out, "I give, I give."

"How many times did you dip your spoon?"

"Just the one time, I swear," Chuck replies, clearly unwilling to hold out any longer. Matt was the only wrestler out of all five of us and he's scrappy as hell when it serves him.

"Not twice?"

"Scout's honor."

"You and Jax have to stop saying that—neither of you were scouts."

A moment later, Chuck comes out and gives me a look. "You couldn't have kept him distracted?"

"I'm not a mind reader. How the hell was I supposed to know you were planning to sneak in?"

"When am I not?" He crosses one ankle over the other and leans against the desk.

"Touché. You going out tonight?"

"Maybe," he replies, so he's got plans for sure. "You?"

"It's the fire meeting tonight so we're grabbing wings after. I'm picking Sam up," I say, attempting to be casual.

"Look at you blushing!" He slaps his leg as his face lights up. "You finally asked her out?"

"I didn't call it a date," I say, feeling the need to clarify this isn't going to be our first date. No, it's going to be something special.

One eyebrow raises and he oozes judgment in a way that only Chuck Landen can.

"Shut up," I grumble.

"Just don't let her put you in the friend zone."

Doubt creeps into my mind, reminding me of how easy she was around Jax.

"On second thought, don't overthink it," Chuck says. "Listen to your gut."

My mind races about how I'm approaching the most-perfect human being I've ever encountered in an attempt to date her. If only I had half of Chuck's confidence. Unfortunately, Maisy shredded whatever I had to bits. I just hope that, if she's interested, Sam really is everything she seems to be.

Chapter 3
Sam

The five outfits that lay neatly organized on my bed have my complete attention until the ticking from the antique alarm clock on my nightstand reminds me I'm not ready. Tommy will be here in fifteen minutes and he's never late, which means he might show up earlier than he said.

My nerves keep creeping up and it takes a few breaths to settle them so I can avoid breaking out in a full sweat.

Not. A. Date.

Tommy Landen has his pick of people in this town. He has to. Yes, Jacksy has his own charm that seems to draw in people left and right, but Tommy... He's the full package: smarter than anyone I know, sweet, kind, thoughtful, and so sexy. I could get lost in those sparkling blue eyes of his for days.

Shaking my head to remind myself that this is not a date, I refocus my efforts. He's simply being a kind friend to me, just like he is with Avery and Courtney. Nothing more. So, if this isn't a date, what do I wear to a work function that will turn into drinks and apps?

The pencil skirt is too work-centric, especially for this small town. I put that and the blouse I paired with it back in my closet.

It's not hot enough today to have a/c on, so the bar won't be freezing.

The two sets with pants go back to the closet as well.

Okay, that's progress.

The flowy skirt with a high-neck sleeveless top with strappy tan, but sensible, heels would work with a casual blazer with the sleeves rolled up for the meeting and would look casual without it after. Or I can wear the long slacks-like shorts with the button down navy shirt with eyelets paired with my tan ballet flats.

My eyes bounce back and forth for another minute and I realize I'm chewing my thumbnail. Again. I turn around and grab the bottle of polish from my bathroom counter to touch up the chip I made. I look back at my bed.

"Just pick one, Samantha," I mutter, blowing on my nail.

With a rare burst of courage, I let myself consider that maybe, just maybe, Tommy might be thinking of this as a pseudo-date. Grabbing the shorts ensemble, I hang it back up, deciding to wear the flowy skirt.

Only ten minutes, which means I need to be waiting at my door to leave in five. I release a quick breath to steady my nerves and step out of my robe to get dressed, making sure that nothing is out of place. A childhood memory of having my skirt tucked into my underwear pops into my mind and I smooth the fabric down and check myself in the mirror as I add my jewelry.

"That's not gonna happen again, Samantha, and you know it," I say to my reflection.

Worst-case scenario is that Tommy will notice before anyone else and fix it himself just like he does for his two besties. Which means I'll be friend-zoned.

I snort. It's not like I'm *not* already there.

My brown suede work tote is laid out on the table with my three options I already decided against for tonight. I stack my clipboard, planner, and printed agenda before slipping them in along with my little canvas bag with my flare-tip markers, sticky-notes, and tabs. My keys get clipped inside and I zip my phone in the pocket.

And I promptly pull it right out since I need to know when Tommy arrives. My hand shakes almost imperceptibly. Closing my eyes, I focus as I breathe in, and then breathe out.

It's a meeting, where you're not presenting, followed by drinks with new friends. You'll know most, if not all, of the people there.

In, and out. Over and over until my hand vibrates because a message came through.

Tommy: I know I'm a little early, so take your time if you need more, but I'm here when you're ready.

A smile spreads across my face. I like a guy who doesn't show up late, or forgets me altogether. Which is what my second-to-last ex did. Was I that forgettable?

Either way, Tommy's here now, so even if it's just a mutual friendship, I'll take it. My heart knows that Tommy Landen is a catch no matter how you get to have him in your life.

Oh no. What if he asks me to be his wingman so he can pick up someone else at the bar? No, that's ridiculous.

Shaking my head, I turn off all the lights in my apartment except the one I always keep on near the door, flip my keys out of my bag, lock the door, and am on my way. Making sure the front door fully latches, I give it an extra tug.

And then I see him. A genuine, unrestrained smile lights up his face and I know it reaches his eyes even though they're behind his aviators. My heart skips a beat. Waving, I let myself return the smile without reservation. His white cowboy hat sits on his head and I haven't decided if I like him better with or without it. Tommy could wear a fruit basket and look amazing. He casually steps away from the passenger door and opens it for me.

Another skipped heartbeat.

Oh my goodness he smells so good. It's almost torture to walk past him without brushing my fingers against his.

I step up into the passenger seat, making sure my skirt doesn't catch on anything so I don't make a complete fool of myself. By the time I'm settled and buckling my seat belt, he's getting into the driver's seat with this hat in hand. He gently places it in the back seat and runs his hand through his not-too-short light brown hair that has one piece that likes to fall over his forehead no matter how many times he tries to move it away. My fingers itch to brush it back just once for him. After placing his aviators on the dashboard, his bright blue eyes are fixed on me.

We just sit there as I hold my breath, staring at each other, that warm smile on his lips. Lips that I would love to…

"Thanks for driving me," I say, breaking off that train of thought and remembering to make my lungs work. "I know it's a small town, but I swear, just last week I got lost."

Something softens in his gaze, making me melt a little. "Anytime, truly."

My heart squeezes and my stomach flip-flops as I'm already mentally shaking myself out of the daydream I'll think about tonight after we have our group drinks.

"I'll have to pick you up sometime," I say, trying to make it seem like I'm not some damsel in distress who refuses to learn how to drive around this tiny town.

"If we're meeting at Barnett Farms or at Jackson's house, then you can pick me up. Otherwise, maybe we can agree to let me do the driving so you don't go fifteen miles out of your way for a meeting one mile from your place."

His wink doesn't help the swarm of butterflies that seem to have taken up permanent residence in my belly whenever I'm around him.

That sounds long-term.

But it's just friendship and convenience. It has to be.

Tommy and I are just friends.

Chapter 4
Tommy

Worry creeps into my mind about how she might feel about me driving her to meetings and town events. She works too hard to do the right thing. The proper thing. I know, in my gut, that she's not going to want this town to think that she's bouncing from brother to brother.

But I know that, if she'll let me, I'd like to be the one to pick her up for meetings, to take her out for drinks, to be the one to walk her to her door. If I fuck this up, she'll just see me as Jax's pathetic younger brother who has a crush on the new girl. I'll miss whatever minuscule chance I might have with her. Maybe I just need to be direct, but not too direct.

She ducks her head as she pushes some of her blonde curls behind her ear. "Fair enough."

Wait, what?

"Does that mean I get to pick you up for the monthly movie night subcommittee meeting, too?" I ask, trying to not push my luck.

Sam looks surprised. "You're going to drop me off at a meeting you're not going to?"

"Why wouldn't I be going?"

"You're not on that subcommittee," she says, her brows furrowing.

"Maybe I just requested to join," I say, flashing her a smile as I start the truck and turn the radio low.

"I didn't get an email."

"You aren't the chair of that committee and the rules state that requests to join should be sent to the chair who will bring them to the subcommittee before the next meeting."

Her mouth falls open. "You're joining the movie night subcommittee?"

"Well, yeah, someone needs to help you bring movies into the mix that aren't in black and white."

That smile. There it is. My chest swells with pride knowing that I might have had something to do with it. And, let's be honest, I joined so I could see her more.

"I could use a partner." She blushes, like she said something wrong.

Before she can hide her face, I hold my hand out to shake hers and say, "Then you've got one."

Her bracelets make a soft jingling sound when she places her hand in mine. It's soft and fits perfectly. Her eyes take in our shake and then bounce to mine.

"Perfect."

"I think we've chatted away most of our extra time if we don't want to show up late," I say, grimacing at the transition.

"Of course," she says, looking at the building and pulling her hand away. "We wouldn't want to keep anyone waiting."

"We would've had a good excuse," I say, giving her one more wink before putting my sunglasses back on. I leave my hat in the back seat so I have one less thing to fiddle with as I drive.

"Chatting in your car is considered a good excuse?" she asks. "Now I'm curious what a poor excuse would be."

God, why is it sexy whenever she pulls out phrases that senior citizens use?

"Whippin' shitties?" I venture.

She coughs, laughs, and then asks, "Pardon me?"

There's that phrase again. Fuck, I love that she says *pardon* of all words. "You know, whippin' shitties, or donuts?"

"I definitely do not know what that is," she says emphatically.

"I suppose city folk have other forms of entertainment. But sometimes, those of us in small towns and in the country, we pass the time by driving in empty parking lots and whippin' shitties. You drive fast, slam on the brakes, and crank the wheel to spin you in a tight circle," I explain. "We also go mudding."

"You do this?" One of her brows is raised in skepticism.

"I *did*. It's a good way to make your tires go bald fast and you might tip your truck, which is a bone-headed thing to attempt."

"Dare I ask about mudding?"

The way her nose crinkles has my heart jumping in my chest, but I try to play it cool and chuckle. "It's literally taking your truck,

SUV, or ATV, but not a sedan like yours, and driving into a muddy field."

"Driving in the mud, truly?" she asks, concern and confusion on her face.

"Well, you're not going five miles an hour. You're messing around and getting mud everywhere."

"Everywhere?"

"Everywhere," I say, not thinking about my truck. And before I second-guess myself, I embrace Chuck's advice and say, "We'll have to go sometime."

"Mudding?" she asks, her voice a little breathless and her cheeks flushing with the barest hint of pink.

"Mudding. You game?"

"You'd like to take me to spray mud all over your truck?"

"All over everything," I tell her, not overthinking everything.

She has an almost-inaudible gasp. "Okay."

"Okay." I try to keep a smirk off my face and am sure I'm failing as I turn at the intersection because I'm loving how she's relaxing more. "So what do city-slickers do to pass the time?"

"Go to the movies or hang out in people's basements."

"And…" I say, gesturing with my hand for her to elaborate.

"And I don't know, play truth or dare? That's about all we did," she says.

"What about the evenings at the country club, the cotillions, and the daily tea service?"

A real laugh escapes her. "We had no such things!"

"There weren't country clubs?"

"I mean, sure, those exist, but we didn't go there."

It's my turn to give her a skeptical look. "Then did you wear your formal gowns to the movies?"

"What formal gowns?" she says, still giggling.

"I was under the impression that everyone in the city is required to have several formal gowns for regular events, especially cotillions." I manage to keep a straight face, earning a snort from her.

"Where do you think I grew up?" Her laugh is contagious and I have to fight to keep my mock-serious demeanor.

"I *know* where you grew up," I reply. "Now, where did you wear these gowns?"

"I don't know, prom?"

"That's it?" My exasperation pulls another round of giggles from her.

"That's it."

I sigh dramatically, pulling up to the building.

"What?"

I put the truck into park and turn my head so I can see the flush on her face, the sparkle in her eyes, and the smile on her face. God, she's gorgeous. "I'm so disappointed."

I finally crack when she belly laughs at the expression on my face. Nodding at her water bottle, with the Landen Acres sticker that I never fail to notice, I ask, "What's your fuel of choice tonight?"

She smiles. "Just water."

"Brave woman."

"What about you?"

"Water."

"Brave man."

"But," I say, "I might have something else."

I reach down behind her seat and show her two iced coffees, passing the lighter one to her.

"Oat milk," I explain.

She has a look in her eye that I know I'll strive to see again. The one that's surprise mixed with a tiny bit of awe.

"Thank you," she says shyly as she takes it from me, our hands touching and my entire body feeling the electricity.

Chapter 5
Sam

I swear my fingers have a mind of their own. My brain tries to be polite and not make contact, unlike someone with an unrequited crush might do. But no, they grab the cup just below his and my index finger practically smothers his pinky.

Cheeks burning, I fight to not react. I just keep looking into his eyes, which have completely ensnared mine.

"Oat milk?" I ask.

A twinge of doubt enters his expression. "Isn't that how you take your coffee?"

I smile, hoping to reassure him and not look like my heart is melting into a puddle at the thought of Tommy knowing how I like my coffee. It doesn't matter if it's hot or cold, it's always with oat milk.

"It is."

"Whew," he says. "For a moment, I thought I had messed up something pretty elementary."

"There's nothing elementary about knowing how someone takes their coffee," I reply, thinking of all the times friends and even family have panicked about getting my order wrong and accidentally getting me something with dairy in it.

He raises his eyebrow. "It sounds like someone set the bar pretty damn low."

"The bar?" I feel like this conversation is coded as confusion stirs inside of me.

"Yeah. If you're even mildly impressed by my coffee observations, just you wait for what else is coming."

"What's coming?" I ask, purposefully trying to breathe normally because internally I might be freaking out just a little bit. It sounds like he's talking about setting the bar low for... dating.

"You'll see soon enough." He frowns. "I hope."

"What does that mean?" Nice one, Samantha, way to not sound pathetic and needy.

"It means you have to be interested. I don't want you to ever feel pressured about anything."

Opening my mouth to say something, totally unsure of how I was going to respond, he looks at the clock on his dash, breaking our eye contact.

"We'll both be late for the meeting if we stay here much longer, and I know you like to be early to get a seat in front," he says, rubbing his free hand on his jeans. Is he nervous? "I bet that's where you sat in high school and college, too."

"Of course I did, that's where you can see and hear the best." Curiosity gets the best of me. "Where did you sit?"

We get out of the truck, both carrying two drinks. I'm happy that I grabbed this particular tote since it hangs easily from my shoulder.

"The side of the room, but not in the back or front."

"I can picture high school Tommy Landen in class, actually." It fits what I've learned about him. He's full of life and joy, but he has a reserved side without quite being a wallflower.

A mental image from the "Date a Cowboy" auction night. I remember how hard it was for me to concentrate on the script I was reading of Tommy's admirable qualities, and I'll admit I had to really pare them down so his list wasn't twice as long as every other bachelor's there. The struggle to not just watch him move across the stage like he owned the place was very real. He didn't walk, he strutted. He turned in time with the music, winked at Mrs. Fields, gave Courtney a little wave, and then I was brought back to reality. Or what I thought was reality. Tommy and Courtney really do seem to be friends and not more.

"Allow me," he says, pulling me back to this moment. Of course he got the door.

"Thanks," I say, attempting to not blush. I don't know the last time a guy did that for me. I mean, one I was really dating. Jackson did, but that wasn't even close to dating. He introduced me to everyone, sometimes more than once, so I wasn't floundering with names, and then he stepped back and let me talk to everyone. Those were some of my first meetings and Tommy was absent for most of them for some reason.

I pause.

"Sam?"

If I go out with Tommy, are people going to think I'm basically jumping from one brother to the next with no thought?

The Landens are one of the most well-respected families in Greenstone. Quite possibly the one with the most influence.

Everyone's going to think I'm—

No. You didn't *date* Jacksy. You were each other's helper and you carpooled a couple of times. And Tommy hasn't asked you out, Sam.

"Everything okay?" Tommy asks, his brow knitted in concern.

I mentally give myself a shake and plaster on a smile. "Never better, I just thought I left my highlighters back at my place."

"We can head back so you can get them. We won't miss anything vital, I can promise you that."

Pushing down the guilt that wants to surface, I wave him off as best I can while holding two drinks. "No, they're in my case, I remember now."

"Okay, then let's see if Sharon has music this year to help keep us all awake." He gives me a warm smile, but there's a little concern lingering in his eyes. Not judgment. Lord knows I'm an expert at spotting that in a man's eyes.

Tonight isn't even a date. We're going out with a group after a council meeting, seriously, Sam. It's time to focus on the meeting that's about to start.

The conference room door is propped open for everyone and this time we're in a smaller one with only one table instead of two pushed together.

"I'll grab chairs for us," Tommy says as he sets down his drinks and nods his head for me to set my things down next to his.

"Thank you," I tell him, remembering my manners.

Stop trying to panic over nothing, Samantha Davies.

Plus, you didn't date Jackson. You went to things together so you could network and he didn't look like a grump in the corner. But what if people think I'm taking advantage of the Landen brothers somehow? My gaze darts around the room, trying not to get too paranoid.

Tommy is already talking to Mr. Barnett as I smile at Hank and give Sharon a wave. Taking a slow breath, I focus on unpacking my things and laying them out neatly on the table.

Without interrupting my organizing, Tommy tucks a chair under the table for me before he sits down. He even situates things so I can be in the front. I glance back at him, still chatting with Mr. Barnett who puts his chair on the other side of Tommy.

As usual, Tommy pulls out three different color pens and his hardback and travel-sized notebook. I have to bite down a little on my lip to not smile at how organized he is. This isn't the first time I've noticed he always seems to have a notebook in his front pocket and from our work with Avery on our co-op, I know that he color-codes notes and reports.

"Sam?" Tommy's voice pulls me back into the conversations happening around me.

"Pardon?" I ask reflexively, my feet shuffling a little so I'm facing him as I hope I didn't miss anything too big.

He gives a little smile. "Have you tried these?" He holds up a Barnett's Farm jar filled with pepper flakes. Just the thought of the spice they're packing has my gut twist in warning.

"Oh sorry, my mind was elsewhere. No, I haven't. They look incredible. How long do you have to process them before they're ready to go out?" I ask Mr. Barnett, diving right into engaging in the conversation.

"It's pretty efficient now that we have special trays so we can do them in big batches in our ovens," he replies.

"That's a great system to have in place."

He beams at me. "That was Chase's idea."

"Smart son," I say.

"That he is."

"If I can have your attention, I'll get this show on the road," Sharon calls out to the seven of us.

I look down at my chair that's touching Tommy's as well as the corner leg of the table. How do I sit without falling on top of Tommy?

Chapter 6
Tommy

Holding back a chuckle, I give Sam a second to figure out how to get in her seat. When Mark sat next to me, I didn't realize how much I ended up crowding her space, but I didn't have any choice. Now I can see the gears turning in her head, and it's adorable.

If it was at all appropriate, I'd pull her right into my lap.

If she wanted that.

Before she starts to panic, I pull her chair out and she steps to the side, allowing me to bring it farther so she can sit down without maneuvering through the little gap between the chair seat and the table.

"Thank you," she whispers.

"Any time," I say, helping push it in as she sits down.

I reluctantly take my hand from the back of the chair. Sharon's presentation begins and I avoid groaning because it's the same opening slide as the last two years. Instead, I flip open my notebook to a fresh page and grab my blue pen, noting that Sam has a heading already written with highlighters and pens. Without wanting to distract her too much, I gently nudge her elbow while she uncaps her black pen. She looks back at me with her deep blue eyes and I mouth "nice" as I nod to her notes.

A crease appears between her brows so I tap the heading. She looks back up at me with a huge smile on her face. One of her genuine smiles, the unguarded kind where she isn't smiling because she thinks it's expected. She turns so she can watch Sharon and a blush creeps up the back of her neck. That feels like a step in the right direction.

I can't let that go to my head. Maybe people see her organizational side and she hides her artistic skills.

After noting the meeting and the date, I start flipping my pen through my fingers. Besides jotting down the code numbers that are relevant to permits, I don't really need to write anything else.

We're about twenty minutes into the presentation and Sam is already turning the page.

Yeah, she definitely always sat in front for every class.

Granted, if she was my teacher, I'd be fighting for a spot in front. The things I'd study about her...

Every now and then her eyes wander to my right hand and the pen that I'm barely thinking about. Shit. Is it annoying her to have me fidgeting over here while she dutifully takes notes?

I do my best to hold the pen still for the rest of the meeting, which means I end up doodling. At least I'm not snoring like Mark. Even with his daughter being one of my best friends, I don't feel comfortable nudging him awake, maybe Jackson would feel more comfortable doing that than me, so I fake a cough, extra loud, causing him to startle awake.

Hank, across the table, smirks and pretends to be watching the presentation.

"Any questions?" Sharon asks.

Sam's hand shoots up.

"Oh, um, yes, Sam?"

"I was curious about provisions regarding setups outside of those you outlined. What do we do if we get requests that don't follow examples?"

Sharon gives her a smile, "I'm sure you will at some point. You can always call me to make sure we have everything properly handled."

Sam makes a note. "Thank you, I always appreciate specific instructions. That was my only question right now."

God, she's cute. And I'm definitely going to remember that she likes instructions.

"Thank you for keeping us up to date so we can handle whatever requests that inevitably come through."

"Of course, Hank," Sharon replies to him, looking a little relieved to be done.

"I think that's everything for tonight unless anyone has other business?"

We all shake our heads.

"In that case," Hank says, "let's get out of here early tonight. I've got the first round of wings for those going."

Sam looks a little lost. I lean in and whisper, "We always do this after the fire presentation. He buys the blazin' wings and then heads out."

"Really?"

"Yeah, I said it was a group."

"I don't picture Hank with a pile of spicy wings in front of him."

"Don't let the comb-over fool you," I say, earning a quiet giggle. "The man might not eat them, but he loves this tradition."

We pack up our things and everyone walks out together. Sam seems to hesitate a moment before walking to my truck.

"Everything good?" I ask.

She takes a quick inhale. "Of course."

I get one of those partial smiles. And then I see that Hank is watching her. Not weirdly, just observing. Is she worried about being seen with me? Is this the kind of thing I missed with Maisy? I don't open the door for her and go right to mine.

"I'm sorry if you're uncomfortable riding with me. I can bring you back to your car if you'd rather drive separately."

"Oh," she says, looking torn.

"It's okay either way. I won't be offended. I promise."

"Thank you." She takes a breath. "Before I moved, I never walked in or out with someone from a work event. But I've done it before and I'd like to do it again. With you."

Ouch, I didn't fully need a reminder that Jax showed up with her to a few things.

"I just had a moment where I was worried that Hank might think I was being unprofessional. But there's nothing unprofessional about two people carpooling."

"No, I don't think there is. We're being eco-conscious."

"Definitely."

I breathe a little easier and pull out of the spot.

"Are you ready for the wings?"

"I'm not sure I'll be able to eat any of the first round."

"Not a blazin' girl?"

"More like an almost-mild girl," she says, looking like that might be an issue.

"Ooh, you're not going to like the ones Hank gets then, but we can make sure there's a basket of the sweet chili wings for you."

"Okay, even that sounds too hot," she says with a nervous laugh.

"It's as mild as they make them, and it's a very sweet heat."

"Alright, sweet chili it is, I guess." She makes a face that has me snorting.

"On second thought, you might need plain wings," I say, throwing the truck in gear.

"They'd do that?" she asks.

"Why not?"

"I guess not every place I've been has been accommodating to special orders like that," she says, shifting her iced coffee around in her hands and looking out the window.

"Where have you been going?" I ask, suddenly feeling protective.

"Oh, more so in the city, I suppose. I haven't really been out to eat much here, actually. Just official functions so the food is already set for the most part."

"We'll have to remedy that."

She chews on her thumbnail for a moment before nodding and saying, "That sounds lovely."

"We should go to a new place each week and I'll let you know where ahead of time so you can check out the menu."

"I do like to do that."

I just give her a smile because if anyone has paid attention to this woman for more than two minutes, they would have been able to guess that.

Chapter 7
Sam

Why does Tommy look so good driving?

I can't seem to make my heart calm down.

Since he parks a little farther from the entrance, we have more space to get out of his truck, so I don't have to focus too hard on how to slide down. But being used to my low sedan plus the fact that I'm wearing a skirt isn't a great combination for remaining casually graceful. In the time it takes to gather my things, let alone my exit strategy for the second time tonight, Tommy is already opening my door before I can reach for the handle.

"You can leave anything you want in the truck," he says.

"I suppose it would be silly for me to bring my water bottle into the bar."

"If you'd like, you can leave your notebook and pens here, too. You shouldn't need them."

"Fair point," I reply, stepping out of the truck and pulling out just about everything so my bag only has my keys and wallet.

"I think that's better," I tell him.

"As long as you're good," he says sincerely.

My heart flutters again. Usually any guy I'm with doesn't notice what I'm carrying or if it's too much.

Get a grip, Samantha.

"Shall we?" I manage.

He shuts the door and hesitates for a moment, then shakes his hands at his sides like he's unsure what to do with them.

"After you," he says.

Maybel's is about half full tonight. I've only been here one other time when Hank brought me for dinner with his wife and children, celebrating my first day on the job.

I feel Tommy's hand gently press against my lower back causing a shiver that I can't hide.

"Our table's this way," he says, leaning down so I can easily hear him over the country music playing on the speakers. "Hank calls ahead each year."

"I didn't realize this was truly an official ritual," I tell him. "Hank told me about going out for drinks after this meeting, but it sounded less mandatory than this is turning out to be."

"Definitely not mandatory, but a nice way to unwind after Sharon's presentation. She even joins us."

He lifts his hand to wave at Hank and Mr. Barnett and my skin is left feeling colder than before he touched me.

"Are you going to finally beat Mark's record tonight?" Hank asks Tommy from across the table as Tommy pulls out a chair for me like there's nothing to think about.

"I swear mine were spiked with ghost peppers last year," he says.

"What's Mr. Barnett's record?" I ask.

Tommy waves his hand at Mr. Barnett who shakes his head. "Mark, please, there's no need for formalities."

"Of course, Mark," I say, trying to undo the lessons drilled into me from birth by teachers and even my parents.

"I've eaten eleven wings before needing anything to cool the heat down. Tommy made it all the way to six last year before he had tears in his eyes and was practically begging for mercy."

Hank and Mark laugh and I look at Tommy, loving the shy blush on his cheeks.

"It's true," he admits. "The year before I made it to eight before I caved. Last year was pitiful."

"Who else has been close to the record?" I ask.

"Sharon only competed two years ago and she got to six and Hank—"

"Hank doesn't even try," my boss says.

The waiter comes by and Hank places an order for the spiciest wings on the menu with an assortment of other appetizers. He looks around and asks if we'd like anything else.

"An order of plain wings, please," Tommy says, raising one finger to get his attention. My heart flutters against my will. Just because I've always ordered for myself because I can't handle spicy foods or dairy, doesn't mean I should suddenly have butterflies over the guy who remembers and feels confident enough to order the right thing.

"And a pitcher of light beer and a pitcher of cola. Anyone need diet?"

We all shake our heads and our waiter takes the menus from everyone.

"Sharon, how are the new recruits working out so far?" Mark asks.

"Really great potential, but we have some big shoes to fill. Figuratively and literally," she smiles.

"How many positions are open?" I ask.

"Just two for our station, but we cover a broad area, so the Greenstone location houses more than usual. We're one of the few paid rural stations in the state, but we also train the volunteers."

"I didn't know that," I tell her.

"We're fortunate to have the resources right now to replace both retirements. One might not be full-time, but we're trying."

My mind is already processing this information and I'm already thinking of ways to help make sure the region gets funds to at least keep their previous staffing numbers.

Tommy shifts in his seat, drawing my eye. He pulls out his notebook from his front pocket and one of his pens.

"Write it down," he says, setting the notebook in front of me and placing the blue pen on top. "Your stuff is in my truck, so get your ideas down. Then you don't have to worry about forgetting them."

A smile tugs at my lips. I should be surprised at his thoughtfulness and his attention to detail. But this man seems to know what I need so I don't fixate.

"Thank you," I tell him, opening the notebook that's warm from being against his leg. For some reason, that makes this feel intimate. I don't usually have a reason to write in someone else's notebook and I know that this isn't his diary or anything along those lines, but the warmth makes me think that there might be more than meeting notes in here. I use the ribbon to open to a fresh page and jot down the list that has already formed in my head.

He goes back to talking with everyone as I go into the zone, letting my thoughts come out on the page. I finish when our pitchers are delivered with plenty of glasses. Tommy grabs the beer, pours five glasses, and passes them around.

It's only now that I realize Tommy and I are the only two people sitting side by side. Our table is a square and it didn't feel funny to sit here, even before Sharon arrived.

When was the last time I was this comfortable with someone?

Chapter 8
Tommy

God, that smile.

Sam stops writing in the middle of her second list, the second list she has used my notebook for, and she looks up right into my eyes. I hold her gaze and watch the left side of her lips softly rise. I don't dare ask what brought this on. She opens her mouth, about to speak—

"Should the pile of wings go in the middle?" Keith, our server, asks. I *don't* glare at him for unknowingly cutting off Sam.

"Yes, please," Hank replies. "These two have reputations to uphold."

Keith finishes placing the apps around the table and when he gets to the plain wings, I point to Sam so they get placed in front of her, earning me another shy smile.

"Thomas," Mark says solemnly.

"Markus," I say, bowing my head.

"May the best man win," Hank says, passing us each a plate.

"I should've thought twice about driving you here tonight, you might not want to ride with me after you see me with tears streaming down my face," I mumble, thinking aloud.

"Oh, I think this is going to be wildly entertaining," she says with a twinkle in her eye, scooting the plate closer to me.

"Tell me how many to eat."

"Pardon?" she asks. She couldn't be cuter when she says that word, either.

"How many wings should I eat?"

"How is that up to me, Tommy Landen?" She laughs.

I can't imagine the look on my face when she's laughing and saying my name. If Chuck were here, I'm sure he'd tell the whole table what's so obvious to him.

"Last year I did worse, so I need motivation," I tell her.

"And how on earth does me picking a number motivate you?"

"You're not the only one who does well with instructions," I say quietly so only Sam can hear and those blue eyes widen. "Just trust me, it will help me."

She pauses. "Do you want to win this year?"

I nod.

She looks at Mark who already took his first bite and is letting out a deep breath. "One full dozen."

"Done," I say and grab the wing on top. The vinegar in the sauce hits my nose before the pepper smell and I look at Sam watching me as I bite down, knowing it'll be a little bit before the full effects of the heat are felt.

I finish off the first one and grab my second right before Mark. It's never a race for who can finish first, and some years we've drawn it out, but I feel like something's on the line. That if I can pull this off, it'll be a sign to officially ask her out. I can practically hear Bryant telling me that's some stupid-ass logic. But there's almost a panic in my chest that this is my big shot. That tonight is the subtle shift.

Oh God. I'm on my third wing and the spice is starting to hit. Still, I reach for my fourth.

"It's okay to only eat three. I swear my eyes are going to start watering from just being near a sauce this spicy." Sam's frown is adorable.

"Someone has to dethrone Mark," I say between bites. My lips are already tingling.

"In your dreams, Tommy," Mark says.

Sharon reaches out and carefully takes one of the wings and the bleu cheese dressing. "Since neither of you will be needing this any time soon, I'll help myself to a reasonable amount of spice," she taunts.

I'm pretty sure Mark and I both glare at her because Sharon, Hank, and Sam all start laughing at once.

The distraction helps because I'm already on my sixth. I ignore Mark and focus on the wing in my hands and the woman next to me. The woman who, between giggles, is encouraging me. And then she shifts to face me better and her knee is barely resting against my thigh.

Twelve of the hottest wings in the world sounds pretty manageable right about now.

"You were amazing back there! How did you manage so many after never getting close to that before?" Sam asks as we reach my truck and I open the passenger door for her.

"Maybe I had the right cheerleader with the right instructions." I can't help myself and give her a flirtatious wink.

"I was cackling half the time," she says, sitting down.

"I think I'd eat another dozen to hear you laugh like that again."

She looks surprised. "Really?"

"It'd be worth it," I say, closing her door before I really let my mouth run.

My lips tingle from the sauce but all I want to do is kiss her until I can't see straight. Taking a deep breath as I walk in front of the cab, I try to pull it together a little more.

"Well done, Tommy," Mark calls out from his truck.

I wave to him and say, "I'm sure things will be back to normal next year."

"I don't know, we might have a true competition on our hands."

"We'll see. Drive safe."

"You, too." He gives me a wave and drives out of the parking lot, towards Barnett Farms.

I get into the driver's seat.

"Everything okay?" Sam asks, nodding towards Mark's taillights.

"Of course, I think he was happy to have someone who could keep up with him for once."

"You definitely did."

I pull out of our spot, already knowing the drive will go too fast.

"Did you have fun tonight?" I ask.

"I did." I can hear that she's smiling.

"Good. That meeting is truly the worst one we have each year but going to Maybel's helps."

"Oh, I didn't mind the meeting," she says.

I look over at her to call her bluff, but she's blushing. Biting back the sarcastic retort, I change course. "I'm sure Sharon would be happy to hear that."

"She was very thorough and I feel like I have an idea of what should happen if we get a request like that. I think I would have panicked or told someone that it wasn't possible to shut off the sprinkler system otherwise. Sometimes, I freeze up if I don't know what to do next."

"Which is why you love instructions?" I ask.

"It sounds silly, but even in social situations it helps to know what I should or shouldn't do or say. I know it's odd." She waves it off.

"But that's also just one of the reasons you're perfect for the job," I tell her, risking a glance to find her staring at me.

Pulling into a spot in front of her building, I put the truck in park and turn towards her.

"Before you say something to contradict me, let my words sink in. You really are the perfect person for this position and you prove it daily simply by being yourself. Hank doesn't beat around the bush or give unnecessary compliments and he regularly sings your praises."

Her eyes search mine in the dim light from the dashboard. I hold her gaze and wonder what's going on in that head of hers.

"Truth or dare?" I ask her.

Her nose scrunches as she considers the repercussions.

"Truth."

"What are you thinking about right now?"

"That I'd like you to come up?"

Well, that's not what I expected.

Chapter 9
Sam

"If you're asking, I'm accepting," Tommy says.

He kills the engine and looks back at me.

Oh no. I didn't just *think* about asking him into my apartment, I actually did it.

And he said yes.

"Um, let me grab all of my things," I say, gathering up everything and stuffing it into my tote. I hope I didn't just tear any pages.

Tommy gets out of the truck and walks around, clearly coming to my door.

I take a deep breath.

This is not a date. It's a work function.

I need a distraction badly.

"Truth or dare?" I ask him, having no clue what I'll think of.

"Truth."

His response is so simple, so easy going. I envy how he can go with the flow. My last ex wished I could do that, too.

"Um, have you been in the building before?" I ask, gesturing to the main entrance to the apartments. Way to go, Sam. Very smooth. Why am I so terrible around guys I like when I should be flirting?

He barks out a laugh.

"I didn't know what question to expect, but it wasn't that one," he says. "Yes, I have. The last time was probably hauling some of Caleb's things when he moved here."

"So you don't need a tour, then."

"I'll always take a tour from you."

I'm definitely blushing. We've made it into the lobby and I go directly to the stairs with Tommy about half a step behind me, his boots clicking on the tile floor in the entryway.

Before I'm able to conjure up the potential flaws he'll find once he enters my place, we reach my door. "This is it, home, sweet home."

The handle makes a soft sound as it unlatches and I open the door. My entry light is still on, of course, and Tommy quietly follows me in and takes off his hat and boots before I have a chance to reach down and slip out of mine.

He smells so darn good. It's a combination of cedar and a little garlic, which should smell terrible, but of course it doesn't.

"It's nice in here," he says, looking around. "Pretty much as I pictured it."

He's pictured my apartment?

"What doesn't quite live up to your expectations?" I ask.

Tommy looks at me with eyes that I swear could stop my heart. "Nothing about you hasn't exceeded my expectations, Samantha Davies."

I have to remind myself to take a normal breath before I physically swoon onto the floor. Is Tommy Landen actually flirting with me?

"Truth or dare?" he asks.

"Dare." My heart is pounding with the anticipation of what he might say.

"I dare you to select the first movie that pops up on your TV for us to watch."

It's so absurd that I can't stop the giggle from escaping. I can't even be a little disappointed at myself for misreading what felt like a possible kiss because he wants to stay for a full movie. Not an episode of something, not a quick board game, but a movie.

"Are you trying to give me the easy ones?" I ask.

"We both have to sit through the whole movie, so it might be torture."

"Fair enough," I say, turning on the TV and clicking on the movie.

It's a rom-com.

"Ooh, we got lucky, this one is good," he says.

"You've seen it?"

He shrugs. "Courtney and I watched it in theaters."

A little prickle of uneasiness hits me for just a moment. I know that Tommy, Avery, and Courtney are best friends, so it's not odd that he'd go to movies with them. But the idea of him going to one with just one other person makes me a touch jealous. "We can pick something—"

"And ruin your dare? Absolutely not."

I give him a smile and walk into the kitchen. "Make yourself at home. Can I get you anything?"

"Water would be lovely."

"Okay," I say, getting two glasses, dropping in some ice, and taking them to the faucet. Once they're full, I grab some blueberries and crackers. It's not the sexiest combination, even though this is definitely *not* a date, but not having snacks seems wrong.

When I come back to the living room, Tommy is seated, watching me with an easy smile. He already has two coasters on the table. This has to be one of the most enticing scenes I could have walked into. A man who thinks ahead and puts coasters out.

Oh, I'm in too deep.

"Should I hit the lamp?" he asks, nodding to his left.

"Sure," I squeak, immediately grateful he already turned to switch the light off because I know I'm blushing as if this *was* a real date.

It's not like we're going to be in the dark making out like teenagers. And I have the kitchen lights still on along with the entryway. But, as I sit down on my couch, which normally seems roomy, it feels so much more intimate without that lamp illuminating the space.

He looks completely at-ease. And completely sexy. His jeans are a relaxed fit with a worn but crisp look. And I bet he gets his shirts right out of the dryer because there aren't creases from being ironed, but they're not wrinkled either. My eyes travel up his arm as he reaches for some blueberries. They're toned without being massive, much like him. Subtly strong.

I let out a little sigh.

"You okay?" he asks, looking a little concerned.

He definitely heard the sigh, then.

"Fine, totally, fine. You?" I reply much too quickly. Way to play it cool, Sam.

There's a pause as his gaze searches my face. The crease between his eyebrows relaxes as the start of a smirk appears. "Never better."

"Shall we begin?" I ask, turning my face towards the TV.

Tommy relaxes against the couch with a soft chuckle. "We shall."

"Excellent." I grab the remote and start the movie. And then uncertainty hits me.

How the heck am I supposed to sit?

Tommy's all casual and comfortable and this is a two-seater so by the time we're both lounging, there won't be much wiggle room. I should have bought a different couch. A bigger couch. One that affords more seating arrangement options.

Specifically for the occasion when my crush happens to come up after a work event.

I can't lean back because then it'll look like I'm trying to seduce him and he's been a perfect gentleman. A perfect friend.

"Truth or dare," he says, interrupting my spiral.

I look at him, which is my first mistake because he looks like he's right at home here.

"Dare," I say, likely my second mistake.

"I dare you to relax and let that brain of yours enjoy this movie."

I open my mouth to respond.

And close it.

"How do you…"

"…know what's going on in your head?" he finishes for me. "Just a lucky guess."

He puts his right arm across the top of the sofa and pats it. "Come on. This is your place, just tell me what I can do to make you more comfortable."

"It should be the other way around, you know," I point out.

"Maybe, but what *should* be isn't always what happens."

Isn't that the truth?

Chapter 10
Tommy

Don't push her. The goal is to do things completely right with Sam.

Now my arm is stuck on top of the couch like I'm going to drop it over her shoulders. Not that I haven't dreamt of it.

"You're right," she says, taking a strengthening breath and on the exhale, she stiffly melts into the couch. Somehow. It's absolutely adorable how hard she's trying to relax and be proper at the same time.

"Truth or dare," she whispers, eyes glued on the first scene.

"Truth."

She fiddles with her nails for a moment before purposefully flattening her hands on her thighs.

Still looking forward, she asks, "Where do you...want...your arm?"

Even with the lamp off, I can see the blush creeping up her neck and onto her cheeks, giving me the confidence to give her the full truth.

"Around you," I say, quickly adding, "only if you are receptive to that, though."

Damn it, I can feel myself blushing as my heart races.

She swallows visibly and bites her lower lip. Shit, the things I would do...

"I would be," she says, her voice still quiet, her eyes now staring down at her hands.

Thump-thump. Thump-thump. The thundering of my heart drowns out the sound of the rom-com. She looks nervous, like she's worried she said the wrong thing. Her cheeks, even seen through this dim lighting, are crimson.

The immediate urge to bring her confident side back out has my hand snaking down so I can wrap my fingers around her bare shoulder. It shouldn't be legal for someone to have skin this soft.

She smiles and I give a little tug and say, "I think you'll be more comfortable over here. I know I will be."

That seems to help her relax. Having instructions might be a love language in itself for her.

I can do that, I think, tucking her against me.

"Sam," I say.

"Yes?" she asks, still nervous.

"Relax," I whisper.

"Sorry."

I take my free hand and put two fingers under her chin so she's looking at me. "You have nothing to apologize for."

Sam swallows hard and her eyes drift to my lips and snap back up to my gaze.

"Okay, I can relax."

"You sure? Do you need anything else?"

"You're the guest here, I should be asking you that," she says, swatting my abs.

My fingers drop her chin and capture her hand, causing her to let out a little gasp. Oh God, now I want to know how else to get her to make that sound.

Our eyes lock and she shifts a little. Just enough to make it easier for her to face me. My body sings at every individual point of contact as I lace our fingers together. I tip my head down an inch, ignoring how painful everything is in my pants at this point. She tilts her head back a little more, her breath brushing across my lips in tantalizing waves.

Bam!

Sam squeals and her whole body starts, squeezing my hand instead of pulling hers away.

I groan, forgetting that this movie starts with a door slamming right when we meet one of the main characters. Maybe my blood will start flowing to my brain for a few minutes and give my dick a break.

"Time to watch?" I ask her.

"Probably," she says with a soft laugh. "Will I jump out of my skin again?"

"I don't think so. But I assume this means we're lucky it wasn't a slasher film?"

"Oh that would not have been good. I would have kept my eyes closed for most of it and would probably hum so I wouldn't hear much."

"I'll be sure to keep that in mind for future movie nights."

I tuck her back into me and this time she relaxes and rests her head on my chest, our hands still woven together. I memorize everything about this moment. My head relaxes against the back of the couch and I feel my smile grow as I breathe in her perfume that has a subtle floral scent that I can't quite pinpoint.

I'm definitely not washing this shirt for a while.

Chapter 11
Sam

How can I be so comfortable and so stressed out at the same time?

Tommy feels like heaven and smells even better. He probably shouldn't smell good after wolfing down twelve hot wings in a bar that, unsurprisingly, smells like fried food. There's a little bit of that lingering on him, but the cedar and mint combination is coming through tenfold with my cheek resting against his chest.

Well, it's on his right pec, to be specific.

Now I'm wondering what this pec looks like.

And his whole torso... and back.

Who am I kidding? I want to know what this man looks like in his birthday suit.

And for once, I'm thinking there's a chance, because this feels like a date.

I don't think I talked him into anything. Did I?

No, Tommy's got the biggest heart, but he wouldn't do something he wasn't comfortable with.

I let out a little sigh as his fingers lightly trail from my elbow to my shoulder and back down, leaving goosebumps in their wake.

Looking down at our hands, I realize that mine isn't sweaty. For all that my brain is wondering about what the heck we're doing, and not doing, something with Tommy soothes me. And turns me on. Especially since I can feel his abs. He's not flexing or anything like that, but they're definitely there.

From years of working on the ranch...throwing bales of hay, riding horses, moving feed, and who knows what else.

We shift every now and then, and I pull my feet up onto the sofa, but things are easy and unpressured. And then the movie ends and I realize I have no plan or protocol for what comes next.

"So?" Tommy asks.

So, what? So are we going back to my room? So what now? So...nice to see you?

"Um," I begin, totally unsure how to tell what I was thinking he might have meant.

"What'd you think?" he asks, nodding toward the rolling credits.

I let out a nervous laugh. Of course that's what he was wondering.

"Where'd your mind go?" he asks, amusement sparkling in his eyes as I sit up so I can face him.

We disentangle and I run both hands down my face, groaning.

"It was really cute," I tell him, attempting to avoid his second question.

He pulls my hands away from my face. "Please don't feel like you have to hide, not from me."

There's a gentle command in his eyes. But I still feel like I have complete control of the situation. How the hell does he do that?

"No hiding, I can do that. But you might have to remind me every now and then," I tell him.

His eyes soften and he smiles. "I can keep that in mind. But I should get going, it's technically past my bedtime."

That answers the bedroom question.

"Of course, same here." As if I'm going to fall asleep after he leaves. My head is already spinning.

Tommy grabs the glasses in one hand and the snacks in the others. I stare for a moment. He has some big hands.

And now I'm thinking about what else might be comparable in size as he walks to the kitchen.

Man, he has a cute butt. Especially in those jeans.

"You can just—"

"Truth or dare," he says, cutting me off.

Narrowing my eyes at him because I don't know where this is going, I take the brave route. "Dare."

"I dare you stand there and let me put this all away."

My mouth falls open as I take a breath to speak. But nothing comes out.

Tommy looks smug and watches me.

The only sound I make is a pathetic squeaking one because my brain is not sure that it processed his last statement correctly.

"Do you accept?" he asks.

At least his prompting pushes my brain into an automatic response. "Yes."

"Excellent," he says, looking at the bottom of the glasses. "Dishwasher safe. Do you hand-wash these anyway?"

I shake my head. *What is this man up to?*

He opens the dishwasher and I groan because it's half-full. Which means dirty dishes. He's seeing my leftovers.

It's not like he's rifling through my dirty clothes, I remind myself.

Tommy pulls out the top rack, placing the glasses next to the three already there. He leaves the same amount of space between each one as I did and puts his hand on the end of the rack to push it in and pauses.

I look up and find his eyes on me.

"What are you going to change?" he asks.

"What do you mean?"

"When I leave, are you going to move these into a different place?" he clarifies.

"Actually, no."

"Okay," he says, closing the dishwasher until it clicks. He reaches for the cracker box, with those big hands of his, on the counter. Instead of grabbing the bag right away, he looks inside the box for a moment and gently unfolds it. He pours the crackers back into the bag, refolds it just as it was, and closes the box. The mixture of attraction and confusion at what I'm witnessing is unbelievable. No one has ever done anything like this before.

"Would you like to point to the cupboard where these belong or do I get to explore?" he asks.

This is the most bizarre dare I've ever experienced. I'm sure that Tommy would be incredibly amusing while trying to locate the right spot, but my hand has a mind of its own and points to the one next to the fridge. Half a heartbeat later, he's looking inside and setting the box in the one open space.

"What will you change when I leave?" he asks.

"That box sits on its side because it's easier to see the flavor from the top flaps." I cringe. I shouldn't have said that. It's better to keep those quirks quiet.

"Ooh, smart." He tips the box over and pushes it back in.

What? That's his response? Nothing about me being neurotic like my ex said?

As my brain tries to go down a rabbit hole, Tommy already has his face in the fridge. The door shuts and he pours the blueberries gently into their container.

"I don't think I need any pointers for where this goes." And he winks at me.

About blueberries.

Actually, he winks at me about putting blueberries properly away in my fridge.

Oh my, I have never been more attracted to another person in my entire life.

Chapter 12
Tommy

This is definitely a date, and you can kiss on a date.

But it was connected to a work function. With her boss. No kissing.

God damn it, my head is a mess. I have Chuck's voice screaming at me to make a real move and a little voice, that's fucking persistent, telling me to take it easy. I got to hold her for almost two hours for crying out loud. The smell of her lightly floral perfume on the collar of my shirt drifts up to my nose as a reminder and I'm sure my chest smells even better where she rested against me.

Closing the refrigerator and glancing at her hands, I'm reminded of how much softer they were than I could have imagined. Grabbing the plate and bowl, I put them into the dishwasher, feeling her eyes following my every move. "Alright, final judgment."

She hesitates and bites her lip.

"Don't hold back on me now, Sam."

"The bowl goes on the top rack," she says, scrunching her nose and looking adorable.

Nodding, I move the bowl to the other rack where it seems like it fits the best.

"Perfect," she says.

The smile on her face has nerves exploding in my gut. She's relaxed with me here. With me learning how to load the dishwasher the way she likes. In ways that would be normal if we were together.

Part of me wants to tell that little voice telling me that I want to give her a great first date to shut the fuck up so I can pick her up, set her on the counter, and kiss her until we're both gasping for air.

I let out a little sigh, knowing that letting her see me as someone who isn't just interested in a quickie, but who wants everything with her, is what she needs to feel all the way to her bones.

"Well, it's past my bedtime, so I better be on my way."

"You've mentioned that," she says, letting out a small laugh.

"I guess I did," I reply as lamely as I feel.

Why couldn't I have an ounce of Chuck's swagger?

She leads the way to the door and I slip my feet into my boots and put my hat on, feeling like a middle school kid on his first date.

It's not a date, I remind myself.

"Truth or dare," Sam says, looking down at the deadbolt as she unlocks it.

My heart pounds. "Truth."

Still looking down, she asks, "What are you thinking right now?"

"That tonight wasn't a date."

"Oh," she says, turning her head fully away from me.

My left hand reaches in front of her until it rests on her right hip and gently guides her so she's facing me. My other hand goes under her chin, tipping her head up until her eyes meet mine, the embarrassment written plain as day on her face.

Once her eyes lock with mine, I continue, "That because it wasn't one, I don't get to give you a proper kiss goodnight."

Her mouth parts and her eyes soften.

"And I hope that when I ask you on a real date, you might say yes," I finish.

My head tilts to the side and I hold her chin gently in place. I don't have to bend down terribly far, which is a nice change, Sam is the perfect height for me. It takes every ounce of self-control to only place my lips lightly on her cheek. I linger for a moment, savoring her sharp intake of breath, the feel of her skin against my lips, and the smell of her.

"Goodnight, Samantha Davies," I whisper, forcing myself to release her, put my hand on the doorknob, and stand to my full height.

Her eyes slowly open and trail from my chest to meet mine, giving me time to take in the flush on her cheeks.

"Goodnight, Thomas Landen," she whispers back.

Reluctantly, I open the door, tip my hat with my free hand and command my feet to take me to the hallway. I only turn around once to send her a smile, taking one last look at her watching me from her doorway. The stairs ground me in reality and I pause just for a second, briskly rubbing my cheeks. I whisper, "It's time to bring your A game, Tommy Landen," and take the steps two at a time.

The air is chilly outside as I walk to my truck without staring up at her window to see if she's watching me leave. At least not until I get to my door.

She's at the window, giving me a little wave.

As I wave back and get into the driver's seat, my phone buzzes. Smiling, I pull it out of my pocket and then my heart feels like it's on the pavement. I squeeze my eyes shut tight to fight off the nausea that usually hits when Maisy decides to reach out because I'm flooded with shame.

After a moment, my breath comes steadily and I start the engine. Sam doesn't need to see me deal with Maisy's crap, but I doubt she can still see me with the headlights on, so I roll down my window and wave once more at the woman of my dreams while I pull out of the parking lot.

"You've got this," I reassure myself, trying to keep the building panic that I'm nowhere good enough for someone as incredible as Sam at bay. Doubts rush my brain. Every little comment about how charming, sexy, and mysterious my brothers are I've heard over the years. All the reasons Maisy had to cheat on me for so long...and for me to remain oblivious.

My thoughts unwillingly go to the latest set of texts I got from my ex saying she was moving back soon. Maisy truly has nothing to say to me that I want to hear anymore. I know I'll eventually look at the message because she might be telling me she's never coming back to Greenstone and I can breathe easy. Or that she'll be here in a few days and I can get our first face-to-face meeting since she left out of the way once and for all. I toss my phone to the passenger seat, turn up the radio, and drive home, focusing on the amazing night I just had, letting the smell of Sam's perfume on my shirt keep me in this moment.

Chapter 13
Sam

Talk about an exit.

Holy cow, my heart is still pounding.

I need to leave the window, he drove away a full minute ago, but I swear my brain and body are both trying to figure out what all happened. For a moment, I thought I misread everything and that my worst fears of having a chance with Tommy Landen were almost within my grasp and then torn away.

Well, being friend-zoned is definitely not at the top of my list, but I'd rather have that and clear boundaries than thinking he might feel the same and turn out to be completely wrong. The embarrassment alone would be enough to create an awkward rift that I'm sure would never be filled and I wouldn't even have him as a friend.

Finally, I move to the couch and curl up against the spot that smells like him, the cedar lingered the most. I know that I must look like some love-sick puppy right about now, but I haven't felt this comfortable with someone, so cared for, so loved. Not that he loves me or is even thinking too much about things, but he seems interested. I can't remember the last time I was held like that.

Intrusive thoughts keep trying to, well, intrude, on my moments of bliss. Reminders of Brad, in particular.

Nope, we're not going there.

And I'm sure Tommy is attentive in bed. He is in everything else he does. Maybe I'll finally figure out how to have good sex.

A laugh bursts out of me at the absurdity of that thought.

But I sober quickly, now trying to not go down a rabbit hole for why I've never had an orgasm with anything, or anyone, inside of me. I've read enough to know that not everyone has the same g-spot sensations, but that doesn't mean I haven't tried to figure it out. And apparently I'm really good at faking it.

Why do I have a feeling Tommy isn't going to be satisfied with me faking it? I'm both thrilled and terrified at that prospect.

Pulling out my phone, I go with my gut, for once, before I can overthink things.

Sam: I enjoyed our not-date. Cheers to the hot wings champion of the year!

Something about Tommy makes me feel brave, and I'm going to lean into that. I'm going to stop hiding.

Maybe not stopping altogether, old habits die hard and all...

But still, this fresh start in Greenstone might mean more than just doing what I love. It might mean a happier Samantha, too.

"Sam," Hank calls out. "You've been working without moving for at least two hours. We can't have you developing carpal tunnel anytime soon."

Wrapping up the sentence in the email I'm replying to, I look up. Oof. The last time I looked at the clock on the wall was almost three hours ago.

"I guess I was in the zone," I tell him.

"You're easily the most efficient person we've ever had, but you need a break. Why don't you take a long lunch and start now?"

Hank holds up one hand as my mouth opens to protest. "I insist. Until we get the budget approved, you'll have blown through your entire year's worth of duties by the end of this month, we have to spread things out and I won't let you work ahead without getting compensated, Sam."

My cheeks heat at the mention of how far ahead I am. I used to be paranoid about how much I was doing each hour and found when I hide the clock on my computer, I get in the zone so much better and my productivity almost doubled.

"Thanks, I'll take you up on that and I'll be back by noon."

"Twelve-thirty, please."

"Twelve-thirty, then."

I'm already packing up my binders when Hank clears his throat.

"I'll just take my binder for the co-op," I tell him, setting two of the binders back on my desk.

"You do unplug after you leave for the day, right?" he asks, not for the first time.

"Of course, but if I don't have something to take notes with and I get an idea, I fixate on it until I can write it down, so I promise my binders not only help me stay organized, but they really do help me unplug."

He nods and says, "Good."

"I'll be back soon. Can I get you anything?" I ask.

"This is your lunch, Sam, not time to run errands for the office, but I appreciate it all the same."

My tote is ready so I leave out the side door of our suite which takes me right to the parking lot. My sedan chirps as it unlocks and seeing that the sky is clear, I decide to see if the cafe has any tables open on their back patio.

As usual, there are only a few cars on the roads, especially since most people aren't taking their lunch breaks yet, and there are a few spots open in front of the cafe. I park, grab my tote, and walk into the calm space. Sarah is at the counter, cleaning the espresso machine, when the bell above the door jingles.

"Sam, lovely to see you! I don't think I have a group order that came through," she says with a frown while unlocking her tablet.

"I'm just here for lunch, I have a longer break today."

"Oh excellent," she says, looking back up at me. "Would you like your regular?"

My heart warms. I have a regular order that the owner knows just like those born here in Greenstone.

"Yes, please. If there's space, I'll sit out back," I say, smiling at her.

I pay and while Sarah pours me an iced coffee with a splash of oat milk, I look at the mural along the wall. Something about it draws my eye every time I'm here. Maybe one day I'll meet the artist, Fiona.

"That sounds like a great plan with this weather, I'll bring your food out when it's ready."

"Thank you so much," I tell her, taking the coffee and weaving my way through a few tables, only seeing a few people seated, and they're either on their phone or their device. The door to the patio is propped open and a soft breeze is coming through. I already feel the tension from work dissipating as I set my tote on a chair next to the table in the corner.

My watch vibrates.

Tommy: Can I pick you up for the meeting tonight?

I pull my phone out and start typing, my heart fluttering.

Sam: Of course. Can I pick up beverages this time?

Tommy: You can.

Tommy: Can I take you out for dinner on Thursday?

Tommy: To be perfectly transparent, I'm asking you on a date.

I couldn't hide my smile if I wanted to.

Tommy Landen just asked me out on a date.

Chapter 14
Tommy

I think I laid the groundwork well for this. But I'm definitely floundering now that I sent the text. I push my phone just out of arm's reach on the desk so I don't send her more messages while she thinks things over.

It's only eleven. Huh, she usually doesn't text much until her lunch break.

My phone vibrates just before I'm about to sit on my hands since I have more questions. Legitimate, normal questions, not panic-induced babbling.

Sam: Decaf for you?

I groan. Of course she's answering the messages in order.

Tommy: Surprise me.

She's typing.

My leg starts to twitch as I stare at the three dots that don't go away.

Shit, did I totally misread everything the other night? She sent a flirty text that night and I replied, doing my best to ignore Maisy's message.

The dots leave the screen and I frown, now worrying that I messed up. Maybe I didn't mess up. Maybe I'm just not the guy for her. I wince at the physical pain that brings to my chest.

Rubbing my sternum, I try to ease the building pressure.

Calm down, Tommy Landen. You know she stresses about her words. Don't assume the worst in her just because—

The front door swings open with much more force than is necessary and Bryant comes in caked with mud from head to toe. He looks like he's about to murder someone.

"Dare I ask?" I venture, grateful for his timing.

He kicks off his boots and I see his jaw clenching over and over, still fuming.

"No."

Well, I didn't expect to get much more of an explanation from him, especially looking like that.

"Want coffee ready for when you're clean?" I ask.

He takes a deep breath in through his nose. "Please."

"On it." I reach for my phone and slip it in my jeans as I walk to the kitchen. Since it's after eleven, the other guys will be in soon for lunch, so I brew a full pot. I consider setting out the whiskey, but they're all going right back outside with the animals, so they can't partake.

My pocket vibrates and my nerves return tenfold. I take a deep breath before I pull my phone out and unlock it.

Sam: Sorry for the delay! Hank called to remind me to not work right now. For full transparency, I'm saying yes to going on a date with you on Thursday. Where would you like to go? I'll start studying the menu on my break!

Nothing could stop my smile. Not even Matt and Caleb barreling through the front door. They're not quite as caked as Bryant, but whatever went down didn't leave them unscathed.

I burst out laughing. "Do I get to know what happened now?"

"We were going to try getting someone on the new mare today."

Caleb waves at me, "We attempted to get my ass in the saddle. As you might have guessed by my appearance, I didn't make it."

I rush a few steps over to him, "Shit, are you okay?"

Matt swats me away. "He never got a boot in the stirrup, he's okay. We had a helmet on him the whole time, too."

"Did the doctor give the okay for him to ride a horse that has only recently gotten used to wearing a saddle?" I ask, looking at them both suspiciously.

"I was cleared to ride." There's a stubborn set to Caleb's jaw as he says it.

Matt smacks Caleb in the chest. "Are you saying you were, in fact, cleared for all styles of riding? Because that's what you've been inferring."

Caleb closes his mouth as he stares at my youngest brother whose face goes through about ten different emotions before he lets loose.

"What the fuck are you trying to do? Do you want to go back to the hospital for another month? I was there with you, and I'm not going to let you do something bone-headed just because you're bored or think you have something to prove to the cowboys traveling with the rodeo," Matt fumes.

"And what, I wasn't there? I was the one in the goddamn bed, hooked up to monitors, getting my ass wiped by nurses while in a neck brace and two casts."

This is definitely not something I want to get in the middle of. These two have been friends for a long time, but we were all surprised that Caleb's one person who could come to the hospital was Matt. Not even his agent had access to him. I mean, this whole thing has to still be hard on him. He's made a small fortune in the rodeo circuit and we're six months out from his last ride, and he still can't let loose like he seems to be born to do.

I walk back to the desk and I hear Matt's voice soften. Turning up the speakers, I drown out their conversation and return to the one on my phone.

Tommy: Sorry, apparently the new mare wasn't keen on the idea of someone riding her today and people are coming in hot for lunch. I know we just went for wings, but what if we did Maybel's? Their Thursday evening chef always has something new to try and last week it was an Italian beef dish. You game?

Sam: Oh my, is everyone okay?

I can imagine her confused face at the thought that a horse might not be ready to have a person hop on its back, let alone the time it takes for them to be comfortable with a saddle. She's typing immediately.

Sam: Maybel's sounds great. I should be done well before 2 for the next while until Hank can present the justification for more tasks for my position, so I'll have more time for co-op and dinners.

Sam: I mean, if you want to have dinner again.

The dots pop up and go way over and over while I type my reply. I can practically see the blush on her face as she tries to backpedal assuming there will be more dates.

Tommy: I think just bruised egos over here.

Tommy: Perfect. How about a matinee before dinner since you're off early? I can sneak out. I happen to have an in with the guy who runs the office at Landen Acres.

Sam: Oh good, I'm glad there's no lasting damage. How long does it take to be able to ride a horse?

Sam: A matinee before dinner sounds perfect. You pick the show and tell me what time.

Tommy: I promise to not pick anything that I know will make you jump.

Tommy: You should come out sometime in the afternoon after you're done and see the horses we have. Maybe Friday?

Wow, that was smooth. If Chuck were reading over my shoulder he'd smack me upside the back of the head for being desperate. But I suppose I am. I'm desperate to be around her. Desperate to hold her again. Desperate to breathe in that floral perfume and have it linger on my clothes.

Desperate to kiss her.

Chapter 15
Sam

Butterflies explode in my stomach.

Friday?

I get to see Tommy tonight for the subcommittee meeting, one that he recently joined for reasons I won't allow myself to examine. Tomorrow for a real date. I re-read the text just to make sure it wasn't in my head. Nope, not in my head.

Tomorrow, I have an actual date with Tommy. Math-loving, horse-riding, cowboy-hat-wearing, thoughtful Tommy Landen. The man who held my hand and tucked me against him for an entire rom-com. The one who tells me not to hide. The one who knew I'd want to write my ideas down right before his annual wing-eating-contest.

The one who sees *me*.

Sam: Friday it is. Will we be outside or inside? I'm not riding that mare, am I? Am I riding any horse? I've never done that...

Tommy: We'll be calling you a cowgirl before you know it. But no, you won't be riding the new mare...not even Caleb managed getting close enough today.

A sense of relief washes over me. Logically, I know that no one would ever put a novice on a mare an award-winning rider couldn't mount today. But I don't know the etiquette around horses. There seem to be rules, but you can't shake a horse's hoof. Well, I suppose you can. But not the way you would with a person.

Sam: Thanks for not throwing me into the deep end.

Tommy: I'd never.

Tommy: Not that you're a person who's meant to spend her life in the kiddie pool, but we don't have to go from zero to what sounds like bucking-bronco-level on day one. We'll explore and take our time.

My cheeks burn at his casual confidence in me. He doesn't speak to me like I'm incapable due to my inexperience. He doesn't push me to do something I'm not ready for. He just seems to know that I'll get there.

Sam: Am I correct that rhinestone boots won't do the trick on Friday?

Tommy: You might want your turquoise boots, if you're okay with them getting dirty.

He remembers my other pair of cowboy boots? Or cowgirl, I suppose?

Sam: Jeans and a flannel shirt?

Jeans I have, but a sturdy flannel shirt is something I'll have to pick up. I have, what someone might consider, "work appropriate" flannel where the material is thinner and the buttons are delicate. I think my long-sleeve shirts that I clean in would be sturdier, to be honest. I add a note in my phone to stop at the general store.

Tommy: Jeans that aren't ones you love. If you don't have a flannel shirt, come in a t-shirt and you can wear one of mine.

Reading that one a second and third time, my heart skips a few beats. I have to bite my lip to keep my smile slightly in-check in case someone comes out here to claim a table.

Sam: I just might take you up on that.

Tommy: Much better than a stiff new one. You won't be able to relax.

Sam: I'm not sure I'll really relax around animals taller than me...but I'll try.

Tommy: I'll keep you safe, I promise.

Sam: Oh, I didn't doubt that for a second.

Tommy: Excellent - just wanted to make sure. See you tonight?

Sam: Text me when you're on your way and I'll have drinks.

He likes my message and Sarah comes out with my turkey and cheese panini with a salad on the side, no onions.

"Thank you," I tell her, already putting a napkin on my lap and setting my phone to the side.

"You're welcome. Let me know if you need anything else."

I take my first bite of the panini and it's delicious, if a little hot. Instead of pulling out a notebook or a binder, I take Hank's advice and relax. It takes a moment to turn my brain off of work and the co-op, but I manage to let the tension in my shoulders dissipate.

This town is truly starting to feel like my new home. Of course I had high hopes when I applied. I remember my shock when they reached out to tell me they wanted an interview and that shock only grew when they offered me the position.

This town is gorgeous in its quaint ways. People might be private, but they're kind and they're here for each other. No one has been short with me or unwelcoming. I can tell when I've asked too many questions, but that's nothing new.

I consider texting Avery so she can meet us at Landen Acres on Friday, but maybe I'll just let her know the next time I go… Yeah, that sounds like the better plan. Tommy said we'd be seeing the horses, so I'm not sure how much time we'll spend chatting about the next steps for the co-op.

Rolling my shoulders back, I release the remaining tension from sitting at my computer for so long. Shifting my chair so I'm alongside the table, I put my plate on my lap and my iced coffee within reach. Without spilling all over my blouse, I tip my head back so the sun is shining on my face between bites until everything is gone.

Of course there are cafes in the city, but the lack of constant sound surrounding me is heavenly. I hear Sarah stacking dishes inside, the occasional ring of the bell as customers come in and out, but there are birds singing. They're not drowned out by the noise of traffic.

I suddenly sit up, my eyes wide, reaching for my phone in a panic. I have a date with Tommy *tomorrow* and I have to find something to eat that won't make me ill.

But when I unlock my phone to find a message from Tommy. It's simply a link to the menu at Maybel's. And just like that, my stress is gone as I study my options for tomorrow.

Chapter 16
Tommy

Bryant comes through the door and this time, he's only slightly muddy.

"At least you didn't get kicked today," I say.

"I suppose there's that." He sounds exhausted simply putting his boots away. "Please tell me I remembered to put the steaks in the fridge last night."

"They're thawed out. Want me to do anything to them while you go soak? You look terrible."

He waves a hand in dismissal. "Nah, I'll be down in plenty of time. Jax is at his place so it's just the four of us, right?"

"I have to leave before six, so just talk Caleb into staying and he'll replace me."

"What do you have?"

"Didn't get to talk much to your wolf-dog today?" I joke. Bryant's not chatty on a good day. And today was *not* good for them.

"Someone's got to keep tabs on you, Chuck, and Matt," he mumbles.

Huh. I didn't expect that.

I clear my throat at the thought of Bryant feeling like he has to fill the shoes of both Jackson and our father. "There's a meeting for planning the next few city movie nights. I joined the sub-committee."

"Why?" He doesn't ask it with judgment, just confusion and curiosity.

"It's good to be involved, we need to have at least one movie in color this summer, and I might be picking up Samantha for it."

"Finally."

I want to ask him how he knew anything but he's already walking past the kitchen to his room.

She said yes to a real date *and* to coming here on Friday, I might as well warm my brothers up to the idea of me bringing someone around again so they don't treat her like Courtney and Avery.

Oh God. Why did I invite her here in the afternoon? And why this week? All four of my brothers are going to think I can't set up a real date. I run a hand down my face in defeat.

Chuck is never going to let me live this down.

As if on cue, Chuck's cackle and Matt's groan carry through the window just before the front door opens. Matt's face is bright red, while Chuck looks smug. Caleb brings up the rear, looking sheepish with his hands buried in his front pockets.

"How're the girls?" I ask Chuck, sensing Matt would prefer to not have attention on him.

"Amazing. But that's not surprising because they are mine," he says, giving me that cocky grin and his stupid toothpick flip that seems to charm the boots off any woman in a thirty-mile radius.

My eyes roll entirely by reflex. "Ugh, your brothers are immune to your swagger. Save it for the vet when half the herd gets a bug."

"Oh, there's plenty for her," he says with a smirk.

"I thought she wasn't dating anyone," Caleb pipes up, his boots off.

"I'm working on it," Chuck says.

"Seriously? Don't you dare piss her off." Matt smacks Chuck across the chest.

"I said I was working on it, not mauling her." He rolls his eyes. "She won't even realize she's falling for me."

Three of us sigh in unison.

"You all know I would never jeopardize the ranch or my ladies. I'm not being rash." Matt narrows his eyes at Chuck as he continues to defend himself. "Seriously. Have I ever given anyone a reason to doubt me?"

Three sets of eyebrows raise in his direction.

"No, really," he explains. "I haven't once been a dick to someone I was dating or hoping to date. And everyone else knew exactly what we were doing."

"Just don't fuck things up. She's amazing for this town," I say.

"Ye of little faith." Chuck saunters to the stairs, going to his room.

"Can you stay for dinner?" I ask, turning to Caleb. "Bryant is making enough for all four of us, but I have a meeting that I'm leaving for soon, and you could likely use a pile of protein after dealing with the mare today."

Matt musses Caleb's hair, making an odd picture since Caleb's older. "He's staying. The man can burn soup and is not to be trusted to cook edible food for himself."

Caleb tries to hold back a smile. "I suppose I can let Bryant bribe me with his grilling skills. Maybe he can give me some pointers."

"Maybe you'll be part of the dinner rotation here," I say.

"No, you're not learning from Bryant. You'll never eat a vegetable with any color for the rest of your life," Matt says.

"That's fair," I agree.

"Okay, maybe I'll just stick with lessons from the Landen brother who already keeps me healthy."

Matt blushes again.

"Why don't you two get cleaned up? You can snag a pair of my sweats if you'd like, you and I are closer in size," I say to Caleb. "Actually, you should just keep a few sets of clothes here. You could keep them in one of the extra bedrooms."

It's clear he's about to protest so I put a hand up.

"You're starting to work here more and more. Plus, we con you into eating with us a lot, so you can crash here when you like. Just think about it." I pat Caleb on the shoulder. "I'm going to grab a bite now before my meeting."

As I turn to go into the kitchen, I catch a glimpse of Matt looking confused. But he clears his expression right away and he goes upstairs with his buddy. *What the heck was that all about?*

Before anyone can give me shit about my meal preferences, I grab leftover rice, chicken, and some fresh veggies, making a quick fried rice.

For some reason, I'm feeling calm about tonight. Maybe it's because it's not a date. Or another non-date.

Oh shit. Is this a terrible idea to be on so many things together? She seems interested, lord knows why. But she seemed genuinely disappointed the other night before I finished saying that it hadn't been a date, but a work thing.

Or is she just interested for now?

The clamping of my stomach has me shaking my head. I don't let myself go down that old road. Fuck, because of Maisy, I have doubts creeping into my head that didn't exist before shit went south.

It's high time I get over the damage she left me with.

Chapter 17
Sam

I can't believe I almost put the wrong binder in my tote for the meeting. Now I'm double-checking that my pens are in there, too, before going to the kitchen.

Sarah gave me two iced coffees to-go, just without the ice before I left, so I take them out of the fridge along with my ice tray. I smile as I loosen the cubes and put five in Tommy's and four in mine. Filling the tray back up, I pop it back into the freezer and my bracelets jingle.

Making my mind up to wait outside, I take the drinks, my tote, and my sunglasses to the door and slip on my strappy sandals. I leave the light on just inside the door, pull out my keys, and throw the deadbolt, somehow balancing the coffees with one hand. Tommy wouldn't have an issue holding both in one hand. They're huge.

A flush creeps up my neck and my cheeks.

Now is *not* the time to think about the size of anything on Tommy Landen.

I open the front door to the building and Tommy's truck is about to turn into the parking lot. He waves at me and, instead of pulling up right in front of me, he parks in a spot, gets out, and opens the passenger door for me.

"You didn't have to do that," I tell him.

"And miss a chance to say hello?"

"I'm about to get into your car, we could have chatted in there."

There's a sparkle in his eye. "I know, but then I wouldn't have been able to open the door for you."

I hold my tongue because I'm quite sure he could have leaned over to pop the passenger door ajar for me. I've had plenty of experience with that.

"Thank you," I say, realizing that we're only standing a foot apart and he's slightly in the way of me getting in, but I don't mind in the least.

"What'd you grab?" he asks.

"Half-caf."

"Can't go wrong there." He holds out a hand to take them. "Here, you hop in and I'll pass them to you to put in the cup holders."

"Thanks," I say, watching him put both in one hand.

"What?"

Oh my, I'm blushing.

"Nothing," I squeak. In an attempt to avoid a no doubt awkward conversation, I quickly step into the cab of his truck. Even in my embarrassment, something about this seat is feeling more and more comfortable. It's a silly thing to be thinking, especially right now.

"Okay," he says, drawing out the syllables. Our fingers touch as I transfer them to the holders and the best kind of shiver rolls through me. My door shuts and Tommy makes his way around and gets into the driver's seat. As usual, he smells amazing.

"You have everything you need?"

"Yep," I reply, knowing my cheeks are less red at this point. I hope so.

He turns on the radio, playing country music at a low volume so we can talk about our days as if we didn't text every few hours. Everything is easy. Comfortable.

Well, it's comfortable when I avoid looking at his hands.

What the heck has gotten into me? I'm not someone who has ever obsessed over the size of a guy's *thing*, so why do I keep thinking about Tommy's?

He clears his throat.

"I'm sorry, did you say something?" I ask, seeing that we're already parked.

"No, you seem to be deep in thought."

How embarrassing.

"How long have we been here?"

"Not long," he says with a smile. "But you're okay?"

I breathe in, letting that cedar and garlic smell center me. "I'm okay, truly."

I leave off the fact that I'm now curious what his, well, his penis looks like. If I want to see it, I better get used to at least thinking the word. It's not like I have to say it.

I snort out a laugh, imagining myself asking Tommy Landen if I can see his penis.

"Did I miss something?" he asks, a curious look on his face.

Busted.

"Um, nothing, just remembering something funny from work."

"Uh-huh," he says skeptically, watching me a little longer.

I squirm under his gaze until he puts a knuckle under my chin so I'm looking him in the eye.

"No hiding, remember?"

I swallow. Maybe it's not such a crazy question. For later.

"It's something to be shared after tomorrow, if ever."

"Samantha Davies," he says. "Are you blushing about our date?"

Hearing him say it out loud tonight has me feeling all sorts of things. Things that are most certainly *not* helpful to feel before walking into a room with your boss and a few other people.

I clear my throat the way I assume a trained debutante would and say in a terrible southern drawl, "Now why ever would I do that, Thomas Landen?"

He breaks out laughing until he snorts. My nerves and excitement have me giggling like a proverbial schoolgirl.

Hank walks in front of the truck to go into the building and we both quiet down to the occasional chuckle.

"We'll make a true cowgirl out of you, just you wait and see." He reaches across the center console and tucks a piece of hair behind my ear. "I have an extra-early morning tomorrow, so I'm afraid I'm going to have to drop you off and head right home when this meeting is done."

He must see a little disappointment in my face. I realize that I was planning on him coming over again after the meeting. Or at least hoping that he could.

"It's probably for the best though," he continues with a little smile, "because tonight is *not* a date. Tonight is a work event. And we can't have our first kiss tied to a work event."

His eyes search mine for several heartbeats. His hand is still on my cheek, and I manage to find my voice, somehow.

"Who made that rule?" I ask.

"The guy who wants to do everything absolutely right with you."

Chapter 18
Tommy

Of course I'm ten minutes early for our date, but Sam is always ready with plenty of time to spare so it shouldn't be an issue. We'll get to watch more previews this way.

Who am I kidding? I feel like a kid in a candy store who can get anything that fits in his basket.

I unbuckle and pocket my phone, deciding to just use the buzzer to let her know I'm here since I'm too antsy. When I'm out of the truck, I shake out my limbs to try to calm my nerves and then shut the door. Before I can buzz her place, someone pushes the door open.

"Hey Tommy, what are you doing here?" Caleb asks.

"Picking up Sam for a movie," I say, trying to not make it sound like a date.

"Nice," he says. "Head on up, I've never seen her late for anything so I can't imagine she's not ready."

"Where are you off to?" I ask, passing into the building.

"Groceries. Your brother now sends me lists each week."

That sounds like Matt. "You guys hanging out tonight?"

"I think I might be able to convince him to keep me from destroying my dinner tonight." He winks as he walks to his old pickup. I've always been confused about that truck. This guy brought in cash hand-over-fist steadily for almost a decade before his injury, but he's always had that beater. I take the stairs two at a time and when I reach the hallway for the second floor, I hear it roaring to life. I'm surprised the windows don't shake.

Sam's deadbolt is thrown so the door is cracked open, which is odd. I knock all the same, not wanting to intrude.

"I'm in the bedroom so you can come back here!" Her voice is muffled and it sounds strained and my heart races.

My mind wars with itself, trying to figure out if she's in danger or not.

No, not likely, she sounded calm, like she was expecting someone.

My gut sinks.

No.

No. I clench my fist to ground myself. She isn't waiting for someone else. Sam isn't Maisy for fuck's sake. She's not already seeing someone.

There's a reasonable explanation for this.

Trust her.

I open the door while taking a deep breath to try to reset myself and I'm enveloped by the smell of her perfume. It's not overwhelming, but it gives my heart a different reason for beating as fast as it is.

Quickly stepping out of my boots and walking to her room, I'm about to tell her that it's me, because I'm not sure what's actually going on, when she says, "I can't thank you enough. Tommy's going to be here soon and these hit out of the blue."

I'm in her bedroom doorway in two strides and at her side in three more. She's curled completely in a ball around a pillow on top of her bed with her eyes shut tight in pain.

"What's wrong? Do you need to go to the hospital?" I ask, looking for injuries and afraid to touch her in case I aggravate something. I swear under my breath as she lets out a groan that sounds suspiciously like the word *no*.

"Sam, what's wrong?" I try again.

"No, no, no." Her eyes stay closed so tightly that her nose scrunches up. "You aren't supposed to be here yet. You aren't supposed to see me like this."

"What do you mean *like this*?" I ask, panic building that something's terribly wrong. "Sam, I'm about five seconds from scooping you up, putting you in my truck, and taking you to the hospital."

Her eyes fly open and it's clear she's cried recently. A primal-like rage fills my chest, something that's so unlike me. If someone made her hurt like this, I'm ready to throw them into a wall.

"Oh my goodness, no! This is mortifying."

I fall to my knees in front of her, putting my hand on hers, which are holding the end of the pillow in a death-grip. "Please tell me what's going on."

Another groan escapes her. "They're only this bad about once a year and I have meds, but I forgot to get more when I moved."

My thumb traces a small path on the back of her hand as I wait.

"This is so embarrassing," she whispers, still clearly in pain. "It's cramps."

Her eyes close again, and this time not from pain.

"Hey," I say, gently. "No hiding, remember?"

One eye opens and she must see something reassuring. The murderous feeling in me has subsided and my gears are already turning.

"I may have four brothers, but my two oldest friends in the world get cramps. And even if they didn't, there's nothing embarrassing about them."

"Of course that's what you'd say," she says, her facial expression softening before scrunching up again. "I'm ruining our date."

"You most certainly are not. In fact, I heard that Maybel's is booked for a bachelorette party."

"It was not," she says, attempting a smile.

"Okay, maybe not, but let me get you settled and then give me twenty minutes in your kitchen." I stand up and look around, already making lists in my head. "Do you have a heating pad?"

"I have a hot water bottle."

Of course she would have something a grandmother would keep on hand. God, I want to kiss this woman so badly.

"Where is it?" I ask.

She starts to uncurl herself from the pillow, wincing. I put my hand on her hip. "Just tell me where to get it."

"The cupboard in the bathroom on the top shelf."

"Stay put," I tell her and I walk out of her room to the bathroom, turning on the hot water in the sink before opening the upper doors to the cupboard. It's right where she said, of course.

Once it's filled with steaming water, I screw the top plug in and wrap it in a hand towel I find on another shelf.

Thankfully, she's right where I left her.

"You don't have to do this. Greta from down the hall is bringing me something."

Ah, so that explains the ajar door and the strange greeting.

"I don't have to, but I want to," I tell her, only lying a little. I actually feel like I *need* to take care of her. Like she's mine to take care of. Or that she could be if she let me. "Hold this between the pillow and yourself."

She lets me tuck the hot water bottle in and I unfold the throw blanket at the end of the bed. The small amount her face relaxes has me feeling more and more confident that I'm being helpful. As I adjust the blanket, I realize that half of her hair is in curlers and that she's wearing a robe and slippers. Images of her joining me for breakfast dressed just like this pop into my head. Wow, that's something I haven't done in a long time...I fully pictured a future moment with someone.

Kneeling once more, I lean the rest of the way over so I can place a kiss on her cheek and that's when I notice a fresh tear.

"What happened? Did it get worse?" I ask.

She shakes her head. "This is not how our date was supposed to go. We had plans and those plans ended with a kiss." Covering her face with one hand she adds, "I'm sorry, I'm all over the place right now and whining, apparently."

My shoulders relax, I tilt my head down so it practically mirrors hers, and she peeks at me through her fingers. "Who said the plan was that we had to wait until the end of the date?"

And then I weave my fingers through hers and carefully tug her hand away from her face. She searches my expression as I close the gap and ever-so-gently, finally, kiss Samantha Davies.

Chapter 19
Sam

If a person could melt into a puddle from the sweetest, softest kiss in the world, that's what I would be right now. It's like he knows I can't handle more than this and the tenderness he's showing has fresh tears filling my eyes. He's one hundred percent perfect.

And here I am tucked around one of my pillows with curlers in half of my hair, dressed in my robe. And my date is kneeling before me when we're supposed to be on our way to a movie before going out for dinner. And I'm crying.

But he's kissing me like this is simply a tiny change in plans versus my once-a-year, life-halting cramps ruining our first official date.

Holy cow, this man can kiss.

Nothing steamy is technically happening. But...wow.

Tommy breaks off our kiss and leaves one more on my forehead. He glances up at my hair and starts taking out my remaining curlers.

I'm mortified.

My hand is gently swatted away before it can get close to my hair and Tommy shakes his head.

"Your job right now is to think about where you're going to be comfortable while I'm raiding your kitchen. If that spot is right here in bed, that's just fine, but I need you to tell me so I can get you situated before I get a few things started." He takes out the final curler and walks them to the bathroom where he's clearly putting them back in the heater.

I sit up, my abdomen feeling like it's in a vise grip, and mask the sound I make by asking a question. "What can I do?"

"Hold on, cowgirl," he says lightly, but without hiding the worry on his face. "Your face is pale."

"I want to help," I protest.

Tommy looks at me, then the bed, and then looks outside the room.

"How comfortable would you be on the couch?"

"More. Being able to sit up a little can help."

One second I'm curled up on my bed, and the next I'm being held in two strong arms. Tommy carries me to the couch, setting my legs down first so he can grab a pillow to put behind my back.

He gently lays me back, putting an extra pillow under my knees so I can stay tucked in my little ball of misery. It's a whole lot better than the blinding pain of standing.

"Okay, now you need to not move, but you should be able to see what I'm doing and I'll ask when I can't find something. Got it?"

I look up at him standing there with his hand rubbing the back of his neck and his eyes checking my face for signs of something.

"This is pathetic," I say, keeping the whine out of my voice.

"No, this is you needing to stay put and me knowing how to make things a little easier, so please let me."

"Okay," I reluctantly say.

He nods and goes right back to the kitchen, opening the fridge and then the freezer and moving some of the contents.

"What kind of dairy can you have?"

"Things like cheese and yogurt, but not a lot of either."

"Got it. I'll steer clear from even those for tonight." He closes the freezer and comes back into view while typing something on his phone. "Will you be okay if I stay in the kitchen?"

Another wave of pain that's almost searing hits and I hold perfectly still, holding my breath.

"Whoa," Tommy says, closing the distance immediately. He looks me over as if he can find the pain to soothe it away.

I suppose if anyone can, it would be this man.

"On second thought, I'm going to stay right here until you can take something," he says, looking decisive.

I make a sound of disagreement and take a shallow breath. "I'm fine, really."

Of course a tear picks this very moment to fall again. Before I can try to hide it, Tommy's palm is cupping my cheek and his thumb is brushing the tear away.

"No," he says softly before his face screws up a little. "How about I stop talking about raiding your kitchen and wait right here with you for Greta to drop the meds off?"

The pain is ridiculous and I want to scream at the timing, but I can't help feeling like the luckiest woman in the world to have Tommy here, wanting to have our date. Even though I'm going to be terrible company tonight.

"Sam?"

"Oh, sorry. Yes."

"Where'd you go?" he asks.

He sees my hesitation clear as day.

"Don't hide," he reminds me, his eyes soft as he sits on the end of the coffee table in front of me.

"I was just thinking about how you're not running for the hills."

He snorts out a laugh. "Again, someone has set the bar far too low if this is winning me brownie points."

There's a knock at the door and I sigh in relief at the sound.

"I'll get it," Tommy says, kissing me on my forehead as he stands. That cedar scent is stronger today and I take a moment to appreciate being calm enough to soak it in.

Greta's surprise is evident even from the couch when it's not me at the door. Moments later, Tommy pockets the meds, grabs my water bottle from the kitchen, and, when he's back at the couch, sets a coaster for the table. This man is racking up brownie points tonight. I reach out and take the water from him with a smile. I think I'm going to cry again because he doesn't even think twice about caring for someone. Nothing about him says he expects anything in return, or that this is any sort of a burden.

He takes out a little container and pops off the lid. Again, how this man thinks about all the little things completely baffles me. One of my hands is holding my bottle and it would have hurt more to move around to set it down just so I could have two hands to open the container, but he just does it. He's the first guy I've dated, even though this is just our first date so I don't know that we've officially dated at this point, who was sympathetic to this. Everyone in the past just left me to my own devices.

Oh no, the tears are coming. I let him drop the two pills into my hand and quickly take them, hoping the cold in my mouth will somehow offset the waterworks.

It doesn't.

Tommy is on his knees, once again, cupping my cheeks like I'm the most precious thing in the world which, combined with the pain that persists, sends me into full-on crying.

"What happened?" he whispers.

"How are you this wonderful?" I ask, blubbering and trying to find something to wipe my nose with before it runs. Somehow, I think even if I had mascara running down my face and was blowing my nose constantly, Tommy would still be here. He'd stay to help while I was sick versus just leaving me to my own devices, which is heart-warming and a little terrifying.

Chapter 20
Tommy

Two feelings battle inside of me: relief that borders on the edge of laughter because she's not in more pain, and anger that she's crying because someone wants to take care of her when she's hurting.

"I don't know who you've dated in the past, but I can promise you one thing, Samantha Davies: I won't let a single day go by without you knowing how lucky I am to be with you."

Okay, maybe that was a bit overbearing. We're not officially together, but Jesus Christ, her past relationships must have been with complete tools.

Sam scrunches up her face. "I'm sorry, I'm just a complete mess."

"Why would you ever need to apologize for that?"

Her eyes well up again and I change tactics, trying to get her out of this headspace of someone showing common decency being amazing.

"Truth or dare."

She takes a sharp breath in and pauses, her eyes finding mine. "Truth."

"Are you okay with the idea of us being," I give myself a moment to not put too fine a label on things, "a thing?"

She searches my face, like I might be trying to walk her into a trap. I want to throttle her exes. But then, she nods.

"Yes?" I ask, needing to be sure.

"Yes," she whispers.

"Perfect," I say, leaning over and kissing her again. Her lips are incredible and her breath hitches just a little, even though these are some of the most chaste kisses two people can manage. I pull back, my hands still cradling her face.

"You have one job while I'm cooking."

She opens her eyes with a questioning look.

"Relax right here. Okay?"

"I can do that," she says, her eyes clearing up.

I grab the remote that's on the other end of the table and put it in her hand. "And pick out something for us to watch."

"Okay."

"Do you need anything else? Another blanket or tea?" I ask, trying to make sure I didn't miss anything.

"No, everything is perfect," she says.

"Liar," I say.

"Well, as perfect as can be while dealing with cramps." She thinks for a moment. "You're going to be less than twenty feet away."

"Alright," I kiss her once more and turn around before I crawl behind her on the couch and hold her, trying to take away some of the pain. Courtney used to have terrible cramps every month before she went on birth control and I guess I've just gone into autopilot from taking care of her.

Once I've done a preliminary search of what she has on hand, I ask if chicken and rice soup will be okay.

"That sounds so amazing right now," she says, her head resting on the back cushions.

It doesn't take long before I've found everything I need to lightly season two chicken breasts. She even has the same stock Matt likes to buy, so I know what I'm doing. Her oven takes longer than expected to heat up, but that's the only quirk I've found so far. Everything feels natural moving around in her kitchen.

It feels right.

Not Sam sitting on her couch, curled in a ball with a hot water bottle. But cooking for *us*. Maisy always rolled her eyes when I wanted to stay in and cook, not that I'm great at it, but anything she saw as "domestic" in her mind was a waste of time.

I'm not expecting Sam to have zero faults, that would be completely unrealistic and unreasonable. But all of her hesitations so far revolve around not wanting to be a burden and not wanting to ask something of anyone else.

That thought settles in and reassures me that I'm not: A) putting Sam on some pedestal that no human could ever live up to; B) "finally" having a rebound; or C) desperate to show Maisy I've moved on before she comes back to Greenstone.

This is the first time I've thought about being with someone whenever Maisy returns to Greenstone. Until now, I've assumed that I'd still be single because trusting someone seemed like too much and I'd just ignore her. She'd find someone new to fixate on soon enough. I've had plenty of time to truly know how wrong Maisy was for me and the more time I spend with Sam, the more I'm certain that she is nothing like my ex.

As I put the chicken in the oven, I realize that my heart didn't squeeze and my gut didn't drop thinking of my ex. I let out a breath of grateful disbelief because Maisy's hold on me hasn't been about me still harboring feelings for her in a long-ass time. But the damage of knowing how long she felt it was okay to keep me around *and* how long it took for me to recognize what should have been glaringly obvious was far worse.

This shouldn't be some major revelation on my part, but holy shit I feel like a weight has lifted from my chest and I do what I should have done months ago: block Maisy's number.

There isn't anything I need to know. God, I'm not sure the last time I even opened a message from her. Probably four months, at least. It's time she doesn't have access to any of my time or my thoughts.

Taking a deep breath, I lose myself in the little things I'm doing like wiping down the counters and putting things away that I won't need later. When I go to join Sam on the couch, I take in the scene in front of me and say the first thought that pops into my head.

"What did you do?"

Chapter 21
Sam

The look Tommy gives me is downright comical. I'm still uncomfortable, but the edge has been taken off so I can think straight. I even added the meds to my shopping list so this doesn't happen again. But he doesn't know that. All he sees is that I'm now in a sweatshirt, which I was attempting to hide by staying under the blankets. However, I needed to pause the show I was watching so I could greet him and low-and-behold...a very non-robe-wearing-arm came right into view.

"You had one job," he says with mock sternness.

"Actually, two jobs, and I did one of them," I counter.

"You didn't stay put. How did I miss that?"

"The meds kicked in about five minutes ago and I had to go to the bathroom. You were in the zone, so while I was gone, I changed for our date. You know, 'slip into something more comfortable' as the saying goes."

He blushes.

"No, truly something comfortable!" I pull the blanket back and show him the oversized sweatshirt and my lightweight navy leggings that feel like I'm wearing nothing so there's no added pressure on my abdomen. His gaze lingers a moment before he clears his throat.

"Alright then. You do look more comfortable. Not just clothes-wise," he says. "Should we start the movie you picked out?"

I smile and nod as Tommy closes the curtain so we don't have any glare. Then he settles in behind me on the couch.

This man.

"Is this okay?" he asks, resting a hand on my hip.

I nod against his chest, breathe him in, and snuggle close. Part of me wonders if I should be wary of how comfortable I am around Tommy, that his motives aren't what they seem. But he's never done anything that puts me on alert, the man has zero red flags, and I've never heard anyone in this town even hint at something negative about him. If anything, his consistency, openness, and kindness pull me in and wrap me up.

Twice during the movie, Tommy refills the hot water bottle and he kisses the top of my head when he returns to his spot behind me, pulling me close against him. He's got a little layer of softness to him that feels incredible and if it wasn't so early in the evening, I could totally fall asleep right here without a problem. I'm less and less aware of the rom-com I picked out and more and more aware of every place we're making contact. These ridiculous cramps always hit several days before my cycle starts and I have a tendency to feel a little...*more* and Tommy's presence is amplifying that.

His thumb makes lazy circles on my hip and when he settled in this last time, I might have let my sweatshirt ride up just a little. Which means those circles are tracing patterns directly on my skin, increasing my heartbeat as I try to hold perfectly still and pretend like I'm not ready to flip over to see what he's really capable of.

The credits roll and he gives me a little squeeze. "Stay here and I'm going to put the rice in and dinner will be ready in just about ten minutes."

He dips down to kiss me before giving me a lovely view of his cute butt in those not-too-tight jeans.

Tommy moves things around and calls out, "How are you feeling now?"

"If I'm curled up a little I feel good, actually." I test stretching my legs out so I'm almost flat and immediately regret it. "Yep, if I stay like this I'm okay."

Tommy comes back into view and leans against the end of the counter looking like he belongs here. One of my kitchen towels is casually tossed over one shoulder and his arms are crossed over his chest, accentuating his shoulders and waistline. Something about the sight has me feeling more confident than ever so I give him a dare that *I* want. "I dare you to kiss me without holding back."

His jaw clenches and his Adam's apple bobs as he swallows. "You forgot to let me pick truth or dare."

"Would you prefer a truth?" I ask, nerves creeping in.

"I wouldn't." He grips the counter so hard that his knuckles are turning white. "You're feeling up for that? Just kissing with you staying semi-curled up?"

Well now I want more than *just* kissing but I'm not about to push my luck and make these cramps ten times worse, so I nod.

The muscles in his jaw work once more as he pauses, his hands still glued to the counter.

"You're sure?" His voice is rougher this time and I feel like we're balancing on the edge of a cliff and I'm about ready to beg him to jump off with me.

"I'm sure," I say, my heart pounding, my voice breathy.

And then he pushes off the counter. There's a look of pure desire in his eyes as he strides over to me, tangles one hand in my hair as he leans down, and kisses me like I'm the first rays of sunshine he's seen in a decade. He's powerful and sure as he gently lays me on my back. Using his free hand, he hitches my leg around his waist so I'm not lying flat and uncomfortable. The way his mouth moves so smoothly with mine already has me shuddering with need.

Here I thought sweet kisses from Tommy Landen were the best thing in the world, but, oh my God, I think I've died and gone to heaven. My fingers reach around and grip the back of his flannel shirt so I can pull him closer and get more of him.

Jesus, his tongue darts out against my bottom lip and I realize this is the first time he's used it. For once, I don't stop and wonder what the other person is thinking about me and I let my instincts take over, opening and allowing him to take everything.

Chapter 22
Tommy

One tiny part of my brain tells me to take it easy, that she's in pain, but my body soaks up every message she's sending my way that she's more than okay with what we're doing. Her lips part for me and our tongues touch for the first time, setting every nerve in my body on fire.

Her tongue is fucking perfect each time it darts out to find mine. Her mouth is fucking perfect with her soft lips and equally soft noises that escape. And she's fucking perfect.

Her hair is silky and getting absolutely tangled in my fingers. Both legs are wrapped tightly around my waist and I can't stop touching her thigh. These leggings are so damn thin and I can't get enough.

And then there are her hands. Christ Almighty, she's gripping the back of my shirt like she's riding a bucking bronco, pulling me flush against her so I can feel her breasts against my chest. If I rock my hips just a little, she'd know just how much she turns me on. I'm in sensory overload with her perfume, her little squeaks, her responsiveness, and just *her*.

Samantha Davies dared me to kiss her without holding back and it's more than I ever imagined. Each time I pull back just a little to make sure this isn't too much for her, physically or emotionally, her mouth chases mine, her nails press into my back, and her legs clamp down.

Suddenly, the most obnoxious sound comes from the kitchen. It's a herd of cows mooing.

Damn it, he did it again.

I groan into her mouth. "That's the timer on my phone."

"Why cows?" she asks.

"Chuck likes to record the cattle, sometimes the horses, and changes my alert sounds to them." I sigh.

But Sam just laughs, keeping me against her so I can feel every shift in her body.

"I'm glad one of us is amused," I say, unable to keep the smile off my face.

"I don't have any siblings who could play pranks like this, especially into adulthood," she says. "So this is hilarious."

I close my eyes for a second because every single time she says or does something that only our parents, or grandparents, would, I just want to kiss her senseless. Why does it turn me on when she refers to us as being in "adulthood"?

"Fuck it," I murmur, trying to ignore the cows and tightening my grip on her hair and claiming her mouth with mine. I'm done holding back with her. I'm done not showing her that every fucking thing about her is so sexy.

She gasps in surprise, but then one hand grabs my shirt and the other shifts so she can weave her fingers into my short hair. The way our mouths move perfectly in sync has my blood surging below my belt with abandon and my dick is painfully hard. I can feel precum leaking out even with the damn cacophony of cattle getting progressively louder.

I slow things down, silently cursing Chuck. My timer alert is usually pretty soft, a rippling brook, chimes, birds chirping, so I truly could have ignored it for a while. But this is just ridiculous and it's only going to get worse.

"What was that for?" Sam asks, her lips bright red and her pupils dilated.

"Just for being you," I say truthfully. "I need to shut that damn thing off before your neighbors complain that you have your own herd."

I give her another peck and carefully lean back so I can pull her into a seated position.

"Don't go anywhere," I say, dropping one more kiss on her lips before standing up and adjusting myself. The relief to my ears is immediate when I'm in the kitchen and I hit the button on my screen to silence the alert. I suppose nothing resets you from making out to eating soup like the sound of cattle.

"Who else works with the cattle besides Chuck? He can't be the only one who goes out there."

I ladle the soup into two bowls and add them to the tray with the rest of our dinner. "We hire some guys in the summer to stay in the buildings wherever the herd grazes near. I mean, there are houses stocked with non-perishables, but sometimes they move daily so it doesn't feel like a home."

"Have you done that?" she asks.

"Yeah, we've all done it over the years and when someone needs to be gone a few days or is sick, one of us goes out. Chuck is the one who usually goes though, since he's the one who handles everything for them."

"But you all work with horses, too?"

"Everyone but Chuck," I say, carrying the tray to the low table. "He has his own horse, of course, and can step in when needed, but somehow, the cattle are his world. His personality and reputation might make him seem like a playboy and a goofball, but he's dedicated to them year-round. If he has to travel for something, he has multiple contingency plans in place if something happens to one of his herd."

"I don't think I've heard someone talk about Chuck this much who wasn't trying to recreate his dance moves." Sam smiles. "You're proud of him and it shows."

Looking down at my bowl, I feel a blush hit my face. "Ask him about 'his ladies' sometime and, while he'll sound completely cocky, you'll see what I mean."

"And you are clearly the one who handles the books for all the animals." She dips her spoon in and lets a small bite cool.

Nodding, I blow on my own steaming spoonful. "Everyone tracks certain things, but I do the ordering, the taxes, the payroll, the bills, the calendars, and schedules. My brothers like to joke that I handle anything that has a number in it. But really, it saves us from bringing in some suit from the city."

"That's amazing you're able to do that for the ranch. I know so many small businesses have to hire someone to handle it." Her eyebrows furrow.

"What are you thinking?" I ask, taking a bite. It's still hot as hell, but it's my ultimate comfort food that both Courtney and Avery have requested since we were younger and they didn't feel good.

"The co-op." She pauses, her mind churning something over. "How many people here could use a central person to handle some of that, who truly understands the intricacies of farm- and ranch-life?"

"I couldn't take on everyone's finances."

"Not you, though you would be amazing. But look at how Greenstone came together to bring Rebecca in and how we're talking about a retainer system through the co-op so everyone has consistent costs and she has a consistent income. What if we had someone who could compile the needs of the ranches and the farms to get better deals on larger bulk orders, but who could also help handle other finance tracking and processing for taxes? It could be someone who lives around here and everyone could pay in just like with Rebecca while getting those services and benefits. And then they wouldn't be paying a suit from the city, as you called it, who knows the tax breakdowns, but wouldn't know all the little things making the ranch run that could be write-offs, for example."

Sam pauses and looks up at me. I've just been staring at her in wonder. She's constantly thinking about ways to preserve the great things about life here while making things better and easier.

"I love it," I say.

She blushes. "A lot of details will have to be considered before we can even bring it to the members, but it might have enough merits for them to explore it."

I put my hand on her knee and give it a little squeeze. "They'll love it, too."

She smiles while looking down at her soup. Taking her first bite, she lets out a sigh.

"This is amazing, Tommy. I don't know what you did, but this beats Maybel's." Her eyes widen in horror. "Not that Maybel's isn't great!"

I peck her on the cheek and stand up to grab her notebook near the door. "Don't panic. I always think staying in and having rice with anything is the best."

"Okay, good. Because I mean it, this is perfect."

I catch myself before telling her how perfect she is, thinking that I've made my feelings pretty clear already and I don't need to make her feel smothered on our first date.

Chapter 23
Sam

There's no way Tommy's leaving already. I watch him walk to the door, completely curious. I'm still a little ruffled after potentially offending Maybel's, but his response was so genuine that I believe him. I didn't realize just how often I assume what I say or do will be a deal-breaker.

Of course he's bringing me my notebook.

Once again, he knows what I need and doesn't hesitate to give me that. He's so natural about everything, so at ease. I can easily lose myself in the possibility of this being life. Of a life shared with him.

Oh boy, I need to slow that train of thought down. He's sweet, charming, understanding, and completely sexy, but that doesn't mean this is a 'til-death-do-us-part thing.

Tommy hands me the notebook and reaches into his pocket for a pen. "Go on," he says.

I enthusiastically uncap the pen, which is dark green, and start jotting down the basics. We're going to need someone qualified, of course, and they'll ideally live around here already. Someone both the farmers and ranchers feel they can trust.

"The buy-in could be per-acre for farmers and per-head for ranchers," Tommy says, rubbing his chin. His knee touches mine and a wave of heat washes over me from simply thinking about what it felt like to make out with him. His hands, his weight, his lips.

Focus on getting the list down and out of your head, Samantha.

Although I sure wouldn't mind if he kissed me breathless again before he leaves tonight.

We talk through a few more details that I jot down and transition into easy conversation while we eat our soup. Before long, he gathers the dishes and insists on handling them before we have dessert.

"I've already shown that I'm capable of handling dishes here, remember?"

"Yes, but I can stand now," I say, fairly confident in the statement.

He leans over to kiss me. "Excellent. I'm still doing the cleanup."

"Am I allowed to empty the hot water bottle?"

"Of course," he replies, balancing the tray so he can offer me his hand. "I just get the kitchen tonight."

"Deal," I say, my fingers running over his palm before he helps me stand. He gives me a concerned look. "It's not like I'm going for a run, I can handle this mission."

This really is perfect. Any pressure on tonight was purely in my head. Tommy doesn't have expectations, and there's nothing to stress about. I don't feel like I have to placate anyone when I'm with him.

This is definitely a new feeling. But it's freeing to be fully seen just as I am, and I could get used to it.

By the time I freshened up, Tommy is closing the dishwasher. Even the pots are clean and put away. Who is this man?

"Are you ready for dessert?" he asks.

"There's dessert?"

"Of course. Do you usually not get dessert on a date?"

"No I do. I'm just surprised since we're just, you know, here."

"This is our first date. We're doing this right." He winks at me. "Back to the couch with you, I'll be right in."

He moves around the kitchen, like he knows where everything is, which I guess he does by now. A warm feeling settles over me. Instead of the tray this time, Tommy walks over with two bowls in one hand and spoons in the other.

"More soup?" I ask.

"No," Tommy says. "Chocolate oat milk ice cream."

"Thank you," I say, taking a bowl from him. "What are you having then?"

"The same." He shrugs.

"You're having non-dairy ice cream for your dessert on our first date."

"Yeah," he says like it's normal.

"You are something else."

"So I've been told." He flashes me a smile, making my heart flutter. "Eat up."

"You picked my favorite flavor," I say, staring at my dessert.

"I hope so."

"How did you know?"

"You had the one with brownies in your freezer last time, too."

Looking up, I can see that he has already eaten half of his. "You remembered?"

"Of course. Why wouldn't I?"

I just stare at him.

Tommy chuckles.

"What's so funny?"

"Whoever your exes were made what I consider to be the bare minimum look extravagant."

He's not wrong there. But now I want to know what he thinks *extravagant* might look like.

"Truth or dare," I say.

"We should keep things tame tonight, truth."

"What's something that you'd like to do but aren't sure about?" I ask, twisting my fingers in my lap.

"So much for keeping things tame." He winks at me and my face is on fire.

"Oh, I didn't mean—"

"It's okay. I'm going to assume you did."

My eyes must betray how mortified I am because his fingers weave through mine, stilling their movements.

"We're both adults who are going to be fully consenting to anything we decide to do, and we might as well talk about things so we know who's comfortable with what."

Well, he has my full attention.

"As long as neither of us is getting injured, if it's something you'd like to try, I'd be open to it." He pauses. "I'd like to keep things with just you and me, if you're okay with that?"

Did he just ask me if I'm comfortable with a monogamous relationship? And why does he look worried?

"Um, I'm good with that. Just the two of us," I manage. He nods, the wrinkles on his brow relaxing and a slow breath leaving him. I've heard that he had a nasty ex and I've never remembered her name, but I wonder if she's the reason he was clearly stressed about it.

"That was a terrible response for your truth, you know. There wasn't a single thing you actually noted." Trying to get him to relax has me feeling more confident in pushing him in a playful way.

He smirks, his eyes locking with mine. "I suppose I can get specific, for the sake of truth or dare, of course."

Something tells me I'm about to get more than I bargained for.

Chapter 24
Tommy

The tension is almost out of my body as my brain shifts away from the thought of possibly sharing someone when I'm a one-person-kind-of-guy to all the things I want to do with Samantha Davies. I know she saw that asking that question was a big deal to me, but her reply was genuine, if not a little surprised. There's no way she was more surprised than me when she asked what I wanted to do…

"I want to take my time getting to know your body inch by inch. I'm going to memorize everything about when and how you come," I say, leaning in so I can trail kisses down her neck as I whisper against her skin. "And I'm going to study your body every damn chance you give me. I'm going to know exactly how to make you shudder, make you gasp, and make you writhe even before getting you naked."

Her head tips back and I use my free hand to shift the neck of her sweatshirt so my lips have access to her collarbone. I've never wanted to leave a hickey so badly before. I want physical proof that this is real, that she's here with me, melting into my kisses, her fingers holding my hand in a death grip like she's afraid I'm going to disappear. I have a feeling she wouldn't be fond of needing to cover one up for work, though, so I just breathe in her perfume, the floral scent is stronger closer to her ear and it's driving me mad. I want to rub against her like a damn cat just so I have it on me all night back at home.

The tip of my nose trails back up her neck, nudging her earlobe, and I leave a barely-there kiss behind her ear. Her response is immediate. A gasp combined with a little whimper escapes her.

"Exactly like that," I say, kissing down her jawline while guiding her mouth to meet mine.

When our tongues touch, something is released inside of her and she drops my hand and her fingers are digging into my back, pulling me on top of her as she falls back against the couch. I lift up so her legs can wrap around my waist before settling most of my weight against her, reveling in the feel of her underneath me. Each breath she takes presses her breasts against my chest, erasing whatever space manages to get between us.

My now-free hand grips her hip, encouraging her to grind against me. When she's taking care of that movement, my fingertips brush her bare skin just above the top of her leggings. She moans and I swear the vibrations carry from my lips directly to my dick as if her mouth was there.

"You are the sexiest fucking person in the w—"

Her tongue is back in my mouth before I get to finish that thought and she shifts underneath me so her core is rubbing against my sensitive tip that's pushing against the edge of my belt buckle. The sound I make is some cross of a grunt, a moan, and a choked sigh, but I don't care. She doesn't seem to, either. If anything, she's now tugging me harder so I'm completely settled on her and rolling my hips into her.

I wrap my hand around her to lay flat on the small of her back the next time she arches into me. Her skin is warm and soft and she presses her back down, trapping my hand right where it is. She makes a little sound when I nibble on her lower lip, and I pull back to look down at her. Her lips are bright red and swollen, her cheeks are pink, and her pupils are dilated. Fuck, she's everything I imagined and so much more.

She's looking at *me* like I just unlocked something deep inside of her. Her chest is heaving and she licks her bottom lip, driving me mad. I shift my hand from behind her so I can brush her hair off her forehead. Her eyes search my face and I don't give her time to start wondering if something is wrong before I press against her and slowly kiss my way from her cheek down the side of her neck.

Focusing on every reaction she has, I kiss softly along her collarbone, paying extra attention to when goosebumps follow my path. Tugging on her wide sweatshirt neck, my lips caress her shoulder and dip down her chest as far as her sweatshirt will allow. I moan against her skin when she presses her breasts up and my fingers release the thin material, brushing over her nipple.

Her gasp at that light touch has my head spinning. I nuzzle the tip of her other breast and trace the peak with my nose, cupping the other. The whimpers coming from her are driving me crazy as her fingers press into my scalp, keeping me right where I am. My lips tease her, even through the fabric of her sweatshirt and bra, drawing out and cataloging the different sounds and twitches from her body. The way she responds to my touch is mesmerizing and it's a little while later until I finally untangle my fingers from her hair and barely trace her throat while carefully using my teeth to pull at her nipple.

"Ohmygod," she pants. "What are you doing to me, Tommy Landen?"

I chuckle against her breast, causing her to squirm under me, and place kisses as I rub my nose against her sweatshirt lower and lower on her belly. "I'm just learning."

"Learning what?" she asks, moving her hands to my face and pulling me up.

"You," I say as I kiss her, my tongue claiming her mouth as one of her hands anchors me in place by grabbing the back of my neck. She gives everything she takes and it's not for a few minutes until things slow down.

"As much as I'd like to stay and continue this, I'm afraid I'm going to have an even harder time leaving."

"You have another early morning?" she asks, our foreheads touching.

"Every morning is early on a ranch."

"It sounds like such a different world than mine." There's a little worry in her eyes even though she's hiding it in her voice.

Hoping I don't scare her off, I say, "A world you can be part of in any way you'd like."

A soft smile lights up her face. "A world I get to see again tomorrow."

"Tomorrow," I echo, nodding and giving her a slow kiss.

I reluctantly sit up, grab the remote, and scroll through a few movies until I find the rom-com we watched the night I could barely feel my lips from those damn hot wings. I let the opening credits play and turn to look at her confused face. "Now, your job for the rest of the night is to relax so you're feeling ready to ride tomorrow. I've got the dishes and you stay put."

She sits up and I'm not good at hiding my surprise because she simply raises an eyebrow at me and says, "I'm going to have to lock the door behind you so there's no harm in standing now."

"Fine," I say dramatically, earning a giggle from Sam. "I suppose I can allow that."

Maybe one day I'll have my own key so she won't have to lock up after I leave...

Chapter 25
Sam

I follow Tommy into the kitchen without even an outward wince from pain, which is clear progress. Well, it's *my* kitchen, but something feels less like it's *only* mine when he's around.

Ignoring the whispers of doubt that try to rise to the surface, I enjoy my view of Tommy perfectly putting the bowls on the top rack of the dishwasher.

Once again the man is ridiculously sexy while doing domestic things.

With his large hands.

That were recently causing so many involuntary reactions as he explored my body.

And barely anything happened that was skin-on-skin. Hell, most of what he did to make me almost lose my mind was on top of this gigantic sweatshirt. But between what his fingers were doing and that mouth of his, he can spend all the time he'd like studying my responses.

Something about him gets me out of my head and puts me in the moment, allowing me to be fully present without constantly wondering what I'm doing wrong or what I'm going to have to fake to make sure he's happy. No, Tommy Landen watches, feels, and hears every little thing my body does and it pulls out *more* from me. It was like he was trying an experiment three different ways to see how the results differed with one small tweak.

And it was sexy as hell.

The cuffs of my sleeves hang past my palms, so I bunch the fabric in my fists and bring it to my nose, needing to know if it smells like whatever he puts in his hair.

Tommy catches me just when I know it not only smells like his hair, but like *him*, too. He gives me a curious look as the dishwasher door clicks shut. In two steps, he's right in front of me, gently weaving his fingers through mine, kissing my knuckles on each hand before lowering them and wrapping them behind my back so he's holding me.

"No hiding," he whispers.

I could correct him and tell him I was trying to figure out if I could spend the night smelling not only like cedar and garlic, but that intriguing fresh scent that's in his hair. Instead, I opt for not hiding myself because I feel embarrassed from having the level of patience of a mosquito, to be able to wait to sniff my clothes. So, I repeat his words and tug his hands farther away from my back causing him to flatten me against the edge of the counter. I lift up onto my toes and it's as if we're magnetically drawn to each other now that we've kissed. We don't wait for anything and we're both more than ready.

He shifts our hands so he's holding both of mine in one of his and my heartbeat, which had only recently normalized, starts picking up the pace. I expect the other to go back into my hair, so he can tangle his fingers into it, but instead, he grips the spot that's not quite butt, not quite hip, and he deepens our kiss. It's almost as if he's pulling me tighter against him, but the only way we could get closer is if we weren't wearing clothes.

Once more, I find myself excited and completely turned on by the idea of letting Tommy explore my body and of us being together. I think the last time I was this excited was back in high school before learning where most guys zero-in, and more importantly, where they don't. But this is the man who pulls out his own notebook at a happy hour so I could write my ideas down. This is the man who dared me to allow him the chance to clean up after our first non-date. This is the man whose only concern tonight was making sure I was comfortable. He doesn't run, he doesn't mansplain, he doesn't assume. He stays, he listens, and he asks.

He sees me.

The real me. The one with systems in place and instead of mocking me, he checks to see how I do things. He pays attention to details and remembers the little things. He makes things better, easier. He kisses me like I'm the most beautiful woman on the planet and he's the luckiest guy to be here.

And he tastes like my favorite ice cream right now.

I'm not sure how long he has me pinned before his hand loosens its hold and he lets it drag up my side, slowing at my breast but not changing course. He spreads his fingers out between my jaw and my collarbone. His thumb takes its time rubbing its way across my chin so he can hold my face totally in place.

Not one coherent thought is left in my body in this instance. His ability to take control has me wanting to know more, to experience more.

I must make a sound because he chuckles against my mouth, sending a shiver through me. The way his chest rumbles when he does that shouldn't make my toes curl, but it does and they do.

"Think you can hold on until tomorrow, cowgirl?"

"There you go calling me a cowgirl again," I say. "I haven't ridden anything yet."

I'm so wrapped up in him and this moment, that I completely miss how that could be interpreted until he says, "I think we'll have you riding like a pro sooner than you think."

If panties could spontaneously combust into flames, mine would have at this very moment.

"You're very confident," I say, his hands still holding me right where he wants me.

He gives me a grin. "I'm confident you're going to enjoy the experience."

"Are we still talking about horseback riding?" I ask.

That grin turns downright mischievous. "Nope."

Tommy leans down and nips at my bottom lip and kisses me so thoroughly that I'm grateful the counter is behind me to hold me up. My knees feel like they're about to give out and my skin tingles.

But then he releases my neck and his hand trails down the side of my breast before he sighs. He rests his forehead against mine.

After a moment, he shifts so our arms are around each other and I'm tucked against him, my head resting against his collar bone. We stand there, just holding onto one another and my eyes drift close. I'm not sure the last time I've felt this at home with someone.

But then his pocket vibrates. He makes a disgruntled sound as I loosen my hold on him.

"You should see who it is."

His hand disappears into his pocket and the screen of his phone is lit up when he pulls it out. Avery's name appears in his notification. He opens it and almost snorts. Turning the phone around, he shows me a group chat.

Avery: Did you finally kiss Sam??

And then another message pops up.

Courtney: If you didn't, I'm going to lock you two in a closet until you do!

"Um, you might want to reply before Courtney gets more creative with her threats."

"What?" he asks, frowning and turning the phone back to him. "Oh my God, she's like a middle schooler."

"They seem keen on the idea of us kissing," I say.

Tommy closes his eyes and his face scrunches up.

"Are you okay?" I ask, feeling like I said something wrong.

He rubs his free hand over his face. "How was that sexy?" he mumbles.

I look down at myself, trying to figure out what he's talking about and when I look up at him once more, his mouth crushes against mine. It's over a second later.

"I need to actually leave your apartment so we can both be responsible adults who get the right amount of sleep and go to work on time."

I'm thoroughly confused about the moment we just had, but I nod my head. "Alright then. Let's get you out of here before you decide you'd like to learn how my curlers are properly stored."

His eyes widen. "Do you want the truth?" he asks.

"About…"

"About that."

"About you learning how to put away my curlers?" I ask, trying to keep up with where his mind just went.

He leans down so his lips leave a trail of goosebumps from my collarbone to just behind my ear. "If it means spending time with you, I would love to learn how to properly store every damn one of your curlers, Samantha."

Now Tommy Landen is flirting with me about my silly curlers.

I'm a complete goner.

Chapter 26
Tommy

I accept the call as I'm exiting the stairwell.

"Are you keeping tabs on me?" I ask, waiting for their faces to pop onto the screen.

"Definitely," says Courtney.

"Maybe," says Avery at the same time.

"Give me a second to get into my truck."

"No way," says Courtney, her face taking up half of my screen as Avery's lags. "You're not getting off the hook that easily. Spill."

My cheeks get hot.

"Oh, he's blushing!" Avery squeals.

"He kissed her!" Courtney backs away from the screen and she does a series of victory dances.

"Oh my God," I briskly scrub my cheeks, knowing that I'm definitely blushing. "How can you even see my face that well?"

The door to the apartment building closes behind me with a gentle thud.

"That building's entrance has lovely lighting, and you know we pay attention to everything." Avery snaps her fingers in front of her. "Court, get back here."

"I'm sorry, I've been waiting for far too long for Tommy to really make a move. Oh wait, did *she* make it?"

"I'm more than happy to let you two speculate all night and not provide any actual facts," I tell them, starting up my truck and mounting my phone. "And, for the record, it's not like I mauled her, but I went in for the first one."

My cab fills with high-pitched sounds of sheer delight. These two are the best damn support system in the world.

"The *first* one?" Avery asks at the same time Courtney says, "*Please* tell me you two made out!"

I rub my jaw, waiting at the red light. "Um, yes."

There's silence on the other end and I peek down at the screen, barking out a laugh at the very unamused faces staring at me.

"Okay, details." I let out a breath, taking a second to gather my thoughts. It's not like I've had time to replay or process anything. These two have a sixth sense for when to call. "We didn't go to the movie."

"Hot damn," Courtney murmurs.

"No, she had horrible cramps and was actually trying to get ready for our date with them. She was in so much pain and she felt like our date was ruined, so I kissed her, got her settled, and then cooked so we could have our dinner-and-a-movie-date at her place."

"Oh. My. God. You are the fucking sweetest." I can hear Felix meowing behind Avery.

"Anyway, I started chicken soup since that's what Court always wants—"

"Yessss," Courtney interjects.

"Good lord, you two," I murmur before filling them in on the rest of the date.

"You did dishes there again? Oh my God, she's going to ask you to move in soon." Avery leans away from the phone to yell, "Jackson, are you taking notes?"

My oldest brother's voice is faint, "Didn't you already move in with me?"

"Fair enough." I can hear the smile in her voice.

"We already figured you two out, we're focusing on Tommy," Courtney says impatiently.

"Just wait until you turn your dating apps back on," I jest. The dating pool has been slim pickings for her lately.

There's a pause. "What aren't you telling us, Courtney?"

She lets out a disgruntled snort. "I don't even know if there's anything to tell, to be honest. There's a chance I'm going on a date this weekend, but I also know he's going to be out of town for a while. So all of this is to say that my apps are off and if this happens to be a date, it's not like there will be a second date any time soon."

Avery and I just sit there until I break the silence. "Well, who is it?"

"I'm calling a rain check on this one. If I misread this, I'm going to look like a huge ass so I'm going into it pretending it's just a friend thing."

"Do we know him?" Avery asks.

"Yes," Courtney says with a little fake sulk in her voice. "But no names or hints unless it turns out to be a date. And stop changing the subject. I need my details, man!"

"Okay, okay. She's an even better kisser than I imagined, and I promise you that my imagination has been especially fixated on Samantha Davies." I take a breath in through my nose, smelling her perfume from my shirt. "We definitely made out and I realized that things just feel good and natural with her. I can pause to kiss her in the kitchen and she smiles at me. She cuddles with me during movies. And this might sound stupid, but she lets me get to know her quirks. She has a system for everything and when I ask about it, she'll explain it. I mean, she'll blush and look self-conscious, but it's like she's waiting for me to make fun of her for it. I swear she must have dated some complete dickwads before."

"Listen to him talk about her," Courtney coos.

"I know, he's so far gone."

"You know we're on a group call and I can hear you both, right?" I say, trying to deflect a little of their oohing and ahhing away from my evening. The truth is, I know I'm far gone. That even with my baggage and how long I've put off anything resembling dating, Sam just feels right. Now that I know she's interested in me, I can do what's natural. Both girls laugh at me and we fall into an easy silence for a moment.

"You know as well as us that tonight was a big deal for you and we couldn't be happier for you." Avery's tone is soft and kind.

"No matter what happens with Sam, and we both hope it's a wedding and babies and the whole nine yards, you take a moment to celebrate what a badass you've been just for acknowledging your feelings to yourself. Then celebrate the fact that you asked her out because that takes so much more to put yourself out there."

"Thanks, you two," I say quietly, knowing just how right they are.

Chapter 27
Sam

Someone clears their throat and I stand so quickly that I'm instantly light-headed. Once again I was so absorbed in my work that I missed something.

"Excuse me?" someone called from the other side of the counter for our department.

"Pardon me, I didn't see you there," I say, taking care how I walk so I don't fall right over while my blood starts to flow normally again.

"That happens more than you know," she says, not fully joking but pointing out that she's an inch or two over five feet. I can't imagine people wouldn't stop to notice this woman. She's got curves that I've only dreamt of. "I'm Maisy."

"Oh my, where are my manners?" I say, feeling completely out of sorts. "I'm Samantha Davies, but everyone calls me Sam."

I hold out my hand to shake hers and she glances down at it and then proceeds to dig around in her bedazzled handbag.

At least I think she saw it.

I let my hand drop.

"Perfect, just the person I came to see," she says, pulling out gum, unwrapping one piece, and then tossing the remainder of the pack into her bag. "I'm here for a calendar of events for

Greenstone, I'm moving back and there are a few things I don't want to miss."

"Of course, let me grab you one." She's quiet as I walk to the filing cabinet and something feels odd. Very few people come in asking for a physical copy of anything, especially not people under the age of seventy. It's not like they can't, but most adults use the online calendar to sync with their own.

"Is there something in particular you're looking forward to?" I ask, flipping through the hanging folders.

"Not really," she says.

"Here it is," I announce. "These are subject to change, of course, so if you want the most up-to-date information, our website is the best place to confirm."

She picks up the paper, folds it in half, and puts it in her bag while looking at the office behind me. She takes her time blowing a bubble, pulling it back into her mouth before it pops and then makes a series of crackling sounds.

"No, I got what I came for and I'm not worried about a thing." Her eyes take me in for a moment.

In another context, I would have thought she was hitting on me, but this is strange. The entire interaction feels off.

"Well, if you think of something else, feel free to stop by or send me a message," I say in a cheery voice. "It was lovely to meet you—"

I'm hoping she doesn't notice I trailed off because, of course, I already forgot her name. Oh, I'm the worst at this.

She looks me over once and with a tight smile says, "I'm sure I'll see you around." Then she turns and walks away.

What was that about?

And why did she want to see *me*?

Draping myself across my couch, I weave my fingers together across my stomach and look at my feet, propped up by the armrest. I'm not sure why I'm checking the polish on my toes, I'll be wearing socks and boots today. Sighing, I assess the damage to my thumbnail. I definitely chewed it at work.

Stop replaying that scene, Sam. I did nothing that could have offended her or made her feel unwelcome.

It was likely me being so caught up in my work. Who knows how long she had to stand there? The familiar flush of guilt hits me. Automatically, I close my eyes, gently tap my thighs, and breathe.

I did nothing wrong. I was working and simply hadn't heard her. It was an honest mistake, which I corrected immediately. I was helpful and kind and did my job well.

One last exhale to let it all out. My eyes drift open, and I feel a little more centered.

Springing into action, I grab the dark blue nail polish. I touch up my nail and blow on it while pulling out my jeans that I'd never wear to work and toss them on my bed. I've mastered the art of getting ready with wet polish over the years...one of the skills from trying to hide a nervous habit. I run my free hand over the holes I've worn into this pair. One from each move I've made over the years. The left knee is the move with my family when we moved across town to a place that was one level, their dream for eventually retiring. The snag on the back pocket and start of the right knee happened over the few times I moved for college. The full right knee is from when I sort of moved in with an ex. The final snags and one of the belt loops coming halfway off are what I'm most proud of...those are from moving here. I'm not sure why, but I think learning to ride a horse seems like a fitting thing to do in these. Another big event in my life, another move forward.

The pants lay on my bed along with my simple, and I suppose sturdy, brown leather belt. My turquoise boots are just inside the closet, and I set them at the foot of my bed. I open my second drawer from the top and dig one-handed, so I don't ruin my nail polish in record time, shifting shirts out of the way until I get to a plain white V-neck. Since Tommy volunteered one of his flannel shirts, I'm not saying no to that, so this is all I need.

Once I'm dressed and my hair is pulled back into a ponytail, I toss a pair of workout pants and an extra shirt into my tote bag just in case I end up on the dirt. I'm definitely safe in Tommy's hands, but a horse is a huge animal. Can you tip off of a horse? I know that saddles are secured and there are stirrups for the riders' feet, but it's not like there's a seatbelt...

While locking my apartment, I resolve to *not* research if saddles come with seatbelts. I'm a grown-ass woman who already spent way too much time searching for tips beginning riders should know. Sitting on a saddle is going to happen, and it's going to happen today.

After I let Tommy know I'm on my way, I turn on the radio, roll down the windows, and enjoy the wind, the sun, and earthy smells that come with living in this small town and having fields of crops, horses, and cattle surrounding it. The highway is a blur and the turn to Landen Acres is here before I know it. The house comes into view and my heart is racing, but not in an anxious state, an excited one. We've only had one date for crying out loud, but not only do I like *Tommy*, I like *this*. I like this life, I like this place, I like who I'm becoming.

I like not hiding. This place, maybe this ranch even, feels like it could be home.

There are a few spaces where people can park, not with white lines or anything like that, of course, and I pull my car to the far edge, away from the house, so there are plenty of options for customers. I roll the windows up once I'm stopped when I register what's likely one of their dogs coming towards me from near the main stables. I haven't actually met any of the dogs before.

My tote falls off the seat when I reach for it, grabbing the shirt and my water bottle that are now on the floor of the passenger side. By the time I've rerolled the shirt and gotten it back into my bag, a shadow shifts near my window and my whole body jerks in surprise. My mouth is open, like I made some sort of sound, but all I hear for the next few breaths is the whooshing of my racing heartbeat because instead of a dog outside my window, it's a wolf.

And it's in this where I learn that, in true moments of adrenaline, my body neither fights nor flights.

It freezes.

Chapter 28
Tommy

Oh my God.

I jump out of my seat and bolt for the door.

"Gerald!" I yell, jogging down the steps and towards her car. "Go find Bryant."

Of course the wolf-dog comes up for a quick scratch behind his ear and I repeat the command once more before he gives Sam's car one last longing look and trots back to the stables.

"I'm so sorry about that," I say, opening her door. "He's a gigantic fluffball, but he's intimidating as hell when he does this, which isn't often, I promise."

"Who is he?" Sam asks, watching the huge canine disappear into the main stables.

"It's Bryant's dog. He's likely half-wolf, half-dog, but no one knows anything else. His name is Gerald and every now and then he'll check out a car that pulls up. He has a tendency to put his paws up on someone's arms or shoulders so he can look into their eyes, and that can be super weird the first time it happens, but he's been harmless to everyone on or visiting the ranch, and that includes the livestock," I explain, reaching my hand down. "Here, let me take something for you."

She finally looks up at me and shakes her head to clear it. "Pardon me, I wasn't expecting that. I think my brain is trying to catch up with seeing a wolf, even a half-wolf, out here."

Her face scrunches up and she looks at me when she accepts my outstretched hand. "Did you say his name is Gerald?"

"Yeah, Bryant named him." It's hard to read how she's feeling beyond surprised. But she didn't turn around before I could even call Gerald over, so that's a good sign.

She glances in the direction the wolf-dog went and lets out a startled laugh. "It's a good name for him."

Holding out my free arm, she steps close to me so I can wrap her in a tight hug. I rest my cheek on the top of her head and breathe in deep, enjoying that addicting scent that always centers me.

"You always smell so damn good to me," I murmur. "I hope that's not weird to say."

She shakes her head against my chest, then looks up at me. "Nope, not weird at all."

She lifts up on her toes, closes her eyes, and then my lips are on hers, caressing and coaxing little sounds from her. Her fingertips press into my back and her brown tote rests against my hip as it dangles from her elbow. There's an extra tingle that wasn't there before and a pepperminty smell that might be driving me a little wild, and I wonder where that's coming from. I grip the back of her neck so my thumb can trace along her jawline, feeling the shift when she opens for me, allowing me to caress her tongue with mine. Then she erases the miniscule space between us.

Ignoring her open door, I steer her backwards so she's pressed against her car, dropping my hand to her hip and trailing it along the back of her thigh to hitch up her leg. Her fingers lock behind my neck and she does a little jump so she can cross her heels at the small of my back. God, I could die a happy man right now. Relishing every sensation, I squeeze the back of her thigh, trailing up her jeans, feeling frayed holes every now and then. When I cup her ass, my fingers snag on a pocket that has been torn, making me want to tug it off right here. The entire herd of cattle could stampede by right now and I wouldn't be able to tear myself away from her if I tried.

I don't think I've ever seen her with so much as a button out of place, let alone holes in her clothes. Being able to explore them through touch has me pressing against her like there's a way to be closer. As if there was something besides a few layers of torn fabric between us. Her hands shift to my hair, urging me to stay right where I am.

A piercing catcall cuts through the air and something low, almost like a growl, rumbles in my chest.

Sam squeaks and her feet hit the ground.

"For fuck's sake," I murmur into her hair and turn my head.

"Chuck, you're a dick!" I yell in his direction as I cover her ear and tuck her head against my chest.

His laughter carries across the corrals. "Just encouraging my little brother, that's all."

"This is mortifying," Sam says into my chest. "What was I thinking? We're at your place of business and here I am practically groping you in the parking lot."

"I can promise you, every single one of my brothers has done much more not only out here, but in the office, too." I grimace. "You know, where I work."

"Still completely mortifying. How do I hide even more?" She's made herself as narrow as possible, like no one saw her legs a moment ago.

"Come here." I shift so my arm is around her shoulders, keeping her close. She whispers something that sounds like a mini pep talk to herself, shuts her car door, and leans against me as I tug her towards the house. "We can go inside before we even think of dealing with my most obnoxious brother."

"No," she groans but stops, keeping me right there with her. "You remind me not to hide. Plus, I'm riding a horse today, I can be brave."

"You're always brave, but it's okay to drop your stuff off so I cool off before saying something stupid to Chuck."

"That's a reasonable compromise," she says, letting me walk to the house with my hand on her hip, feeling it sway with each step. "Wait, all of your brothers have made out here?"

"I suppose none of us have ever caught Matt anywhere, but yeah, everyone else."

"Huh," she says, her brow furrowed.

"Who were you thinking wouldn't have?"

"I guess I'm surprised about Bryant. He seems more," she pauses, "solitary."

"Bryant may be that, but he's definitely not celibate."

Sam looks up at me with an inquisitive look. "Why does that sound like some sordid tale?"

"He's not the most social person, and he likes to keep things simple, according to him," I explain, bringing her into the office since I didn't bother to log out of a damn thing when I saw Gerald at Sam's window. "So there's a woman he met back in college who lives in a nearby town and they hook up."

"Since college?"

I nod. "I met her a few times and neither of them has any interest in the other, but apparently, when they're both single, they're happy to 'get things out of their system' as Bryant once said."

"But Matt has outsmarted you all and never got caught? It almost sounds like a right of passage at this point."

Once the computer is shut down, I return my full attention to her. "Honestly, he's the only one who hasn't brought anyone here. He doesn't really stay over anywhere, either, but we try to not ask too much, if that makes any sense. I realize that I'm not that much older than him, but since he was still seventeen when our dad died, we've all had to look out for him differently and none of us want him to resent us for treating him like a kid and not just a brother. So, while Chuck will go out of his way to tease the rest of us about our dating lives, a few moments ago was a lovely example of his maturity level half the time, he never says anything to Matt about it. Even when Matt blushes, he'll hold his tongue."

Trying to brush the lock of hair that fell onto my forehead again, I run my fingers through my hair. It's no surprise that I was in such a rush earlier that I didn't even grab my hat on the way outside. Looking up, it's still hanging in its usual spot on a hook near the windows. "Sorry, that conversation took a turn."

"Why would you apologize for telling me about your family?" she asks, standing in front of the desk with her head tilted to the side.

That gives me pause, realizing that Maisy really never cared. God, I was blind to so many things.

Shaking those thoughts from my mind, I walk around the desk to bring Sam into the house. "I suppose you're right. I just get caught up sometimes assuming every girlfriend would be annoyed at listening to me ramble."

"Now it's my turn to be curious about your exes setting the bar low." Her eyebrow raises as she smirks.

"Touché."

Chapter 29
Sam

Tommy holds the door to the house open with one hand and offers me his other. Butterflies erupt in my stomach at the contact as he walks just ahead of me.

"We still need to get you that shirt," he says, his face turned toward me and full of mischief. "I happen to know the place for the perfect one."

"Well, we wouldn't want me to show up for my first lesson in anything but the best," I reply, looking down. "Is this okay?"

He comes to a stop before the stairs, taking his time to take in my simple white t-shirt and completely beat-up jeans. A tug on my hand pulls me against him and he leans down, nudging my ear with his nose, causing my butterflies to go into overdrive.

"You're always perfect," he says in a low voice. My knees almost give out when his lips barely touch the spot under my ear and I feel my whole body flush.

Those gorgeous blue eyes find mine and he gives me a kiss. Before I can kiss him back, or even blink, he turns around to lead me upstairs.

I want to ask what that was about, why the kiss was so short, and how he could go from Mr. Sultry to just walking up the stairs with my hand in his. Like it's normal.

It does feel normal though. My hand in his fits so well and he seems to fit into my structured lifestyle. Now that my brain has fully caught up with the fact that I didn't even get a chance to kiss him back, I want to truly climb him like a tree.

All the butterflies disappear as I remember I was doing just that when his brother saw us. I've never been the girl to show any PDA with the exception of maybe holding hands. But there I was, legs holding tight to his trim waist, anchoring myself to him. I give myself the last three stairs to feel embarrassed and when we hit the landing, I let out a breath and squeeze my free hand into a fist a few times, finding my manners so I don't do that again.

"Do you all live upstairs?" I've only been on the main floor the few times I've been here. We turn to the left and Tommy reaches for a dark doorknob on the first door.

He tips his head farther down the hallway. "Matt's room is at the end and a little around the corner." He looks to the right and says, "Chuck's down that way, close to where our dad's room still is. Bryant lives on the main floor, and, well, you know where Jax lives."

"Actually, I don't." For some reason, I feel like it's important for Tommy to know this.

He pauses with the door partially open.

"He picked me up and dropped me off a few times and we kissed once, but...it was like kissing a cousin."

Tommy looks away and a snort escapes him as he covers his face.

"As much as I appreciate that detail, maybe don't tell Jax that. He's never been happier now that he's finally with Avery, but if he knew that his kissing skills weren't up to par..." His voice drifts off as he starts to laugh, pushing the door open with his back.

"Come on in," he says, his eyes twinkling as he drops my hand and closes the door. "You can put your bag on the bed. Let me grab a shirt."

Looking around his room for the first time, I'm drawn towards his bed, but not because I'd like him to toss me on it. It's definitely a queen and is neatly made. There aren't any throw pillows or a dust ruffle, but I wasn't expecting those. My fingers gently trail along the stitching on the quilt. It looks well-loved and handmade. I turn to ask about it to find him leaning against the wide dresser, arms crossed over his chest and his eyes on me.

"My grandmother made that for my dad. It's the only thing I took from his room. We've all grabbed something, but everything else is still there, just as he left it." He flashes a pained smile, but the sadness doesn't reach his eyes.

"It's beautiful," I say.

With a nod, he turns to the dresser and pulls open one of the middle drawers, pulling out a blue plaid shirt. Shaking it out, he tosses it over his shoulder and closes the space between us in three steps.

"It's only fair that you get a tour of my space."

"Oh, I was worried," I say with mock seriousness.

He stands behind me, putting both hands on my hips. He turns me so I'm facing the bed.

"This is where I sleep." His voice is comically formal. He proceeds to shift me just a little for each 'stop' on the tour. "This is the window where I see the ranch. These are the dressers, they hold my clothes. And this is the closet where the *rest* of my clothes are, if you can believe it."

"I can," I say, unable to stop the giggle that slips out.

"Shush, this is an official tour and is very serious business." He's losing the battle against keeping his smile at bay. "If you could please focus, our tour is about to move."

In an attempt to placate him and his silly antics, I pinch my lips together.

"Thank you, it's nice to know we haven't let any hooligans up here."

My body shakes while trying not to laugh.

"Now, if you'll please take three steps forward, you'll see the door we entered through. That's your main exit should you ever need one. However, should you need an alternate exit, or to use the lavatory, you'll notice we have another door."

He looks down at me, sees my expression that I'm trying desperately to hide to go along with this ridiculous bit, and he bursts out laughing.

"I can't keep that up," he says, his hands coming around to grab mine, finally letting me lean against his chest. His chest's movements jostle me and I turn around and look up at him, loving how his entire face lights up when he's laughing like this.

"But that's the bathroom and it adjoins with the next bedroom that hasn't been used in over a decade after Chuck moved to the other side of our dad's old room."

"You two shared a bathroom?" I ask.

"It was about as ridiculous as you might imagine."

Cupping his cheeks in my palms, I say in mock horror, knowing he loves his brother, "That must have been horrible."

"Oh, it was. Just imagine the pranks he pulled on me."

"I'm not sure I want to."

"You don't," he says, leaning down, erasing all the silliness in that one move and I'm thinking about the fact that we're in his bedroom. "Can I kiss you now? But this time, away from anyone who could interrupt us?"

"Yes, please."

And just like that, his mouth is on mine and I'm kissing him back like we have all the time in the world.

Chapter 30
Tommy

I'm standing in my room with Samantha Davies in my arms and she's already nipping at my lips.

God, this is a dream come true.

Instead of tossing her onto my bed, which I'm not sure we'd leave, I walk her back against the door leading to the hallway. One of her ankles wraps around my leg, twisting us together like a pretzel. Her tongue tangles with mine and my jeans are painfully restrictive as she loops one finger under my belt to make my hips flush with hers. This moment is so many dreams coming true all wrapped into one as I memorize how she feels against me.

My hands have a mind of their own, exploring her sides and feeling the gentle curves of her hips, stopping before untucking her shirt. The V-neck might look plain on someone else, but on Sam, the cut seems to draw my eyes to her chest, her shoulders, and her stomach. It's not tight or see-through, but it fits her perfectly and it's soft as hell to touch, drawing my fingers back again and again.

She gives a little shiver when my hands shift up her ribcage and my thumbs trace underneath her breasts. Another rumble comes from my chest as I feel something thin and likely lacy through the shirt.

"Catch me," she says breathlessly. Her hands lace behind my neck while mine scoop behind her as she takes a little hop, wrapping those jean-clad legs around me. I brace her in place between my chest and the door so my hands can explore these jeans while I breathe in her floral scent. My thumb finds the rip high on her thigh and it rubs her exposed skin before sliding underneath the fabric, tracing almost-lazy circles higher and higher. Fuck, I just want to stay right here until dinner, riding lessons be damned.

My pocket vibrates right as I start to kiss down her neck. A frustrated breath leaves me and I rest an arm against the door as Sam sighs.

"I think we need to shut our phones off the next time we're alone."

"Or just block Chuck's number for a while," I offer.

She giggles as my phone vibrates again. "You should check that, it could be important."

Giving her a little space between me and the door, Sam slides down my body a few inches, which doesn't help the state of my dick, until her feet hit the ground. There's one more vibration as I pull my phone out of my pocket.

"Not Chuck," I tell her. "But it's Matt giving us a heads up that Chuck seems to have less restraint than usual."

My mind tries to go through possibilities for what Chuck might say or do, but I take a deep breath. "Lovely."

"Well, he already cat-called us outside, so it can't get much worse than that, right?" Sam asks.

"Definitely not for you. He'll lay off. But he might be extra-obnoxious with me and the rest of the guys. I promise he's a good guy…he's just a bit much at times. It's just all aimed at me or my brothers."

"I'll take notes about how siblings behave, then."

"Sometimes I forget you're an only child."

"How did you know that?" she asks, neither of us creating more space than I needed to get my phone.

"I listen." My shrug causes the flannel shirt to fall down my arm. Grabbing it before it falls, I hold it up in front of Sam like she's at a fitting. She's going to be swimming in the fabric. "Perfect size."

"Yes, it will be perfect for hiding the entire top half of me." She takes it from me before I can grab it back in mock offense.

I should step back, but my feet seem unwilling to do so. So, instead, I stay rooted right here, watching Sam's arms and shoulders disappear into the sleeves. Her fingers easily roll the sleeves up, exposing first her wrists and then a little of her forearm. My eyes linger on the way the front of the shirt is open and draped over her. The sudden lack of movement catches my attention and her fingers are mid-sleeve-roll.

Something about this has my senses in overdrive. Her floral scent seems stronger and I catch a little lilac in it. And now I can't wait for the lilac bushes on the ranch to bloom.

"I'm sorry, did I do something wrong?" Sam's voice pulls me back into the present, my eyes finding hers immediately. Her brows are pinched and her mouth is in a tense line.

"What?" I ask, completely confused about what she's referring to.

"The shirt, should I take it off?" Her hand is still on the sleeve.

I stare at her, dumbfounded and trying to catch up.

"I," she hesitates. "I don't have to wear it if it's bothering you."

That snaps me out of it. I was staring like a creep and she thought I didn't like what I saw.

My expression softens and I cover her hand with both of mine, making one more fold in the sleeve.

"I'm sorry that you thought that." My fingers make their way to hers, willing her to relax. "The truth is, I might ask you to wear one every damn day."

A gorgeous blush fills her cheeks and she tips her face down. Drawing one hand up, her fingers still woven between mine, I place gentle pressure under her chin and lean down.

"No hiding," I say, giving her a soft kiss. Her eyes are still closed when I pull back and she looks calm, like she's not racing through lists and possibilities that I know run through her mind.

"It's not my natural response, you know," she says, her eyes on mine.

"Oh, I do." She frees one hand and swats my chest as I chuckle. "But I also want you to understand that I want all of you. Not just what you let people see, but every little quirk and everything you consider to be a flaw. I want it all."

"You might be asking for way more than you bargained for." Her weight shifts from one foot to the next.

"You worried that I might scare easily, Samantha Davies?" I wrap my free hand around her waist and steady her against me.

"What makes you so confident that you'll like everything about someone like me?" She says it lightly, but I don't miss the ghost of a wince and the worry she can't quite hide from her eyes.

"My last relationship ended about a year ago," I say, my heart steady. "Things happened that really messed with me, but I also found a new outlook on dating. I'm not interested in something that's not going to work and pretending that it might. What I want is someone whose good and bad can grow with mine. I've been paying attention for a while now and I'm not worried about a damn thing."

She blinks rapidly. "Okay then."

"Okay then."

Chapter 31
Sam

I refuse to be a blubbering mess two days in a row. Tommy's words in his room were so simple and sure and his kiss before we left was soft and tender. He already reads when I need reassurance, when I need to be seen, and when I need time to process.

"Are you ready?" he asks, one hand on my waist, the other on the top of the saddle.

Which is strapped firmly to a horse. I asked him to check it. Twice.

I look down at him from the steps, which is an odd feeling.

"She's truly the best horse for a new rider."

The horse in question is standing pretty still, like she would wait as long as I need until I feel ready. But I was raised to not make others wait, so I reach out and put my hands on the saddle.

"Oh my."

The horse gives a little huff. It doesn't feel judgmental, but since I haven't spent time around horses, I could be wrong.

"That's it, cowgirl, nice and easy."

If I wasn't so out of my element, I might have laughed at Tommy using that nickname as I'm attempting to keep my right foot firmly grounded on the top step while turning my left to get into the stirrups.

"What's the singular word for stirrups?" I ask, trying to take my mind off the sheer size of this horse.

"Stirrup."

"Okay."

Stirrup, I amend in my mind. My left foot is contorting to get into the stirrup.

"Alright," Tommy says, totally unphased by my technical question. "Now, just like we practiced a few minutes ago, swing your right leg over."

"You're absolutely sure the saddle is tight?" I ask, willing away the automatic internal chastisement reminding me that I could be offending him and his ability to do something quite elementary for him.

"I wouldn't let you get on this horse if I wasn't." His voice is steady and sure, not a hint of judgment at my ridiculousness.

Chuck is getting ready to ride his horse out to see the cattle, but, as Tommy assured me, he has been a jokester without giving me a hard time for climbing his brother like a tree right in front of their house and in full view of the stables. Matt is around here somewhere with Caleb, but thankfully they're out of view. I just know at any moment both brothers and the literal rodeo star could come out and just watch me fail spectacularly.

Except, with Tommy right here, my brain is aware of all these things without focusing on them. Instead, it's right here with this horse.

"What's her name, again?" I ask, not trying to hide the fact I'm stalling. I can't believe I already forgot this horse's name.

"Bella, short for Isabella."

"Thank you." Part of me wants to start asking Bella questions about how best to proceed so I don't spook her.

"Sam." My name from his lips helps me focus.

"Would you count to three?" I blurt.

"Of course," he says, giving my hip a tiny squeeze. "One."

I release the air from my lungs in a shaky exhale, willing at least some of the nerves to follow.

"Two."

A steady breath in as I hold my balance and squat down just a little, everything zeroing in on Tommy's next word.

"Three."

Pushing off the step, I'm half airborne, feeling the strange sensation of one foot in a stirrup which is now driving my movements. As expected, the leather saddle isn't a cushioned seat, so when my butt lands, it's a feeling of sturdiness.

I look down at Tommy who is grinning from ear to ear.

"What do I hold?" I ask, wishing for a handle and realizing all of the practicing we did has left my brain.

He hands me the reins, which feel ridiculous for me to be holding. As usual, he must sense my trepidation.

"She's tied up, don't worry. And I'll be leading her until you're ready." He rubs Bella's nose. "Can I help you get your right foot in?"

I was so focused on getting my leg over and what I'm supposed to do with my hands that I missed that one foot feels solidly in its stirrup, while the other is dangling. The blood drains from my face thinking of how easy I could just tip right over.

A gentle hand on my calf jolts me out of that line of thought.

"You're doing amazing."

He guides my foot into the other stirrup.

"Try standing in the stirrups just like we practiced," he instructs, my body reacting immediately.

"Good," he says with a smile, looking at how high I'm off the saddle all the way down to where my foot is pressing against the stirrup holding me up. Somehow. "Everything looks great here. Are you comfortable?"

His blue eyes find mine. I nod at him, lowering myself to a seated position.

"Would you like me to take Bella for a little walk? We're staying inside this little corral."

I look around the enclosure, heart pounding with nerves and excitement. Bella isn't their largest horse by far, but she feels enormous underneath me. My legs feel her body heat through my jeans already. I can tell when she takes a breath just because of the smooth movement. She seems unbothered by me.

Clearing my throat, which feels right from this stress, before I squeak out a "yes". There's something so new and so unique to being on top of a horse. It's terrifying to be at the mercy of a living creature this big, fast, and powerful, but it's also empowering and healing. Giving a certain degree of control away like this is freeing.

I must make a sound of surprise when she starts walking because Tommy looks back to see if I'm okay. I give him what must be a slightly-crazed smile instead of one of confidence because he chuckles softly, leading Bella on. The walk jostles me more than I thought and I use the different techniques Tommy mentioned in the stables for steadying myself. It's not long before I feel the rhythm of her motions. The pattern of how each of her feet touch down and how that shifts me without making me feel like I'm being thrown off. It makes me think that you need to be engaged with the horse for it to be a comfortable ride. There's a mutual respect, and a way to connect that allows you to flow with the horse's movements.

It's easy to see why so many people love this.

"Look at you go, cowgirl."

"I'm not sure I can be considered one just yet," I say, looking around this enclosed space and then down at Tommy who is calmly walking while holding a rope connected to Bella's bridle.

"As someone who grew up around horses, I can officially say the nickname has been well-earned and you'll be wearing a ten-gallon hat in no time."

"I could simply borrow yours."

He stops our first lap and turns to look me in the eyes. "You're ready for that?" His voice is gravelly and the intensity in the question is palpable.

"To wear a hat?" I ask, confused at the turn this has taken.

Realization washes over his features.

"Ah, city girls might not have the same traditions." His hand rubs his five o'clock shadow and he shifts his weight to one foot.

"What have I missed?"

"Wear the hat, ride the cowboy."

Well, that's news to me.

Chapter 32
Tommy

The shock on Sam's face is priceless and I'm half expecting her to say *pardon*.

"Oh," she says, her mouth holding the shape of the word and I can practically hear her mind buzzing.

"You're welcome to wear mine and I'll defend your honor until the cows come home," I say, trying to pull her out of whatever rabbit hole she's about to go down.

She frowns and her mouth scrunches up. "Your cows are home. They live here."

At least she has something new to focus on. I flash her a smile. "Not literally in this case."

Pulling gently on the rope, I get Bella moving again and turn around.

"But you'd be okay with that?" she asks.

Resisting responding with too much enthusiasm, I settle on saying, "I'd love to see you wear anything of mine, anywhere."

She gives a thoughtful *hm* behind me. "Do you have more than one?"

"Hat? I have a straw one for when it's too hot, but not another one of these." I tip my hat towards her and touch the brim.

"And the color? Does white signify anything?"

Shaking my head, I say, "My hats growing up were white because Chuck always picked black and then we'd never fight over them. So, when I turned eighteen, my dad picked this one out for me. It's a little cooler than everyone else's, which is nice in the summer, but I have to do a little more maintenance to keep it clean."

"But a cowboy hat has another…meaning when it comes to who wears it," she phrases it almost like a question.

I glance back and see her eyebrows pinched together in concentration. "Is your brain working in overdrive at learning rules you weren't aware of?"

Sam blinks and relaxes. "You can read me well, Tommy."

"I'd like to think I'm learning." I clear my throat and continue, "The big thing to remember is that these hats are more than just something we throw on. They're a part of us. We take care of them and they can last a lifetime. For someone else to take it is a bold move and for another person to wear it is a big deal. Now, some people might try it for attention or to state intention, but if you see someone wearing a hat that isn't theirs…well, I guess we covered that."

"That makes sense. Now that I think about it, the more instances I can recall where their importance played into what someone did with their hat. It just wasn't enough to prompt a question I didn't realize I had." She flushes and looks around the corral. "We did a full lap already?"

Holding back a smile so she doesn't think I'm mocking her, I say, "We have. You're a quick study, cowgirl."

"I happen to have a great person guiding me, who better not let go of that rope."

"Not until you ask for it, we're going at whatever pace feels good." That earns me one of her unguarded, unpracticed smiles that lights up her face, making her eyes sparkle, and her nose scrunch. I mean it in every way with her, too. Whatever pace she needs, I'm willing to take it with her. Whatever reassurances she might need along the way, I want to give her. Whatever bumps come up, I hope to smooth out. No one else has held my heart like this. I've been wrapped around someone else's finger, but I see that now for what it was, and what it wasn't, and with how critical I've been about anyone to even consider one date with, I know I've done more than my own due diligence in trying to find Samantha's faults in the months before I decided to see if she might be interested.

But her faults aren't deal-breakers, they're simply things that can be balanced. And I can only hope that mine fall under the same category.

"Do I need to steer in here?" she asks, pulling me out of my thoughts. "Does she just keep going in circles because we're in the corral?"

"Are you telling me you're ready for me to step away?" I look back at her studying the reins but looking comfortable on Bella.

"Maybe in a minute, I'm not sure that I'm going to be able to slow her down if she runs, though, but I think I might be able to get her to go in the right direction."

"This corral isn't very big," I remind her. "I promise you she won't be galloping in here. But if she spooks, which is unlikely, I'll jump back in here to calm her and keep you safe."

She nods resolutely. "Okay then. What's next?"

I hold back a comment about her trying to make sure she gets a perfect grade out here, but she's determined to get this right. "I undo the tether and can keep walking next to her for as long as you'd like."

"Won't you get tired?"

"Are you questioning my stamina, Samantha Davies?" I ask, raising my eyebrow. That seems to completely fluster her as a perfect blush spreads across her cheeks. "A few laps in here aren't going to wear me out, I can promise you that."

She lets out a little squeak when I throw her a wink and I shift so I'm looking ahead again. Bella lets out a little snort and I rub her snout, unsure if she's judging my flirting techniques, or if she's praising them.

"I haven't managed to scare her off so far, Bella," I say under my breath. "I must be doing something right."

Chapter 33
Sam

Nope, I need to focus on the giant horse that I'm riding and not think about Tommy's stamina. Or the desire he didn't try to hide in his eyes. There are too many details to catalog and unpack while sitting on Bella.

I notice the way the reins feel in my hand. The leather is soft, well-worn, and well-loved. It's mostly smooth, but there are little nubs that I trace with the pad of my thumb. Next I wiggle my toes in my turquoise boots. I wasn't sure how safe I'd feel relying on these two stirrups to anchor myself, raising up and down with Bella as she walks, but it's surprisingly secure. Even through the saddle and my jeans, I can feel her body heat seep into my legs and, when she's still, each breath expands her massive ribcage, lifting me just a hair. The seat is wider than I expected, which is odd, because the only thing I've really noticed about horses is how massive they are. But their size always seemed more about their height.

A cleansing exhale leaves my lungs as I'm fully back in the moment and focused on this horse, this experience.

"I think I'm ready if Bella is." I refrain from running a hand down my face in embarrassment by squeezing the reins tighter without pulling on them.

What a silly thing to say. Why wouldn't this horse be ready?

"You ready for Sam to lead, Bella?" he asks, rubbing the horse's nose.

And she gives one of those little snorts where her lips flap, tipping her head up for a moment. Like she understood and is saying yes.

Tommy looks back and smiles at me. "I think we're all set. I'll unclip and can stay in here for the first few laps if you'd like."

That's typical Tommy style and it makes my heart melt at his thoughtfulness. I nod, probably looking a little overenthusiastic with nerves coursing through me while determination seems to be winning. This is something I've never done and I *want* to be in this community. I want to know what the ranchers and farmers do. I want to truly understand their attachments to this life, this land. And I want to belong to what has been built here generation after generation and make it more sustainable. To share this with him.

The metallic sound of Tommy removing the tether makes me realize that I'm on my own. It's just Bella and me. Yes, he's in the corral with us, but we're at each other's mercy.

More like I'm at hers.

She keeps her pace steady, unlike my heart, which is pounding. I peek down at my feet, trying to not off-set my balance to make sure my boots are fully in the stirrups, then remember that I'm steering this horse and look up. I check that my hands have both reins the way they were originally positioned and that I'm not pulling back or too much to one side, except to gently lead her with the curve of the circle.

Tommy steps to the center so he's next to the step and he turns as we circle him. His smile is wide and he looks proud of me.

"You're a natural, Samantha Davies," he says, his voice just loud enough to hear over the crunching of Bella's steps. "How do you feel?"

"Terrified and free?" I venture.

"Just enjoy the ride, there's nothing to overthink, you're doing amazing."

I grimace. "Easier said than done."

"Okay then, truth or dare?" he asks, wearing a satisfied smirk.

"Isn't this practically a dare in itself?" I squeak, realizing that this horse is huge and even though she's going at a nice, slow pace right now, one wrong move on my part could send me flying off.

"Truth it is then." Out of the corner of my eye, I see him tap his cheek with one finger as he thinks. I wiggle my feet a little so they're a little farther into the stirrups and immediately pull them back to where Tommy placed them, wondering if I could get stuck in a stirrup. "What did you want to be when you were little?"

My head pops up, my eyes meet his. "An administrative assistant."

He doesn't look surprised or anything, he just asks me what made me want to do that.

"I don't know," I say, my gaze returning to Bella's ears, watching them shift as I speak. "I used to always pretend to welcome people into an office and work at a computer or filling papers or answering phones. I'm sure there were other occupations I pretended to work in, but that was my main one."

"So, you've always enjoyed putting information together and making things happen. That makes sense."

"I guess so." I sit up a little taller, feeling proud that those childhood dreams came true in ways I couldn't have imagined and knowing how much I love what I get to do.

"You ready for another truth?"

"Give me your best shot," I say, feeling a new sense of confidence.

"How long was your last relationship?"

"Two and a half years."

"How long ago did it end?"

"Shortly before I did my final interview in Greenstone." My answers come out naturally, my reflex to be polite and make a good impression outweighing my nerves.

"What's something you've always wanted to do with someone?" Tommy seems to have something ready immediately.

"Watch the sunrise. You're going to have to work harder than that to stump me, you know."

"You've never watched the sun rise?"

"I have, just not with someone."

He makes a thoughtful noise and butterflies erupt at the thought of what he could be cooking up. Tommy pays attention to details like this and he's the type of guy who could make it happen.

"What's the most ridiculous gift you were given by someone you dated?"

"Okay, I'm a little impressed by this question," I relent. "Probably a corsage."

"Wouldn't you have needed to wear those for your cotillions?"

I roll my eyes at him and Bella snorts, seemingly on my side. "I was given one when the guy I was dating in high school broke up with me. He walked up to me in school with it in his hands, gave it to me, and said that we should just be friends."

"What the hell?"

"Exactly," I agree. "The gift would have been sweet for just about any other reason, but it was the most bizarre thing."

Tommy makes a tsk-ing sound before saying, "Those city boys have no manners, apparently."

"That one for sure."

"Alright then, what's something none of your exes realized about you?"

"That I'm really good at faking it."

Oh. My. Goodness. I just said that out loud. My whole body tenses in mortification as I try to think of something, anything, to add to that sentence to make it sound like I was *not* talking about a lack of orgasms.

I realize that Bella has stopped moving on top of my mind whirring. Looking down, I see that I've clearly pulled back on the reins in my panic and my legs are pressing into her sides. At least she responded to my panic by stopping and not leaping over the corral?

I suppose if she had jumped, if I could have managed to stay in the saddle, I would be riding somewhere that I could hide.

But no. Tommy's low whistle cuts through the thoughts pinging back and forth in my head.

This is a whole new level of mortification.

Chapter 34
Tommy

If the shade of red her face is turning is any indication, Sam's mind is spiraling trying to find a way to take back what she just said. But we're both adults and if those fools don't know what it feels like when someone comes, then they're even more pathetic than I thought.

"How many times did you *not* have to fake it?" I ask, my voice even so she keeps talking.

"Oh my goodness, I can't answer that." She looks like she has a terrible sunburn now, the furious blush spreading down her neck and chest. "How do I get her going again?"

"Gently flick the reins or click your tongue."

She does both, of course, needing to do things the best way possible.

"So," I say, letting a little silence fill the space for a moment. "You haven't answered and we're both adults."

"How many times have you faked it?" she asks, groaning, and I hold back a chuckle before she murmurs, "That was a ridiculous question."

"I don't know any guy who has been able to fake the uh, end result. But if you don't want to talk about it, we don't have to."

Sam looks up at the sky with a sigh. "I don't know."

I drop it, curious as hell though. Not because I want to hear just how much her exes failed to know how to find a damn clit, but wanting to understand who she was in a relationship, just what she put up with so I can learn what to look for. I don't ever want her to hide, not from me.

"Probably twice." She barely mumbles the words, but I hear them and choke on my own spit for a second.

I'm about to ask her how these guys could have been so dense but I stop the second I see her expression. It's more than embarrassment about the topic.

"Samantha Davies," I say, waiting for her to look at me. "Are you thinking it was anything other than their fault for not paying attention to your needs?"

She makes a sour face.

"Did any of your exes ask what you like?" My fist clenches behind my back so she can't see my growing frustration at how these guys made her feel. I fight to keep my face neutral for her.

"Why would they need to do that?" Her question is sincere and that tears at something deep inside of me.

"Everyone is different for what brings them the most pleasure. There may be a few things that many guys tend to enjoy, but women, in particular, aren't a one-size-fits-all sort of deal. You have to figure out the little things that work for each person."

Her brows furrow and she looks at the stables. I'm baffled that this seems to be news to her...that she might have thought the "issue" was with her, and I want to make all of those thoughts ancient history.

"We'll get past two soon enough, don't you worry about it." That gets her attention and I give her a wink.

"Pardon me?" She sounds flustered but not ashamed, so that's a step in the right direction.

"I mean, I'm more than willing to learn, as I hope you know by now." One side of my mouth involuntarily tugs upwards. My need to keep her proud of herself overrides any remaining nerves about flirting with this gorgeous woman who happens to be wearing my shirt.

Her lips part and her blue eyes blink rapidly. Bella lets out a soft whinny, startling Sam enough where she refocuses on the horse.

"Do you think you're ready for me to be on the other side of the gate? I'm not moving farther away than that."

Her posture shifts, like her mind is leaving all of those feelings for later so she can tackle the task at hand. Determination replaces her nerves and self-consciousness when she meets my eyes once more, giving me a nod.

Stepping backwards until my back hits the gate, I turn for just a moment to climb a few rungs until I can swing my leg over and hop down on the other side. Sam's eyes dart from Bella to me a few times as the mare keeps her leisurely pace.

"Is this okay?" I ask, leaning forward so my forearms rest on the gate.

"We seem to have found a groove." She flashes me a quick smile before checking the reins once more.

"You definitely have."

After another fifteen or so minutes, Sam has successfully stopped, started, and turned Bella around several times. Her hips move in time with Bella's gait, which makes my mind think of the different ways she might move that way with me. But, best of all, she looks more unguarded by the moment. That unpracticed smile comes out each time she tries a maneuver making her eyes sparkle.

Thankfully, Chuck has stayed in the stables with everyone else doing who knows what. Otherwise, he'd likely be cackling at whatever love-struck puppy expression I undoubtedly have on my face right now.

Sam steers Bella so I can rub the horse's soft, brown nose.

"How are you feeling?" I ask.

She looks thoughtful for a moment before responding. "Like I might be sitting a little funny tomorrow, but I don't mind that in the least."

"Would you like to dismount and brush her down?"

"You'll walk me through it?" she asks.

"Of course."

Her nod is all I need to see and I'm back inside the corral as the three of us move to the steps, Sam beaming with pride at directing Bella to the right spot. I stand next to the steps with one hand on Bella to keep her still and offer Sam the other.

"Do I just take my boot out of the stirrup and windmill my leg over Bella and hope it lands on the step?"

"That's one option," I say, holding back a chuckle at her phrasing. "I can help, too, but once your foot is free, be sure that you feel balanced."

"Can you steady me?"

As if she'd ever have to ask me twice. I'm not fully sure what she wants steadied, so I face her and put one hand on each of her hips, Bella holding her position beautifully. My fingers curl on their own, wanting to take her off the horse and right up to my room. But I wait as she shifts to free her foot.

"You can set the reins on the pommel and use that to anchor yourself as you bring your leg over," I say, walking her through it. "That's it."

She gives a little squeak as she swings her leg over the back end of the horse and my fingers grip a little tighter. She starts to slip from the momentum and I slow her progress so her boot can find the step.

"Can I take my other foot out now?"

I nod, loving the feel of each movement and how there are little shifts in her hips that my hands absorb. With both of her feet on the top step, she stands up straight.

"I did it." Her voice is practically a whisper.

"You did." I reluctantly release her and she turns towards me with the brightest smile yet, putting her arms on my shoulders. I think she's about to jump on me so I shift my weight back to catch her, but I end up pulling her off-balance and we tumble to the ground in a heap.

At least we fell away from Bella who looks back at us like we're both crazy as I make sure Sam is okay.

Chapter 35
Sam

"I think the only bruising I'll have is my ego," I say, trying to make light of the fact that, while attempting to give Tommy a hug and maybe a kiss, we somehow got our wires crossed and ended up in the dirt.

Thankfully, this dirt appears to be poop-free.

But this seems to be a regularly used corral so I can only imagine how much poop gets stepped on and worked into this very patch of dirt.

Poop-dirt.

I feel my ponytail, noticing that a few clumps fall out. The clumps are pretty dry and I will myself to believe that they're only dirt. Plain dirt.

"Are you sure?" Tommy asks, concern in his eyes. "I thought you were about to jump, so I was getting ready to catch you and shifted my stance."

His fingers gently brush something off my shoulder. Something that I try to ignore.

Well, I don't ignore the feeling of his light touch, that gets my brain focused on anything but the dirt and what it may or may not contain pretty darn quickly.

"Is it safe to jump into someone's arms around a horse?" I ask, my eyes drawn to Bella, who looks absolutely massive from down here.

"It would depend on the horse," Tommy says, giving my ponytail a playful tug to bring my attention back to him. He shifts into a squat and offers me a hand. "Bella is pretty calm in just about any situation we've seen her in. Another horse might rattle her if it's pushy, but that's about it."

Butterflies are back the moment my fingers brush his. Then he grips my hand and pulls us both up to our feet where I finally find my manners.

"Thank you."

His free hand tucks a strand of hair behind my ear before he tugs me to him.

"You're welcome," he says right before he gives me a single, soft kiss, making me want to melt against him.

Bella gives a whinny, breaking the little bubble we created.

"We should probably bring her back in?" I guess.

"We should," Tommy says, nodding. "Chet, who mostly works at the small stables near Jax's house, should be here now, and he'll get her taken care of."

Tommy clips the lead back on, speaking softly to Bella, and holds out his hand for me. I weave our fingers together, loving how those butterflies swarm through me as he tugs me next to him before we walk towards the stables.

I watch our boots step almost in synchronicity, listening to the hard earth beneath us crunch. Bella's breathing is steady and the rhythm of her metal shoes has a familiar sound now. Not only that, but just life with Tommy around feels natural.

"You brought a change of clothes?" Tommy asks, leading me towards the stairs that lead to his room after we've taken off our boots.

"I did. I wasn't sure if I wore appropriate attire or if I'd be bucked off, landing in a puddle or trough and needing something dry."

"It's almost a shame you did." He looks back at me as we ascend the stairs, the house as quiet as it was when I got here earlier.

"Pardon?" I'm sure I must have misheard him. He usually is so open and accepting of my preparedness.

He stops us at the top of the stairs, murmurs something to himself I can't make out, and then he cups my face in his free hand and kisses me. This one isn't slow like the kiss outside just a few minutes ago. It's decisive. It's confident.

And it's so damn sexy.

He pulls back before things get too heated in plain view of anyone entering the house, which I appreciate. I've never been able to forget where I am like I can with him. Normally, I'm so focused on what's proper and expected that I'd never dream of any PDA beyond holding hands, but just a few hours ago I was climbing up this gorgeous man trying to get closer to him in full view of his brothers.

His eyes hold mine and his pupils are wide as they take in my face. He looks hungry. Hungry for me.

The supposedly mild-mannered Landen brother somehow seems to be on the same page as me at any given time. My eyes dart from his to the door to his room and he cocks his head to the side, a smirk lifting the edge of his lips as he walks backward, his hand slipping from my cheek to the back of my neck, and the one that was holding mine is on my hip and I slip my fingers through his belt loops.

"When do your brothers come in for the day?" I ask, hoping to not get caught twice in one day, but wanting very much to make out with Tommy for a while.

"Not for a bit," he says confidently. "But we also have established ground rules since we all live under the same roof."

"Oh?"

He nudges the door open with his foot.

"You probably haven't noticed, but not one of us has a shared wall."

"Pardon?" I ask, totally perplexed.

"We've done some soundproofing over the years, but to make sure there's privacy, none of us have rooms next to each other. Even

Bryant's room isn't directly under Matt's." Tommy shuts the door with a click as his lips trail feather-light kisses down my neck.

"So none of you can...hear anything happening?" My words come out breathless and I can feel him smile against my skin.

"Nope, and when a door is shut, it stays that way. If there's an emergency, we knock, but our rooms are our own." He backs me up against the wall next to his closet and I pull him against me, relishing in the feel of the heat from him sinking into me as he kisses his way back up my neck.

"Truth or dare," he whispers into my ear.

I don't know what to expect from this but I'm feeling bold. "Dare."

A nibble on my ear has me gasping as his knee parts my legs. He makes a low sound in his throat that rumbles in his chest and I feel it all the way to my core. "I dare you," he says as he kisses along my jaw, "to tell me everything you're thinking and feeling for the next hour."

"And what do you have planned for the next full hour, Tommy Landen?"

"If you're interested, I plan to have you come for me three times."

Part of me thinks I should be terrified that this isn't going to work, that there's something wrong with me.

"What do you think?" he asks, eyes locked on mine, giving me the confidence to own this decision and let him in. Let him see me bare—not just my body but allowing him to read me and my desires.

And even though I'm scared shitless that this is going to end like almost every other experience, the fact that he's asking and that he's shown me over and over he's here for me, all of me, I nod.

Chapter 36
Tommy

"I need to hear you say it, Samantha." I hold her gaze, willing her to stay with me and not dismiss intimacy as something that's only one-way. My fingers ache to trace the movement of her throat as she swallows hard. To trace every inch of her.

After a few moments, she takes a deep breath and I brace myself for rejection. I know I'm asking for her to put a lot of trust in me and she might think I'm a little overzealous, but I'll be damned if I don't try to show her what she deserves from a partner.

"I'm interested," she says, her voice soft but steady.

I stop myself from starting everything right this second because I need one thing from her still. "And the dare? Do you think you can handle that?"

She winces just a little, almost imperceptibly. "How detailed do I need to get?"

"Enough to tell me if you don't like something for any reason, and if you *do* like something, but it could be even better with an adjustment, I'd like you to tell me that." I pause. "Or you could show me."

Just as I expect, the flush of desire shifts to mild mortification, if such a thing exists.

"But you don't have to do the last one for the dare," I assure her.

"I just tell you if it's not helping, or if it can be better?" she asks.

"Mm-hmm."

"I can try."

"Okay then." I lean in so our noses touch.

"Okay then," she says, closing the space between our lips and I let hers caress mine. Her fingers release their hold on my belt loops and glide up my sides and chest before clasping behind my neck.

She opens her mouth with me, giving me access while tipping her head back. I finally shift the knee between her legs so she's starting to grind down on me and let my hips shift forward, causing her to gasp, stealing the air from me. With her hips in my hands, I rock her, rubbing down on my thigh and my trapped dick, which I'm trying desperately to ignore because this is all for Sam.

The change is subtle when she takes over the rhythm and the pressure, but she's holding herself up with those hands around my neck and only one foot on the ground. As much as I want her to only wear my shirt, I use one hand to pull apart the knot she tied in the front. She didn't button it, just tied the ends together, making her look perfect. God, I need to find a different word for her than that...but it's true, she's fucking perfect.

Ruling out keeping her against the wall, I loop my arm around her and lift so she's fully flush against me, hooking one leg behind my back. She's quick to wrap her other leg around my waist, pressing her core against me, and I imagine what it might feel like to sink deep into her.

Every now and then she makes this sound that's a cross between a gasp and a squeak, driving me insane to find ways to make her do it more. With her in my arms like this, with her holding me tight as I walk us to the bed, it tugs at something deep inside of me, something that's been waiting for her. Bracing the back of her head, my other hand on her beautiful ass, I lay her down and unlace her fingers so I can work my shirt off of her.

"What if I'm not ready to give that back, yet?" she asks, her mouth chasing mine as I pull back to look at her.

"You can wear as many of my clothes as you can put on, or pack up."

"You might run out of things to wear if you let me do that."

"If it means I get to see you in them, I'll walk around in yours if I have to."

Her hand slaps over her mouth, trying to contain her giggles. "You'd never fit."

I shrug, pulling her arm out of the sleeve. "You have some skirts with elastic waistbands, I'll just stick to those and not your jeans."

"Oh my goodness, you'd definitely never fit in my jeans."

"Maybe not all of me..."

When she swats my chest, I trap her hand in mine and lean down, kissing her. Nothing gentle or exploratory. This is a kiss where we know what's coming next and her legs tighten against my hips. Now that both of her arms are free of the sleeves, I leave my shirt half-underneath her and let go of her hand, running my fingers up her arm in light passes. Goosebumps follow the path I take on her exposed skin and I know I'm going to check each place her skin will pebble like this on her whole body.

Those damn noises are back, urging me on. I roll my hips once and balance myself on one arm so my other hand is free to explore her side. Little shivers that could be from attraction or being ticklish cause her to shift the pressure against my dick that sends sparks through my body. A light hissing sound escapes me while I try to rein in my desire. It has been over a year since I was with someone, so anything beyond my hand will likely mean I'm going to finish much sooner than I'd like, and I have to be careful.

Her fingers comb through my hair, tugging just a little bit and for a second, I imagine what it might feel like when I get to taste her with those fingers digging into my scalp. The thought of her letting me go down on her has me deepening the kiss, letting my tongue have a mind of its own. And Sam is so fucking responsive to my touch that she's ruining me for anyone else.

Oh hell, I knew the second she kissed me back the first time that I was ruined for anyone else.

Tugging at her shirt, I untuck it and her hips raise to help, which presses her core against my length causing me to grunt.

"Fuck, you're amazing," I whisper in her ear. "You know that right?"

"So you keep saying," she pants, raising up with me so I can remove her white t-shirt. This is the most I've seen of her and I groan because she's stunning.

Chapter 37
Sam

Tommy's eyes take less than one second to stare down at my exposed skin now that my top half is only in my bra before he's on me again, kissing his way along the fabric covering my breasts.

"I keep saying that," he says, his lips barely making contact as he speaks. He continues his trail for a moment. "Because it's true."

Everything about him is driving me closer and closer to that edge without having done anything in my pants. Looking down at him, I see his cowlick that causes one part of his hair to fall in his face when his hat is off, and I know that I want this, I want him, for as long as he'll have me.

All coherent thoughts leave my brain when his thumb slips under the bottom of my bra, swiping near my nipple. My entire body shudders at the close contact and when he runs that thumb in a circle around it, my back arches on its own volition, pressing myself towards his body. With that one hand, he deftly brings his fingers between my breasts where the clasp is and with a little flick, the tension around my ribs loosens.

Tommy's moan continues as his mouth captures my now-exposed nipple, the vibration from his voice with the feel of his tongue causes a mewling sound to escape me. When his hand flips both cups out of the way, his fingers find my other nipple, rolling it, tugging lightly on it, and palming my breast, the sensation is almost too much.

Holy cow, I've never felt this much pleasure just from staying above-the-belt.

Worry creeps in as I think about the progression of what's to come. What if I can't have an orgasm with someone else very well? What if this doesn't work?

A chill hits one breast when Tommy lifts his head. "Where'd you go just now? Is this okay?"

My mouth opens to respond but nothing comes out, so I nod.

"Tell whatever is going through your mind to take a hike, we have important business to attend to." His grin is contagious.

Soaking in his cedar and garlic scent, I tug at the back of his head and tip mine down. His lips are on mine and I lose myself in the feel of how quickly our mouths move in sync. How eager we both are to connect like this. My tongue finds his and he seems to devour any sound that leaves me. His fingers deftly move from my breast and caress their way down my belly, brushing against the top of my jeans.

"Is this okay?" he asks, leaving kisses down my jaw.

Nerves try to consume me so I focus on the ones of anticipation as I nod. I'm well aware that he's had girlfriends before, but the ease and speed that he has that top button undone has me wondering just how many people the so-called nerdy Landen brother has done this with and I stare at the ceiling. I push down the jealousy that automatically surfaces to make way for the self-doubt. What if he doesn't like any hair down there? What if he likes a lot? Oh God, what if he thinks I smell or something horrifying like that?

"Samantha," he whispers in my ear, which he then nibbles on, pulling me back in the moment. His fingers are at the top of my underwear. I can't even remember which ones I'm wearing, for crying out loud... "What's not working?"

Oh my goodness, he thinks he's doing something wrong.

"Nothing," I squeak out.

He pauses his progress and lets his finger trace a lazy circle right where it is, making me want him more than I thought possible. As he lifts his head so he can look at me, I already know the face he'll be making: one eyebrow raised with a deadpan expression.

And I'm right.

My hand goes over my face and I let out a frustrated sound. "It's not you at all. I'm worried that I'm doing something wrong, or did something wrong, or will do something wrong."

He looks puzzled. "Why would you be thinking that?"

"I don't know! I'm not used to being the center of attention."

"We can stop," he begins.

"Please, for the love of all that is holy don't you dare do that."

That earns me a smirk. "Alright then," he says. "Then we need to change something up."

Sitting up, he looks around the room for a moment. "Stay right here."

It takes so much self-control to not reclasp my bra the moment he steps away, holding up a finger to keep me still. Tommy closes the door to the bathroom and pulls the blinds down over the windows, dimming the light in the room. He unbuttons his shirt on the way back, giving me a glimpse of his upper chest and the form-fitting tank he's wearing underneath.

"This is all about you, Samantha, and I meant it when I said you can tell me the good and the bad. But I also want you to be able to do exactly as you please. All I ask is that you pace yourself because it's been a while for me." He gives a little self-deprecating chuckle but there's a little hurt in his eyes, like there's a reason for this gap for him. All I want is to make that insecurity, or maybe pain, go away for him.

When he's in front of me, I sit up and allow my bra straps to fall down my arms, somehow keeping my mind clear. I reach up and remove his flannel shirt, letting my hands feel his shoulders, his biceps, his forearms, and his fingers before it falls to the floor. My eyes finally lock with his and the intensity of his blue gaze makes my heart race. Just as he did, I pull at the bottom of his shirt to untuck it, feeling heat roll off of him. But before I lift it, I shift so I'm kneeling on his bed, scooting backwards and tugging him with me. Once we're closer to the center of his mattress, I lean back and bring his shirt over his head so he's bent over me by the time it's off his arms.

He catches himself before falling completely on top of me but settles so our skin is pressed together and I whimper.

"Are you ready now, Samantha Davies?" he asks, his nose running along my neck up to my ear.

"Yes, please," I breathe.

Chapter 38
Tommy

We make our way up to the pillow and Sam lifts the sheets to keep us warmer. For the next few minutes, we almost lazily explore each other. Our hands take their time to roam, trace, and tease while our mouths are locked together like neither of us want to break a single kiss.

I shift so I'm on my side and my fingers slide behind her and cup her ass under her clothes. Jesus Christ it's somehow soft and firm at the same time and I fucking love it. And I love the sounds she keeps making because they're becoming increasingly desperate so I finally pull away from our kisses, missing her tongue immediately.

"May I?" I shift that hand so it's moving around to her hip from her ass and hold it there.

She nods, pulling my lips back to hers in a slow kiss, allowing me to breathe in her floral perfume mixed with the smell of horses and leather. The combination is intoxicating. I can barely hear her zipper being undone over our breathing before my fingertips trace the top of her underwear. She shifts her hips just a little to give me better access as I flatten my palm against her belly and allow my hand to slide down.

Fuck me.

With Sam's tongue dancing with mine, her hands in my hair and on the back of my neck, I moan while feeling her for the first time. I'm grateful that I rolled to the side so I don't make a mess in my jeans. God, the slightest pressure from her will have me spent. She's got short curls that give away just how turned on she is. When I press my finger into her seam, parting her lips, she's slick even before I dip into her core once, feeling exactly how tightly she grips it, then bringing it right back out and to her clit.

Rubbing circles next to it, she moves her hips a little, repositioning me without saying a word. When her breath hitches, I kiss my way back to that spot behind her ear that she's so reactive to, nuzzling it while she gives me full access.

"Any improvements to be made, Samantha?" I ask, my voice raspy with my own desire.

She shakes her head tightly and says, "Please don't change anything."

"I'll stay right here until you ask for something else, don't you worry."

As her fingers press harder into my back, I take in every detail as she climbs closer…her chest rising rapidly, her face getting flush, her mouth parting as her eyes flutter closed.

"Tommy," she whispers, "I'm so close."

"You're almost there," I say before rubbing faster and carefully biting on her earlobe so her earring doesn't stab me in the process. Her body tenses more and more.

"Tommy." This time it's more of a squeak and she shudders, coming undone. Right here on my bed. In my arms.

By my hand.

Those little sounds from earlier have nothing on the cries she makes as she comes. I know I'll be replaying them whenever I'm alone. Fuck.

She shifts into embarrassed laughter when she's overstimulated and I dip my finger into her core, soaking it with her release. Then her hands shift to cover face and I roll over her, pulling her hands above her head and pinning them on the pillow, covering her mouth with mine as she sighs.

When I lift my head, I say, "One down, two to go."

"Pardon?" she asks, her eyes wide open.

I repeat myself and she wears a look of disbelief.

"You weren't joking?"

"Why would I joke about that?" I ask, genuinely curious.

"Because just getting this *one* done was pretty epic."

"And you can't have more?"

Her lips part to protest and I raise a skeptical eyebrow at her.

"If you don't like to come more than once, that's okay…" I've never seen her eyes open so wide. "I would love to be the one to get you past your old record. And why not now?"

"So you're just out to break a record?" she asks warily.

I chuckle softly, kissing her neck as she gives me more access. "This is about bringing you pleasure and nothing more. I would watch you come by my fingers alone every damn day."

"Oh my God, Tommy." Sam's voice is full of exasperation as she tries to tug her hands free, likely to swat at me. "That's not funny."

"It wasn't supposed to be," I say, kissing behind her ear and feeling her arch into me. "I wouldn't joke or lie about what my favorite sight is."

"It is n—"

"Oh, I can assure you it is," I say, cutting her off. My teeth run down her earlobe and she lets out a soft whimper of pleasure. "It's okay if you don't believe me, yet. I plan to give you plenty of opportunities to see the joy I get from it."

"Um, I guess I'm not opposed to it," she says, almost as a question, and I lift up so I can look at her. "I've just never done that."

"Well, there's a first time for everything, isn't there?"

She smiles and her blue eyes are brighter when she says, "I guess there is."

I let go of one of her hands, letting mine find her nipple, which is still a pebbled peak. Her free fingers find anchor in my hair to keep my face right where it is as she deepens our kiss. We stay locked like this, breathing becoming more rapid, mouths claiming each other, hips rocking into one another, for a while, just savoring.

"Can we get your jeans out of the way?" I ask, receiving an enthusiastic nod in response.

Sitting back on my knees, I take in the sight of a flushed, topless, and thoroughly kissed Samantha Davies, her head on my pillow, my sheets beneath her, and her fingers tracing part of my headboard. I rub my dick once to relieve some of everything that's building and put my hands on her bare hips, lifting them. She presses her shoulders into the bed and raises her ass as I inch her pants down her body.

Pausing, I hook a finger around her white, sensible underwear. "These, too?"

Another nod, this one more shy, but still sure.

Keeping my eyes on hers, I pull the fabric over her soft skin, reveling in the feel of my hands on her legs. When we're closer to her ankles, I scoot backwards to the end of the bed to pull from the bottom of each pant leg and throw her jeans and underwear on my floor once they're free.

Giving the ankle in my hand a slow kiss, I let my gaze follow the lines of her body, including the glistening blonde curls between her thighs.

"You're so damn beautiful." Instead of kissing my way up her legs, I crawl over her so my lips can find hers as I say, "Every inch of you is perfect."

Chapter 39
Sam

Never feeling more lovely than this moment, I relish the way I'm tingling everywhere and how my lips press against Tommy's. My leg wraps around his only to find it frustratingly clothed in denim.

"What about your jeans?" I ask as his hand roams my breast and stomach, making me squirm in the best ways possible.

"Soon enough, cowgirl."

Who knew a nickname could be so sexy?

"I have plans before my pants come off," he says against my ear. "We'll have time to get the dirt out of our hair before—"

"Oh my goodness," I interject, turning my head to see if I've ruined his pillowcase.

Undeterred by my worry, Tommy lazily nibbles at my ear. "So we might as well get a little dirtier before cleaning up."

Jesus, he knows how to switch off my anxious thoughts at the drop of a hat.

"And would I be able to use the shower here before facing your family again?" I ask.

"Of course," he says. "And it's a new one that I put in a few months ago. An overdue upgrade from the childhood one Chuck and I shared."

His fingers run down my seam and dip into my core, making wet sounds that, instead of horrifying him, seem to turn him on even more. "You're really aiming for three?" I ask, a little dazed at the idea.

"I'm really aiming for three." His breath shudders as his fingers pump once, twice. "I wish you knew how amazing you feel gripping my fingers like this."

Part of me thinks I should hide my face and be embarrassed, but the way his voice has gotten all raspy, the desperation in his kisses, and the groans that leave him only increase my desire. If he can be so open with me, I can do the same, right?

"Inside doesn't do much for me," I explain, trying to be specific but my brain is in overdrive with the ways he's touching me. Being in his bed with him right here makes me feel like I'm surrounded by him. This man who just gave me a damn fine orgasm. His finger finds the rough spot I've explored many times and taps it as he pumps a few more times.

"This, right?"

I nod. "It doesn't feel bad, but it doesn't really contribute?"

"I'll keep my attention right here then." His fingers pull out to rub near my clit and he kisses me, his tongue plunging into my mouth with a confidence that feels like he was born to do this. "You're blowing your dare right out of the water, by the way. I hope you're enjoying it."

Tommy falls into the rhythm he found so easily just minutes ago.

"I definitely am." The climb is faster this time and I don't know what to do with myself knowing that he's lying here with me while he gets no attention. I don't want to ask why it has been so long for him and sound judgmental, but if he's giving me a second orgasm right here, right now, I don't want him to be left empty-handed.

Plus, I'm interested to find out what he's got zipped up.

I loosen my grip on his hair, which he doesn't seem to mind me using as reins to guide his mouth back to mine when I miss it, and my fingers work their way over his pec and down his stomach. His muscles react to my touch and dance under my fingertips. When they trace the sensitive skin right above his belt, he releases a shaky breath.

"I think you're trying to kill me, Samantha."

"I'm just trying to make sure you don't feel neglected. I won't do anything drastic before you're done, I promise."

"I can't tell if it's sexier to think of you keeping or breaking that promise." His voice is a husky whisper in my ear and his warm breath sends shivers down my body.

I pull on his belt and loosen it, bringing my other hand to work the button on his jeans. I feel his hard length through the fabric and am not surprised that he feels longer than average so far but not too thick where I'm worried he'd hurt me from his size alone. The button releases with a *pop* and then I slowly undo his fly. As the zipper opens, he makes a deep sound in the back of his throat.

"I think you're definitely trying to kill me now," he says, his underwear allowing his penis more space. "Remember, you can touch me however you'd like, just know I'll finish pretty damn fast."

"I'll be careful." I let myself explore the feeling of him over the fabric slowly from where his shaft is accessible with his pants still on. I trace a vein running up until I feel the slightly damp fabric over his tip. Knowing that he's leaking from our activities so far enhances the sensations I'm experiencing. Since he's the one in charge and I've only minimally touched him, this is his reaction from pleasuring *me*.

His fingers slip inside of me again, dragging more of my desire up to my clit and I shudder at the sensation.

"Are you close, cowgirl?"

I let a breathy "yes" escape me because everything is building quickly, the desire gathering deep inside of me as he works me.

"Good, chase that for me."

And I do.

My fingers freeze around his penis as my back arches, pressing my chest into his, my nipples relishing the feel of his skin. I close my eyes and my breath hitches in a shallow inhale that fills me with the scent of cedar and garlic. It feels like Tommy is everywhere and I'm wrapped up in nothing but his attention and his need to bring me pleasure not just a second time, but a third. It's that final thought that brings me over the edge and I shatter against him, my hands somehow on his back, clutching him with my nails digging into his skin.

I hear Tommy curse and tell me I'm amazing while he drags out every last ounce of this orgasm until I'm twitching. He slows his fingers and dips them back into my core.

"Fuck, Samantha, what I wouldn't give to taste you right now."

My brain is a little hazy and I hum in response. And then my eyes fly open and I say, "You want to what?"

"I want to taste you so fucking badly." He slants his mouth over mine and lets most of his weight press me into his mattress. I don't think I've heard him cuss this much at one time before and it seems like he's barely holding on.

When his tongue slows and I relax my hands, allowing him to lift up a little, he looks down at me, his desire written all over his face.

"I've never had anyone—"

His groan cuts me off and he rocks against me, making me throb for him once more. How can I be ready for another round so freaking soon?

"I won't ever do anything you're not comfortable with, Samantha Davies." His lips return to mine gently and I'm the one whose desperation ramps everything up. My tongue darts out and he opens immediately for me as my legs wrap around his waist, keeping him pinned against me. I let my hands explore his back and shoulders, noting how he flexes each time he shifts above me. His mouth leaves mine so he can nip my earlobe, driving me up the wall.

"Okay." The word leaves me before I can overanalyze the million ways this could somehow ruin things between us.

Tommy's eyes snap to mine. "You're sure?"

This time I just nod and the sound he makes rumbles in his chest and I feel it all the way to my toes.

Chapter 40
Tommy

I'm the luckiest son of a bitch on this damn planet.

And I know how ready Sam is, my boxer briefs are soaked through from us grinding for only a minute. Grabbing her calves, I tug so she releases her ankles and toss her thighs over my shoulders as I scoot down the bed.

I let out a shuddering breath as I see her splayed out before me, glistening in the dim light. She squirms and before she can feel self-conscious, I give her a grin and hold her gaze as I lower myself and take one long lick. She gasps.

"Fuck, Samantha." I can't say anything else because nothing has ever been so damn addicting as the way she tastes: a little sweetness mixed into a heavenly musky flavor. My tongue explores her, circling her clit, taking leisurely licks all the way up her seam, and dipping into her soaking core.

"Is this okay?" I ask, remembering that this is the first time anyone has gone down on her. God, she dated morons.

She squeaks out an "uh-huh" as she tries to find a place to put her hands. I reach up and catch her wrist and guide her hand to my hair.

"Think of this as your reins, cowgirl."

And with that, I close my mouth over her swollen bundle of nerves and suck hard, flicking it with my tongue. Sam cries out, slaps her free hand over her mouth to dull the sound, and arches her back off the mattress so only her shoulders and ass anchor her. Her fingers dig into my scalp to keep me right where I am. I watch her hold that position as her legs tighten against my ears, making me moan against her because she's so close already, the vibrations from me must only add to the sensations because she makes a sound from the pleasure building. I hold myself from grinding myself against the bed because I'll be coming before she does.

One finger slips into her just before she explodes, biting down on her hand to keep quiet. Her walls clamp down on my finger, drenching it in waves of her desire. Sam starts to writhe on the bed before curling up so both hands are in my hair. Her hair is messy and her mouth is open as she rides out wave after wave of her orgasm, shuddering as each one washes over her.

Her hands tug at my hair and she giggles, falling back against my pillow, sighing. Instead of giving her one last, full lick, I settle on sucking off every drop from my finger, moaning again.

"Thank you," I tell her, letting her legs fall off my shoulders as she lays like her bones are made of gelatin.

"Pardon me? I should be the one thanking you." Her voice is a little drowsy. "Come up here."

Her arms are open and I crawl up to them, careful to keep my erection from brushing up her body. I'm happy to wait for another time.

But she only wraps one arm around me, the other skating down my chest and reaching into my underwear. Her fingers wrap around my shaft and pump.

"Jesus," I hiss.

"I'm sorry, was that too hard?" She halts everything, looking worried.

"Not a bit," I say, leaning in to kiss her. "Everything is perfect."

She smiles against my mouth and within a few more confident strokes, my balls are tightening.

"Shit," I bite out. "I'm going to come."

Taking a moment to adjust the cloth so it can catch everything, Sam's hand is back, gripping me and moving from tip to base. I move my hips to increase the pace and grunt into her mouth as her tongue tangles with mine to the same rhythm. One more thrust and I'm seeing stars as Sam milks every drop from me.

I collapse onto my back so I don't get her messy and take a moment to catch my breath.

"I should—"

"Stay right here for a bit," she says, sitting up and pulling down my boxer briefs. Carefully, she tugs so the sticky material doesn't touch my skin as she takes them off of me. Balling them up, she wipes the spots of my stomach and leg that are messy before tossing it to the ground. I can only imagine the dorky look of amazement I'm wearing right now watching her move so confidently to take care of me.

"Come up here," I say, echoing her words from just a few minutes ago. She grabs the sheet and covers us and I tuck her head into my chest, kissing her wild hair. I tangle my legs with hers and she lets out a sigh of contentment. Soon, our breathing evens out and we drift off.

I've been awake for a bit now, lightly rubbing circles on Sam's shoulder with my thumb. She's half-draped over me, our legs even more entwined, and she's drooling on my chest.

It's amazing.

I feel the moment she wakes up, her breathing becomes shallow and she carefully frees the hand she tucked under my side while she slept. She tilts her head and runs her hand over face. When it gets to her mouth, she bolts upright and stares at my chest in horror.

"You're fine," I say quietly, her eyes darting to mine.

"I *drooled* on your chest!" she whisper-yells, her hands darting towards my chest and pulling them back.

"I'm just going to smear it all over you," she mumbles and starts to get out of bed. Before she can get anywhere, my arm wraps around her waist, tugging her back into bed and nuzzling my face into her hair. Even with a little corral dirt, it smells amazing. And having her on my lap feels even better.

"I think I might be offended if you rush out of bed this fast," I say, letting out a little chuckle.

"My saliva is on you," she whines adorably.

"More than just your saliva, actually," I amend.

An embarrassed groan escapes her, but she softens against me. "If I was grossed out, I could have wiped it off myself. But if having a little drool on my skin, or even on my clothes, means you're in my arms, I'll gladly take it."

Sam turns to look at me. "How are you so sweet?"

Chapter 41
Sam

He leans in, kissing me tenderly as his arm loosens its hold on my waist.

My very nude waist.

I freeze for one second and, of course, Tommy notices. "What happened?"

My nose scrunches up and I remind myself that he likes me for who I am and catch any lie I would have fed him to not make things feel weird. "I'm not dressed."

His eyes dip down and he slowly smiles. "Oh, I noticed."

"You're at least under the sheet."

"The sheet that you abruptly left but are always welcome under," he says, lifting the sheet with his free hand.

"Won't your brothers be coming in soon and get suspicious if we're not downstairs?"

Sighing through his nose while his lips leave feather-light kisses on my shoulder, he relents. "Do you want to shower first or second? And for the record, I'm very open to conserving water but can't make any promises that I won't try to have you coming a fourth time this afternoon."

A shiver zips through my body at the thought of Tommy joining me in a shower. To be able to watch the water run down the panes of his body. "I could go first this time, I suppose."

We stand up and he detangles himself from the top sheet. Bending over, he grabs his flannel shirt and drapes it over my shoulders. "Your robe," he says, tossing me a wink.

Padding over to his drawers, Tommy grabs a pair of athletic shorts and I get a fantastic view of his butt. It's muscled, but soft, just like the rest of him. He catches me checking him out and drops the shirt he had picked up back into the same drawer before walking up to me and tugging me close by the collar of his shirt.

"You better be careful, because I could get very used to seeing you like this," he says. He gives me an open-mouthed kiss, causing butterflies to consume me. "Let's get you clean."

Sighing, I know that he's right. Peeking at the clock, I note that we've been inside for about an hour, so we couldn't have slept for very long.

Boy, I must have been out like a light to have left a little puddle of drool on him so quickly.

As my toes step onto the tiles of his bathroom, I brace for the chill that will hit. But instead, the floors are heated to my absolute delight. Unlike the first time I peeked in here, I take a better look at the bathroom. Everything is tidy, as I've come to expect from Tommy, and it's finished in light gray tones with black accents. The shower is huge with several wall-mounted sprayers, one hand-held sprayer, and what looks like a rain head on the ceiling.

"You did this?" I ask, gesturing to the shower.

He nods. "With a little help, but yeah. We take our sore bodies very seriously here and since we have a few soaking tubs with jets in the house, I decided to go with one hell of a shower system."

"It looks heavenly."

"I hope you feel the same when you're clean."

Tommy walks me through the dials and settings and the shower is filled with steam by the time he sets out a towel for me and gives me one more kiss before leaving and shutting the door behind him. Part of me is curious if there might be signs of overnight guests, but I shake my head at the notion. My mind goes back to his notes about it being a long time for him since he had been with anyone. Anyone remodeling their bathroom wouldn't likely keep souvenirs of bygone lovers.

As I remove his shirt, my nose scrunches up at the thought of anyone who might have broken his heart. I fold it a little more aggressively than is necessary because someone *has* hurt him. It's not like I'm naive enough to think that relationships are puppies and roses, even the ones that end, but it feels like someone really did a number on him.

Someone hurt Tommy.

The man has flaws, I'm sure of that. No one is perfect. But who the hell would do that and why?

I step into the shower and let the water wash away some of my agitation. Fiddling with a few settings, the wall sprayers soon massage my back as I use Tommy's shampoo/conditioner combo.

Reading the instructions, I try to figure out if I'm supposed to leave it in like conditioner or wash it out sooner like shampoo. I settle on rinsing it sooner, knowing that I'm likely going to put a ponytail back in once it's semi-dry anyways. The body wash has a little spice scent to it but mostly smells of the outdoors and I like it.

Trying to not use up all the hot water, I quickly finish rinsing and manage to shut off the water coming from the various nozzles fairly efficiently. Once I'm out of the shower and dry, I detangle my hair with my fingers the best I can and use some of Tommy's lotion.

Hmm, I didn't bring my change of clothes into the bathroom with me. I suppose he's seen everything already, but I wrap the surprisingly soft towel around myself before opening the door.

Tommy is lying on the bed still only wearing that pair of shorts, one ankle crossed over the other with a paperback in one hand while the other is tucked behind his head. He looks over at me with a slow smile as his eyes take in my appearance and sets the book on the nightstand.

"Another sight I could get used to."

I blush at his words but feel emboldened by them. "I could say the same about you."

In one fluid motion, he stands and makes his way towards the bathroom door, which I'm currently blocking. I didn't realize I had stopped walking. His hand tilts my chin up so he can kiss me for a few moments. It's easy and natural with him. That maybe this, us being together, even here in this house, could simply happen.

A voice in my head tries to ring alarm bells that the idea of living in this house, however large and soundproofed, might be too much. Instead of panicking and getting comically ahead of myself, I let my tongue meet Tommy's and my arms drape around his neck. Thankfully, the towel stays firmly in place the whole time.

We slow things down before he convinces me to get back into the shower with him. Not that I wouldn't mind showering with Tommy Landen, but my body is asking me to not go for round four just now. The nap only offset one or two of those orgasms.

Chapter 42
Tommy

Walking out of the steam-filled bathroom to the sight of Samantha Davies gently towel drying her hair at the foot of my bed does absolutely nothing to make me want to take things at that slow pace I originally intended. I don't blame myself because, damn, if there's a chance this is what she wants long-term, I'm all fucking in.

Without being awkward, hopefully, I kiss the side of her neck that's exposed since her hair is tossed to one side to scrunch and grab clothes from my dresser. Of course I didn't even think to bring them into the bathroom with me and I don't want her to feel like I'm flashing her, so I pull up my boxer briefs under the towel I wrapped around my waist. The worst thing I could do right now is scare her off by being too comfortable.

Well, that's not true at all, my brain corrects. I shake my head because there's no way in hell I'd ever pull the kind of shit Maisy did. And even though I might be falling fast, I genuinely believe Sam wouldn't either.

"Everything okay over there?" she asks, a little worry creeping into her expression.

I take a breath and see what's standing right in front of me, letting those doubts that were so automatic the past year melt away. "It is now," I answer truthfully, closing the distance between us so I can wrap my arms around her. We'll talk about our exes soon enough, I can already tell that hers have left their own mark, too. But for now, I can simply be in the moment with this woman.

She drops her towel to the ground and holds me close, just standing here with her head resting against my bare shoulder.

"You smell like my bodywash and shampoo," I say, kissing the top of her head. "I like that, even though your perfume drives me wild."

"Maybe I'll leave my travel bottle here for the next time I use your things so they can mix." She smiles up at me and gives my neck a quick kiss, her hands tightening their grip behind my back to keep me against her.

"You can leave your entire collection here if it means I get to see you more."

Sam bites her bottom lip and blushes but keeps her eyes on me instead of hiding. "I'll have to keep that in mind."

"Good, because there's more than enough space for you," I say, pushing down all the ways my brain is trying to tell me I'm being an idiot for practically asking my girlfriend to move in with me.

And then it hits me: Samantha Davies is my girlfriend.

I think.

At least, she said she was okay with us being official. Well, "a thing" if I remember correctly.

"Hey," she says softly. "Where'd you go just now?"

Instead of taking the easy way out and making some excuse, I think of each time I've asked her to be brave and open with me. To not hide.

"I was just trying to figure out if you're officially my girlfriend or if I need to ask."

She has a shy smile while her eyes sparkle when she says, "You can ask right now if you'd like."

I stand here in my bedroom wearing nothing but boxer briefs and a damp towel and ask, "Samantha Davies, will you officially be my girlfriend?"

"Yep," she replies, her smile growing until her nose scrunches. "Thomas Landen, will you officially be my boyfriend?"

The air whooshes out of me hearing her say my name and boyfriend together. Once I get oxygen back in my lungs, I lean down and right before I kiss her, I whisper, "Hell yeah."

"How many committees are you on now?" Matt asks, his apron was tied neatly in a bow behind his back rather than a tiny knot in front.

"How did you manage that?" I point at the tidy bow.

He grunts, taking after Jax and Bryant even more today than usual. "You didn't answer my question."

"Neither did you."

"I tied it," Caleb says, keeping his back to us while wrapping herbs in cheesecloth for Matt's broth. His ears turn pink at the top and when I look over at Matt, he turns so I can't make eye contact with him. Now I'm curious about more than a bow...but these two have had some odd moments lately, and I don't want to push them.

"Seems much better than the little nub he somehow keeps knotted," I say. "And not many more than usual, but the upcoming outdoor movie night needs a feature film so we're choosing that tonight."

Matt nods and steals a glance at Caleb, who is now fiddling with the satchel that's ready for the pot.

I clear my throat. "I hope everyone can come. It'll mean a whole lot to Sam for there to be a good turnout and I can promise the movie won't suck."

It's Caleb's turn to peek at Matt who is examining the steaming pot. Caleb stands up a little taller and holds out the herbs to my little brother. "Yeah, I bet I can make it."

Even though Matt is a few inches taller than Caleb, he somehow looks up at the former rodeo star through his lashes as he takes the bundle and gives him a half-smile. "Me, too."

Caleb stuffs his hands into the pockets of Bryant's grilling apron and shuffles backwards to the pile of veggies waiting to be peeled and diced.

"We're going to have to get you your own apron for here, especially with how much help you've been while Matt preps these big batches for other families," I tell Caleb.

"I've told Matt I don't need to wear one," he mumbles.

"You do, too," Matt cuts in. "It's not like we're changing into clothes just for cooking, so it's about keeping the food cleaner for everyone else. And Tommy's right, we can pop into town later today and get you one."

Caleb looks over his shoulder at Matt and his ears get a little brighter at the tips. "Fine, I suppose that would make sense."

"Good," I say, rubbing my palms together. "Don't forget to bring extra clothes here, too."

"Oh, I did last week when Sam came to ride Bella."

"Perfect, you can sleep here any time, too."

Matt shifts uncomfortably by the stove.

I know Caleb hasn't been sleeping here, but now I'm wondering if he might be forgoing any of the spare bedrooms in favor of Matt's if he ever does. There's an awkward silence and the two of them are entirely too focused on what's in front of them.

"Alright, I'm going to head out in a few, but I can tell the guys to come in for dinner soon on my way," I offer.

Matt cracks open the oven door and lifts the tin foil lid to check the lasagna he and Caleb prepped an hour ago. He looks relieved to have something more concrete to do. "An hour should do it, thanks."

Chapter 43
Sam

As usual, which might sound silly to consider something a "usual" if it has only been just over a week, Tommy's text tells me he's a little early and I practically skip down the steps to see him. We keep finding time to see each other throughout the week, even when we don't have meetings, but I love that he picks me up for everything.

Except for horseback riding. I drive myself to the ranch for those where I haven't seen Gerald-the-wolf-dog since my first lesson.

Tommy's watching the door as he leans against the side of his truck and has a big smile when I exit the building. A few steps later and I'm in his arms, letting out a little squeal when he lifts me and spins us around. I laugh as my feet touch the ground once more and I raise up to my toes to kiss him. It's quick, like anything where we're remotely in public, but it still sends a shiver down my spine. Our alone time has been minimal since Tommy blew right past the number of orgasms I'd received from someone I was dating and I'm itching for something other than slightly frantic make out sessions soon.

"You ready to go pick out a movie?" he asks, grabbing my hand and walking me to the passenger side of the truck. He opens the door, and the hand that held mine trails along my waist as I heft myself, with some grace, into the seat.

"Are you complaining about the past selections?"

"So someone really did select those?"

"Just you wait until you see the list of what we're licensed to share and you'll be singing a different tune."

"We'll see about that," he says, closing my door. I watch him walk in front of the truck and he looks back at me with a content expression on his face.

"I'd love to know where all of this confidence is coming from," I say.

"I have resources that shall remain a mystery." He puts his cowboy hat in the back seat and runs his hand through his hair, one piece stubbornly falling onto his forehead immediately.

"I'll be sure to take notes on what these resources are."

"I would expect nothing less," he says, leaning over for a second peck and then putting his truck in gear.

"It's supposed to rain a lot tonight," Tommy says while pulling onto the street, confusing me with the shift in conversation.

"Um, yes, I saw that. I guess it's good that the movie night isn't tonight."

"That's true, but I was actually thinking about mud."

"Mud?" I ask.

"Since it'll be nice out and the rain is tonight, tomorrow is the perfect day to introduce you to mudding."

"The practice of driving recklessly and getting mud everywhere?" I ask, my face heating a little as I recall Tommy's words when describing mudding to me not that long ago.

"Not *that* recklessly, but that's the sport."

"It's a sport?"

"More of a recreational activity."

"Okay, so when does this mudding occur and where?"

"After Courtney's morning appointments are done tomorrow, which should be around ten. Jax will be done with his morning work so he and Avery will drive over together and everyone else will be around, ready to go."

"What do I bring?" I ask, pulling out my planner and writing *10am: Mudding* under tomorrow's date.

"Extra clothes, including shoes. Which reminds me... you should start leaving clothes at the house," he says casually. As if me leaving clothes at a guy's house was routine and not something that has me both excited about and worrying over.

What sort of clothes do you leave at your boyfriend's place? Is it the reasonable cotton underwear and a work appropriate ensemble? Is it the laciest bra with the low cut pajamas?

"Okay, I can do that," I say as if this is totally normal and I'm completely aware of what he means by this. I'll wing it and keep things that I grab more casual in style. It's not like we've spent the night with each other, so sleepwear would be presumptuous. Right?

But what if the clothes are so I can stay over sometime and then go to work in the morning? Before I start writing out a pros and cons list for various outfit types, I try to keep the conversation natural. "You should, too."

I have no clue what kind of clothes I should expect, but before I put my planner away, I jot down *clear a drawer* under today's activities. When I look up, I see that we're already pulling into the parking lot for the meeting.

"Sounds good," he says, placing his free hand on my thigh near my knee and giving it a little squeeze. The warmth from his hand seeps right through my skirt and I give myself a moment to wish we were back in my apartment and not going to a meeting. "I have decaf for us tonight, I hope that's okay."

I completely missed the two beverages in the cupholders between us. One looks almost black and the other is tan in color. I pick up the lighter one.

"Oat milk?"

"Of course," he replies, giving one more little squeeze and then taking his coffee and plunking his hat back on his head.

This all feels so natural. When he opens the door, it's like he's never done anything else and when I pause so he can catch up right away, there's nothing that feels awkward or out of place. We simply seem comfortable in not only being around one another, but in how we move together without having to force anything.

Hank greets us when we enter the meeting room and Tommy pulls out my chair and then the one right next to it for himself while striking up a conversation with my boss. I set my iced coffee to the left of the space in front of me then pull out my notebook for this subcommittee where I've recorded every movie chosen for movie nights for the past four years. After the last selection turned out to be a repeat from less than one year ago, I'm eager to not make a mistake like that again any time soon if I can help it. My highlighter and three markers set to the right of everything when I realize I've zoned out of the conversation at hand. Quickly I refocus so I don't appear rude.

"That sounds like one heck of a fishing trip. Did you camp or stay in the lodge?" Tommy asks. They must be talking about Hank's weekend away with his college roommate. Thankfully, I've already been filled in on the fishing report.

"It was. I'm thinking about trying to get the office there for a team-building retreat. There are a few other towns around here who are interested in doing a group mini-conference and that would be a fantastic place for it."

"Just be sure to invite members of any city committees," Tommy jokes.

"I'll be sure to book during their off-season so we can get more rooms and have the subcommittees there, too," he says while chuckling.

Did my boyfriend just get invited to a work event that isn't even on the books yet?

Chapter 44
Tommy

We have to be close to wrapping up this meeting soon. I know I threw them all a curveball when I shared the license I purchased so we could select a movie that would draw more of a crowd, but we're thirty minutes past the scheduled ending time so I won't get extra time with her tonight.

Not that I mind having an excuse to sit next to Sam and have my hand on her leg under the table as we scroll through the top ten titles again. To be honest, I wasn't sure if she'd be okay with any sort of contact, but after her leg rested against mine for half the meeting, I resituated myself so my left arm wasn't on the table anymore. When she started to blush, I pulled my hand back, but she knocked her pen cap off the table right away and grabbed my hand, setting it right back on her thigh before reorganizing her things on the table.

And I'm still trying to contain my smile as I quietly flip back and forth between two pages in my notebook whenever Sam is looking at the screen or taking notes. Thankfully, she's just as attentive during this meeting, even with my fingers tracing circles on her thigh, shifting the fabric of her skirt every now and then.

Hank removes two more titles from the list and we're down to one animated film, two action-adventures, one tear-jerker, and four rom-coms.

"Tommy, what do you think about what's left?" Hank asks me.

"I think something light but a little romance is a good call since we're specifically doing a date night theme and it's an eighteen-and-older crowd. Keep it PG-13 and we hold off on booking Jesse and his barbecue until family night where we'll start things earlier. We talk to Sarah about putting together her more dessert-like baked goods." I do my best to not look at Sam when I share my top choice for title, because it's the one we watched together the first time I was in her apartment. "I've seen that one it's a good one."

"Okay, does anyone else have another option they'd like to consider from what we have left?" Hank checks with the group.

Everyone else shakes their heads.

"Alright, we have our film. Would someone like to talk to Sarah about what she could supply for about fifty people?"

Sam raises her hand. "I can connect with her tomorrow,"

"Great," he says, looking at his notes. "I think that was everything we needed to cover tonight. Our office will handle publicity campaigns, but feel free to start sharing what we chose and cross your fingers the weather's clear so we won't have to reschedule. Thanks, everyone."

Without making it obvious, I think everyone in town knows Sam and I are dating at this point even though we haven't been out in public on a date yet, I take my time pocketing my notebook and pen. Sam's writing down the last details from the meeting and is in the final color-coded highlighting phase. It hasn't taken me too long to figure out that blue is something she wants to remember and yellow is an action item. Or, if she's using colors that would clash with those highlighters, details are green and action items are orange. Instead of using sticky tabs for her notes, she puts paper clips where they would sit, flagging the information she needs to find quickly on the side of the page rather than the top. The only thing she doesn't have with her at meetings are those sticky notes that are transparent so she can add details over her original notes without crossing out what was there. It's fucking adorable.

Everyone else heads out while I offer to stack their chairs so the cleaning crew can vacuum, so it's just the two of us and Hank, who is shutting down his computer when Sam looks around.

"Oh, I didn't realize I missed them leaving," she says, a little frown on her face.

"I promise they're okay," I say as Hank tells her to not worry about it.

She nods and gains back a little confidence. Her habits for social protocol are definitely top tier, but she seems to be giving herself a break instead of having nerves linger in her expression after she missed something.

"Is there anything you need a hand with?" she asks her boss who shakes his head.

"I'm all set, you head out, have a good night, and I'll see you at the office."

"Okay, you, too," she says, checking her space as I stack her chair. "You all set?"

"I am," I say, smiling at her as we walk out together. One day it'll be okay to hold her hand in mine as we leave places. I hope.

"What time do you have to wake up tomorrow?" she asks once we're in the truck.

Sighing through my nose, I start the engine and get out of the parking lot. "Too early so we can get most things out of the way before mudding."

"So you can't come up tonight?"

"I shouldn't," I say, holding out my hand. Sam tucks her tote next to her feet and her fingers slip into mine. Raising our hands, I kiss the back of hers and notice her perfume again. I make a mental note to add it to my list in a minute.

"What footwear should I have tomorrow?"

"Shoes you don't care about and a spare. Make sure you dress in layers and have dry clothes, too. We usually all strip off an outer layer and toss those clothes in a bucket of water to get most of the mud off and then bring it all in to wash. While we're all waiting for the clothes, everyone showers and we meet back in the living room for drinks and watch something."

"I can do that," she says while nodding with conviction. "Can I bring something for everyone to eat afterwards?"

"Of course, anything you'd like." I give her hand a squeeze. "It's never fancy, I promise, so you can show up with nothing or an entire casserole."

"So I should bring an entree?"

"No, you don't have to do that. Avery usually bakes cookies, Matt might have something in the oven before we go out, and then we raid the fridge for snacks."

"How about something easy while watching a show, like popcorn?"

I know she's going to keep trying to think of the right item to bring, and no one ever thinks to bring that, so I say as I release her hand, "That would be perfect."

She reaches into her bag and pulls out her planner, jotting a few things down. As she's finishing up, I park in front of her building and shift so I can get my notebook out of my pocket. Once I get to the right page, I add "perfume" to the bottom of the list, tear out the full page, and fold it in half.

"No pressure, but I thought you might like this for what to leave in my room. They're just ideas," I say, holding the list out to her between two fingers. She takes it while looking a little puzzled. As she reads it, realization appears in her features.

"You made me a list of things to pack to keep at your place?" she asks with a mix of happiness and a little caution.

"I did. You can do whatever you'd like with the list but sleeping with you in my arms for a few minutes might have me addicted already, so I'd like you to be able to stay whenever you'd like."

"And you wrote a list so I wouldn't have to..." She lets the sentence trail off unfinished.

"Guess what to bring? Nope, I wanted you to know you can leave as much as you'd like for a variety of situations, including going to work from Landen Acres."

She smiles and we both lean in at the same time, her hand cupping my cheek and mine at the nape of her neck as we slowly kiss. Taking our time and feeling this moment as we keep taking steps to open ourselves up to this being *it*.

At least I hope we're both on that page.

Chapter 45
Sam

Toothbrush.

He included a toothbrush.

My heart is pounding in my chest like I decided to go for a run rather than stand just inside my entryway while my door bumps against me.

Tommy wants me to have a toothbrush of my own there. And pajamas. And socks, jeans, sweats, and *at least* one outfit for work.

I lock my door and put everything away as I walk into my bedroom, pulling out my duffle and setting it on the bed. It's not until I have everything except my perfume and a few toiletries that he listed that it hits me: I'm packing so I can stay at Landen Acres. Judging by how much is on this list, he's not planning for just one night. This is a list that covers several scenarios for when I might be over as well as what could be happening the next day.

I eye my drawers and shift a few things around so there's one that's completely empty and I sit down to write a list of things Tommy might like to keep here before getting ready for bed.

Per usual, I'm early. It's just my little sedan parked to the side of the house.

A house that I've been invited to leave things at so I can stay over.

But how does their family dynamic work with four of the five brothers living under the same roof? The house is enormous, so I'm sure there's some privacy afforded simply with the square footage, but would I be leaving for work with a Landen brother drinking coffee in his boxers?

Oh my, I'm not sure how I would handle that situation.

And what about other partners? Will there be people sneaking out in the middle of the night? Or will we all sit down and have breakfast together?

Movement catches my eye and, thankfully, stops my train of thought. Tommy steps out of the door to the office, the landline phone held to his ear as he leans against the doorframe. His smile brightens his face and he waves me over.

I turn off my car, grab my purse, and pause. Am I supposed to bring my duffle bag? Did he mean for me to pack everything on the list? Will I look like I don't care if I don't bring it up now? Do I pop the trunk to get it?

When I look back up at Tommy, his head is tilted to the side and he has a quizzical look on his face. Fantastic. He knows something is up.

Why on earth didn't I pack my extra shoes and single change of clothes for today in a smaller bag so I could just bring that in and decide on the overstuffed duffle later?

I'm still in the same position when I notice Tommy walking to my car, slipping the phone into his pocket. While I'm feeling some relief that I can just ask him, my heart starts pounding in a panic because an SUV is pulling up beside me. Jacksy and Avery are here and now I have an audience. At least they're on my passenger side.

Tommy waves at them from in front of my car and walks right to my door, which I open.

"Everything okay?" he asks, a slight frown on his face.

No hiding, Samantha Davies.

"I have a massive bag in my trunk and I didn't think through actually bringing it in and if that's what you wanted when you gave me the list," I blurt. "And now people are arriving and I didn't put my mudding change of clothes in a separate bag so now it's going to look like I'm ridiculously high-maintenance if I need this much stuff for changing after getting dirty and I'm kind of stuck."

Tommy's face relaxes and I think he's trying to not show any amusement. "Did you pack everything on the list?"

"Um, yes?"

He nods once. "Good, let's bring it upstairs."

And then he looks into my car for a moment, his eyes searching, and reaches down to pop my trunk. "Come join me when you're ready."

I get a quick peck on the lips and he's already striding to the back of my car, carrying my bag behind his shoulder like it's not unusual.

By the time I calm my heart and tell myself that this is completely okay and nothing to panic over, he's already getting an enthusiastic hug from a squealing Avery who seems to be bursting with excitement. Jackson's there to tuck her into his side the moment she's free and they share a look of complete adoration. These two were apparently crazy about each other for years but because of Jackson's reputation, her brother Chase never thought he'd be able to settle down. I saw plenty of people try to sleep with him and it was clear they were hoping for seconds, so I don't blame Chase too much, but thinking about how much time they missed out on when they're so happy together tugs at my heart.

Everyone looks over at me when my door closes and I will my cheeks to not turn scarlet while I plaster a confident smile on my face and keep my eyes fixed on anything other than the pastel pink bag.

"Sam, are you ready?" Avery asks, her eyes sparkling.

"I think so," I reply honestly.

"You're going to love it! I haven't been able to go mudding in years. I swear whenever I was home the rain refused to behave." Her excitement is contagious and my nerves settle a little more as we walk to the house.

Neither of them have bags. I suppose that makes sense. He likely has things at this house and she's been one of Tommy's best friends for well over a decade from what I've learned, so it makes sense there's something here for her, too. Amidst the feelings of awkwardness, a little bit of belonging blossoms in my chest. This place is feeling like...it's too early to call it home, but it's becoming a place that's comfortable already. Instead of being scared that it's too soon even for that, I let that feeling grow.

Chapter 46
Tommy

Up in my room, Sam looks more comfortable. A little nervous still, so I drop her bag on my bed and walk over to her and wrap her up in my arms.

"Are you still worried about your bag?" I ask when she hides her face in my chest.

"A little? It's a bit…huge."

I chuckle into her hair. "I'm pretty sure people say to not worry about the size of something."

She looks up with a smile on her face and I kiss her before she can start to worry again. Her breath hitches when my tongue parts her lips and then she melts against me, her hands working their way under my shirt so they're on my back. Those fingers that she had wrapped around my dick what feels like ages ago, press into my muscles and keep me flush against her. As if I need any motivation to do anything with this woman.

She groans in frustration.

"Not quite the reaction I was hoping for," I murmur against her mouth.

"We can't get swept up in this when there are people expecting us to come downstairs. They're waiting."

"We're all waiting for Courtney to get here. Do you think those two aren't making out in some corner right now?" I ask, willing to bet money on that. "Plus, the rest of the guys are still in the stables. If it would make you feel better, we could spend a couple of minutes unpacking that duffle you brought."

Her face becomes increasingly red. "I'm not sure you're going to have space for it all," she mumbles, pressing her face into my chest.

I tip her face up so she's looking at me again. "Why on earth would I have written a list of things that I wanted you to bring here if I didn't have a plan for where it all would go?"

Her eyes squint a little in skepticism as I take her hand in mine and lead her first to the closet, opening one side. I didn't go overboard and make it look like she was supposed to fully move in, but there's a full quarter of the space completely open that I gesture to. "For your work things, any dresses, and shoes."

Those eyes go wide and I take her to the long dresser before she can comment on the closet. I open one of the small top drawers first. "For your unmentionables and socks." Then I move and pull open two of the larger drawers. "For your shirts and then your pants."

Finally, I walk her to the tall dresser, pulling the middle drawer open. "And for your sleepwear."

Her eyes get a little watery and she blinks rapidly.

"Sam?" I ask softly, tucking her hair behind her ear.

"I didn't pack enough," she says.

Tugging her against me, I let out a sigh of relief. "We can make another trip, cowgirl, don't you fret."

She nods against my chest. "I need to find more space for your things at my place. You only have a drawer so far."

Squeezing her a little more, I kiss the top of her head and say, "No worries, I don't want to take over your apartment. There's plenty of space here and I'll pack efficiently for my drawer."

Sam laughs and stretches up, kissing my cheek. "That sounds like a plan."

"Should we at least get your post-mudding change of clothes out of there along with things for you to use in the shower?"

She gives a determined nod. "Yes, please. Then when people aren't waiting, I can empty the rest of this thing and it can stop making me overthink everything."

I interrupt her path to the bag in question with a kiss. "There's nothing you have to overthink with me. I'm here for it all."

Her eyes get a little shine in them once more and she opens her mouth like she's going to say something. But instead of any words coming out, her arms wrap around my neck and she kisses me hard.

Unfortunately, that's when Courtney enters the house. We didn't close the door to my room, so we hear her and Avery scream and Jax's low chuckle. Right on cue, Sam pulls away and looks around for a moment, likely figuring out the most efficient way to get what she needs out of the giant bag. I lean around her and unzip the top to help her get started, kissing her cheek, and she smiles while pulling out the neatly rolled clothes at the top and a smaller bag.

"Should I take that to the bathroom?" I ask as she pulls out a few small bottles.

"Yes please."

"You can lay your clothes out for tonight on the bed if you'd like," I call over my shoulder as I put her supplies in the shower. When I leave the bathroom, I see a neat pile of clothes laid out on the corner of my bed. My heart gives an extra beat or two thinking that it might one day be *our* bed. But will she want to move here? That's a hell of a lot to ask of someone, especially an only child who grew up in the city. Instead of panicking, I realize that I'd be happy for us to get a place in Greenstone if that's what she wanted.

I watch Sam turn to look at me, brushing invisible dirt off her thighs.

"Okay, let's go get filthy," she says, walking towards the door as if that's a phrase that she regularly utters and my jaw drops.

I grab her by the wrist before she gets too far and pin her against the closet.

"What's wro—"

Her question is cut off by my lips on hers and a rumbling sound starting from deep in my chest. My hands can't seem to decide if they should be tangled in her hair or roaming her body while her fingers dig into my shoulders as she meets every bit of intensity I have. She lets my knee press between her thighs and makes a little whimpering sound as she lowers herself an inch so she can straddle my leg.

"Tommy and Sam, are you almost ready?" Avery calls up the stairs, effectively throwing a bucket of cold water on me.

I let out a frustrated breath and kiss Sam on the forehead.

"What was that for?" she asks, her lips noticeably swollen.

"Simply you saying that we're about to get filthy had a few thoughts racing through my head and I might have gone a little caveman on you." I wince and rub the back of my neck, putting everything together. She was talking about mud. Not getting filthy and naked.

"Oh my goodness, I hadn't even thought of that," she says, putting a hand over her mouth.

Way to go, Tommy.

As she watches me, her hand falls away and there's a sexy smile behind it. "But I'm not opposed to you interpreting it that way."

Letting out a pained groan, I gesture for her to lead the way down to the others as I mumble, "I have a feeling this is going to be torturous."

Chapter 47
Sam

They weren't lying that mud gets everywhere. Between the ATVs, golf carts, and random wrestling fights, everyone is covered in mud. I don't think I've ever been this dirty or that I've laughed this hard in my life.

Courtney waves me over to where she and Avery are sitting on a cooler, an extra bottle of sparkling water sitting out for me.

"Thanks," I tell them, a little breathless after being tackled by Tommy just moments ago.

"Does this live up to your expectations?" Avery asks me while the guys start calling out ridiculous rules for some sort of tournament.

"Exceeded them, actually," I say truthfully.

"Good, then you'll help balance things out. The guys can turn into complete douches if there isn't a little estrogen to balance out their testosterone."

I smile at Courtney. She's probably the most blunt person I've met who doesn't seem to cross that line into being rude. She simply doesn't sugar coat things and says what she wants to say without apologizing for taking up space. I can see why Tommy, Courtney, and Avery balance each other out and each bring something to their friendship dynamics.

"I think I can do that."

"Tommy would like it, that's for sure," Avery says, watching Tommy and Jackson wrestle with one arm behind their backs and hopping on one foot per Chuck's last-minute rules. "He finally seems like himself again."

"Thank fuck," Courtney adds. "Don't get me wrong, I completely understand why he has been so picky, but he shut down parts of himself that allowed him to be happy regardless of whether or not he was seeing anyone."

They must note the confusion on my face.

"Sorry, we're all in a weird space of me not having been around much in the past few years with being off at school, so Court and I get oddly sentimental about things. Especially when it comes to Tommy since I could only be there for him virtually so much of the last year." Avery picks at the label on her bottle. "Have you guys talked about his ex much?"

"Not really. Some things have come up for both of us, but we haven't sat down and really talked about our past relationships in detail." It's clear by their tone and expressions that they aren't trying to make me feel inadequate or question why we haven't had these conversations.

"Well, you'll have to talk about Maisy fucking Jones at some point in the near future. I heard she's moving back."

"What the hell? Where'd you hear that and why didn't you say anything sooner?" Avery swats Courtney's leg.

"I just heard it this morning during one of my appointments," she says, rolling her eyes. "Apparently, her rodeo man stopped bringing her on the circuit with him."

"What if she makes an appointment with you like she used to?"

"I'll cancel it," Courtney says matter-of-factly. "I only tolerated her because of Tommy."

My head spins with these little details. Tommy's ex, Maisy, is moving back.

"That name sounds familiar," I say out loud before realizing it. Both girls are looking at me expectantly. "Did she move away recently?"

Avery shakes her head, but Courtney is the one who answers. "About a year ago, she packed up her apartment and had planned to leave a note for Tommy saying she was leaving to be with a guy in the rodeo. But he stopped by to surprise her with flowers and she had no choice but to explain she was leaving him in person."

"She's a real piece of work. Steer clear of her as best you can. She'll try to get under your skin while being sweet to your face, but always have your guard up." Avery's gaze is fixed on Tommy for a moment. "Honestly, just ignore her, if she's not getting the attention she wants from someone, she'll move on eventually."

Questions buzz through my mind faster than I can sort through, but then Bryant shows up and the guys immediately start heckling him.

"Oh this is going to get interesting now," Courtney says, cracking a wicked grin.

Bryant lets out a warrior-like bellow and charges his brothers while Caleb stays just far enough away to not get accidentally thrown down. Even though they had recently been facing off against each other, Jackson and Tommy team up to take Bryant down by his legs while Matt tugs one arm and Chuck jumps on his massive back. Not one of these guys would be considered out of shape but Bryant is somehow holding his own against them as he drags his brothers through the mud along with him.

The girls set down their drinks and grab my hands, joining the chaos and effectively cutting off my spiraling thoughts, letting myself enjoy these moments, this place, and these people.

Who knew mudding would be so fun and exhausting?

I'm completely spent by the time we're walking to the side of the house where everyone starts peeling off their layers to rinse them in a big metal bucket. I'm not sure how long we were out there, but there are clumps of now-dry mud caked in my hair.

Oh I hope everything I rolled in or that sprayed up at me while riding behind Tommy on the ATV was only mud. As much as I love being on this ranch, I don't need to have horse poop in my ponytail.

As I'm peeling off my t-shirt, I nod toward a gigantic stack of firewood and an ax buried in a stump in front of it. "When does that get done?"

"Oh, that's what Bryant does when he's frustrated or stressed," Tommy says, wiping mud from his forearms.

"Or pissed off," Chuck adds, now standing right next to me. "He's out there in waves. When there's a scowl on his face that doesn't seem to leave, he'll easily split logs for an hour a day."

"Thus the enormous supply of firewood available at Landen Acres at any given time." Tommy takes off his pants so he's only in shorts and a tight undershirt. I have to remind myself that it's not polite to ogle in public.

"Poor guy, what has him so stressed?" I ask, peeking at Bryant who is spraying down the golf cart to get most of the mud off.

Tommy shrugs while Chuck says, "Who knows? He has always been pretty quiet, but since we lost our dad, he rarely talks about things beyond the ranch and he'll just step outside halfway through an argument and start chopping away."

He must feel our eyes on him because Bryant looks our way for a second before turning the hose on the whole group. The spray is downright cold, but Tommy grabs my hand and takes off to the front of the house where his brother can't reach us. We can hear shouts and cheers from around the corner as a new battle wages on. I'm still a little out of breath from the shock when Tommy's free hand brushes the hair from my forehead.

"Should we head up and get you clean before the movie starts?"

"Oh my, I forgot to bring the popcorn inside earlier!" My feet crunch on the gravel as I walk to my car while my hand stays tucked into Tommy's.

"What kind did you get?"

"A sea salt, a cheddar, a kettle corn, and a caramel chocolate. No dairy in any of them in case anyone else is curious."

He pulls me against his side, kissing my muddy cheek. "You're ridiculously thoughtful, you know that?"

Chapter 48
Tommy

It's quiet inside the house even when we get to my room. I guess there must be a full-scale water fight happening, but I don't mind missing it one bit knowing that Sam is choosing to be here with me.

Turning towards her after grabbing a fresh towel, I take in her appearance once more. Her hair is in a wild ponytail that has mud splatter throughout. Her face is makeup-free, I think, with streaks of mud that she's tried to wipe off several times. There's a distinct line from where her long-sleeve shirt started and ended because in her tank-top, her chest and arms are clean. The bottom of her leggings, where they meet her socks, are the only dirty spots on her clothes now.

"Offer still stands to save water," I say with a wink as I hand over the towel.

Mischief dances in her eyes. "I was just thinking that I could use some help getting this mud out of my hair, actually."

Unsure if she's joking or not, I take a step closer and put my hands on her hips. "One of my best friends is a hairdresser, so I'm sure I'd be a natural."

While obviously trying not to laugh she says, "That makes no sense at all."

I shrug. "She talks about work sometimes, so there have to be little nuggets that I've absorbed over the years."

She loops her free arm around the back of my neck. "Well, I suppose there's no better time to find out than the present."

I smile as my lips hover just above hers. "I couldn't agree more."

Sam erases the space and I walk us to the bathroom, kissing her until I have her backed against the door to the shower.

"Give me three seconds." I open the door, turn on a few of the shower heads without getting wet so things can warm up, and step back out to find Sam hanging her towel next to mine. "Another sight I could get used to."

She closes the door that leads into my bedroom with a tentative smile. We meet in the middle and her eyes take in my undershirt before her fingers gently grab the fabric where it's tucked into my shorts. Raising my arms seems to be the signal she needed because she gives a tug to untuck it and peels it off my torso. Then she tosses it into the laundry hamper in the corner, like she knew right where it should go because this is her space, too.

My heart thumps in my chest because she looks so at ease doing little things like that. It makes it almost too easy to picture her doing it every single day. Instead of possibly scaring her right off by giving voice to any of those thoughts, they all go right out of my head as her fingers explore my arms, pecs, and then my abs.

"It's not fair if I can't do the same," I say while I pull her tank top up and over her head, counting the milliseconds before her hands are back on me. God damn, it's like my entire body knows every tiny point of contact. Each place her fingers touch lights up.

With her focus on exploring me, I take in the view of her in a sports bra and leggings. Fuck, if we weren't about to get in the shower, I'd drink my fill of this sight, but the steam is already fogging up the glass and people will be in the house soon, so I'd like to make the most of this time. Thankfully, this bra doesn't seem to be suffocatingly tight on her, so I can get my fingers under the band with ease. When I pull it over her head, some of the hardened mud in her hair falls loose and her ponytail becomes even more messy. She must notice because she reaches up to unbind her hair, letting it fall over her shoulders.

I do my best to keep my hands to myself while she does this, so I pull at the waist of my shorts, drawing her eyes to my motions. Or, likely, the very clear erection I'm sporting. Part of me regrets the decision to remove my own clothes, but now, I get to watch her hands glide over her hips and push down those leggings. My shorts pool around my ankles when she stands up straight in only a pair of sensible striped panties.

And God damn if she doesn't look fucking sexy.

I kneel in front of her and grasp the fabric on her sides. Her fingers run through my hair and I tug her underwear down her smooth thighs, all the way down to her ankles before she steps free. I give myself one long look at Samantha standing bare before me and remind myself that she's mine and I'm hers.

I lean in and kiss my way from her belly up to her breasts, giving them each a nibble. By the time I stand, her hands are pulling my face to hers, her lips nipping at mine. Then those magical fingers trail down my chest, tracing around my nipple, which has my hips rolling towards her. She makes quick work of getting me completely naked and takes a step towards the shower.

I open the door and steam pours out as I walk in with her right behind me. When I stop to adjust the water so it's not too hot, she slips her arms around my waist and presses light kisses between my shoulder blades and my dick jumps at the sensations.

"I'll wear protection when we, you know, but I'm clean," I say, my mind a jumbled mess. One arm braces against the wall as her fingers explore my abs, water running down my body as I take up most of the space under the rain head.

"I'm clean, too," she says between kisses as the mounted hand-held sprayer hits her back.

"I mean when we have sex," I ramble. "Not that we haven't done that, yet, but when my..."

What the fuck is wrong with me right now? God, it's not like she hasn't already touched me.

"I know what you mean. We'll use protection when we do...that."

I groan and turn in her arms, bringing her under the gentle water, and push my shaft down, and with one arm, bring Sam against me. I'm positioned between her legs and along her seam without penetrating her. Her sharp inhale and the way her mouth opens a little more has me deepening the kiss before asking, "Did you want to get a little riding done while you're here, cowgirl?"

Guiding her hips, I help her press down on my dick and feel her lips spread over my length. Her hands lock onto my biceps when I rock her forward so her clit presses directly on me. That elicits a small gasp from Sam and her fingers press into my skin as she glides over me, the water adding to sensations that almost overload me.

God, everything about this is incredible. Lifting my mouth from hers, I look down as she slides over my dick again and again. I watch her chest heave and her breasts become stiff peaks. She lets her weight bear down a little more so I'm spreading her folds and she gives a little jump each time the ridge of my dick hits her clit.

But I don't want to chance coming near her entrance, so I turn her around, flat against my chest.

"Is this okay? I ask, my dick pulsing where it's trapped between her back and my abs.

I get a nod in return.

"Samantha." My hand snakes over her shoulder and then up to her chin so she's looking right into my eyes. My other hand lightly traces invisible patterns, getting closer and closer to the apex of her thighs. "I need to hear you say it."

Sam's pupils are wide as she says, "I'm okay with this."

Chapter 49
Sam

I would be pinching myself to make sure I wasn't dreaming if I hadn't just been sliding my lady parts up and down Tommy's penis. Good lord, why does my brain use the least sexy words to describe our most intimate places? But no, that definitely wasn't a dream, it was very, very real. If someone had told me about doing that, I would have questioned if it would actually feel good or be sexy.

Oh my, it was.

And now, Tommy's fingers are almost to my clit while I'm held tight against him with water spraying my chest as he's partially under the rain shower head. After the mud extravaganza, being under the warm water with his body pressing against mine feels decadent. He holds my face in place so he can watch me and kiss me all he wants, his tongue dipping in just as his fingers make their first circle.

My body shivers and Tommy's body absorbs it, keeping me perfectly where he wants me, quickly building that pressure deep inside of me. One of my hands holds on to his neck, helping to keep me up as my knees weaken any time he hits my clit straight on. My other hand is locked onto his forearm where I'm sure, by the end of this shower, he'll be sporting marks from my nails digging into his skin.

Instead of being mortified at the thought that someone might see evidence of us being together, it only adds to the pleasure building. I'm not about to be an exhibitionist, but something about the inevitable marks gives me thoughts of Tommy being mine. Of me laying claim to him.

"God, you're beautiful," he tells me, looking down at my face and my naked body.

For once, I don't want to hide. I don't feel the urge to cover myself. I don't resist the sensations driving me higher and higher. So I push my backside into him a little more, creating a rhythm for him to grind against. There's no way for me to reach him with how he has me pinned, but I'm feeling desperate for him to climb with me.

Because I'm going to peak soon.

"Here I thought we were taking care of you." His breath is hot against my neck while he runs his nose up the side of it. A whimper escapes me.

Again, Tommy Landen is in control. And just like before, he's laser focused on how I respond to his touch, somehow amplifying each sensation. He captures my mouth with his, releasing my chin. His fingers trailing down my neck to my breasts. I raise onto my toes and he picks up the pace on my clit and pinches my nipple softly.

Our tongues meet as our kisses become increasingly desperate. My grip on the back of his neck feels like I'm going to leave a bruise, but I seem to be climbing higher against him as I get closer to my climax. And he doesn't seem to mind one bit.

Tommy's lips leave mine and trace my jaw all the way to my ear, finding that sensitive spot just behind it that has me panting and squeezing my eyes shut.

"I'm so close," I tell him, my voice almost drowned out from the shower.

"Oh I know, cowgirl. Ride it out for me."

Then he nips my earlobe and my whole body tenses as my breath catches. He adds more pressure between my legs and I go off like fireworks on the Fourth of July. The hand that was on my breast wraps around me to keep me upright as I shudder and my knees buckle while the pleasure tears through me in waves.

It's not until I giggle from being overstimulated does Tommy let up, needing to get every ounce of pleasure he can from each of my orgasms.

"Oh my goodness," I say, breathless. "A girl could get used to this."

"Fuck, I hope so," he says, turning me in his arms and giving me what I could only describe as an all-consuming kiss.

Even in the afterglow of what just happened seconds ago, nothing exists besides Tommy and me in this moment. The water spray is gentle and our bodies easily glide as we shift and sway a little. It's almost like a slow dance, except you don't kiss someone like this on the dance floor. At least, not in public.

This is the kind of kiss that no one else gets to see because it feels like a promise. One that we can't put into words right now, but a promise nonetheless. That this is something that has a future and isn't a fling. That this is more than just a good time or breaking records. This kiss is everything.

I open my eyes to see him looking down at me with a combination of tenderness and desire. He looks comfortable and confident in this. In us.

A little voice in the back of my head tries to worm its way into my thoughts that all of this is too fast, too soon. That no one can be this good. Not for me.

But I squash that down, living in this moment. Not letting those usual doubts sour what's going so well.

Tommy Landen isn't a perfect person, but I'm working hard to keep my eyes wide open to what we'll need to compromise in the future. The biggest hurdle I can see right now is that I assume he wants to live here at Landen Acres. But lord, that's not something we have to cover.

"Where's your mind going, Sam?" he asks, interrupting my train of thought.

There's a very hard penis between us right now that I don't want to ignore, so instead of asking him about future living arrangements, I simply say, "To this ranch."

He smiles and clasps his hands behind my back. "Oh yeah?"

I nod as he kisses my forehead. "Yeah. But I have something else on my mind, too."

"What's that?"

My hand answers, reaching between us to grip him. He buries his face in my neck with a long groan.

"Fuck, Samantha," he mumbles against my skin.

"You'll tell me what you want to do differently?" I ask, both hands now working him.

"Please keep doing anything you want."

Chapter 50
Tommy

Her thumb passes over my tip and circles the head of my dick with just the right pressure to make me even harder. Her other hand is wrapped around the base of my shaft, keeping a steady rhythm with her movements, the water helping her to slide along easily.

Even here in the shower and after mudding, I can smell her perfume faintly, especially as I run my nose from her collarbone up to her ear. She makes little sounds of pleasure as she works me like a maestro. The contrast between her pumping my shaft with the way she's tracing my tip is unbelievable.

Her hair is a wet, tangled mess but I weave my fingers into her strands so I can anchor her face right where I can kiss her without changing my position. She eagerly responds to my lips and my tongue, opening right away. Her fingers trail from my tip down to my balls, cupping and caressing them, too.

I moan into her mouth and grab her ass, massaging it and relishing in the fact I can do this right now. God, not only is Samantha Davies in this shower with me at this very moment, but she just let me make her come. And she's about to have me do the same.

Sam carefully uses her teeth and tugs at my bottom lip as my breathing gets shakier.

"Where do you want me to—"

"Just let it happen right here," she says, cutting off my full question.

Since the first time I came by her hands, I had boxer briefs on, but now...now I'm going to be coming on her skin.

The thought sends me closer to my own release as my tongue dips into her mouth finding hers. The strokes are in time with her movements as she continues to pick up the tempo, keeping her grip loose enough to not be painful, but tight enough so I'm not missing where any of her fingers are.

"Are you sure?" I ask, my mind wanting to keep her comfortable while my body barrels ahead like a speeding train.

"I'm sure, cowboy."

Fuck me, that's what sends me over the edge. Her tits press against my chest, her mouth is back on mine, and her fingers squeeze out everything my body can give. I can tell that some hits me but most has to be painted on her stomach and her breasts. Waves of pleasure rip through me and I cuss as the last drops coat her fingers with that picture in my mind.

"You're so fucking perfect," I say, tugging her hair to tip her face toward mine and peppering her with kisses. She hums in contentment and wraps her arms around my back, not bothering to rinse anything off just yet.

If it wouldn't scare her all the way back to the city, I'd tell her right now that my heart belongs only to her. That she's it for me.

That I love her.

But I'd rather follow her lead and move things at a pace where she feels more and more at home with me and with this place.

"What are you thinking right now?" she asks, her eyes searching my face.

"Just that I'm happy. So damn happy."

That seems to be enough for her right now because she smiles. "Me, too."

A few slow kisses later, I reluctantly pull back. "We should probably get clean. I think we might have used up our head start."

Her eyes widen and she looks around the shower until she spots her shampoo. "Oh, we don't want to make everyone wait."

"We don't have to rush, cowgirl." I grab the bottle and squirt some into my palm. "Turn around and I'll get the mud out."

She obliges, wiping down her stomach as I lather her hair. The space fills with the smell of her shampoo: lilac. As I massage her scalp, she makes little sounds letting me know she's enjoying this. I work the suds farther down her strands to dislodge the streaks of dirt.

"Tip your head back," I instruct so I can rinse everything out.

"This feels amazing," she mumbles.

She lets me condition her hair as she uses her body wash and loofah to scrub her body and insists that she washes my hair. When I lean forward she laughs.

"Everything is going to go right into your eyes if you stand like that, Tommy."

Instead of trying to bend backwards, I get on my knees in front of her, kissing her smooth belly.

"I suppose I can work with that," she says, working my shampoo and conditioner into my hair. Her fingers take their time massaging and I let mine explore her back and ass, memorizing the shape and feel of her.

Once we're both clean, I step out for our towels and close us back in the steamy space. I somehow missed that she brought in a second towel which she uses to twist up her hair in. Sam is thorough as she dries herself off and uses her towel to get the drops on my back that I apparently missed. It's sweet and such a detail-oriented thing that she would notice.

I think I might purposefully leave my back wet from now on just so she has an excuse to touch me a little more.

Even though she's using travel-sized bottles of her products, the way they're neatly on the counter, with their labels facing us, feels like it won't be a big shift for her to be here. That our lives can easily come together without huge bumps while we try to figure things out. These moments have been smooth as we watch and learn how the other lives.

I put my face moisturizer on while watching her work her way through a couple of the bottles.

"What is that?"

"My face lotion," I reply.

"It says it has SPF in it, but we're going to be inside." Her eyebrows furrow and her nose scrunches just a little.

"Habit," I say with a shrug. "I can burn pretty easily so I always use it."

She nods. "I burn easily, too."

"At least we know any kids we have will need to wear it."

I hold perfectly still as what I said sinks in. I know that I want everything with Samantha, but when did I add kids to that picture?

Oh God, I should say something.

Anything.

She's unscrewing a bottle of some sort of face product and my brain has officially short-circuited. It's like I'm having an out-of-body experience just watching things happen. My mouth opens to speak and that's as far as I get.

What the hell am I supposed to say? I can't lie and say I *don't* want kids with her. Because now that's all I can picture. Little versions of the two of us running around with her blonde hair and sunscreen smeared hastily on their exposed skin as they barrel out of the house and onto the ranch to see the new foal.

I'm so screwed.

Chapter 51
Sam

My thoughts race with what Tommy so casually threw out: *our kids*. There should be alarm bells going off in my head, right? Not warm, fuzzy feelings.

It's way too soon to be thinking about something so...permanent. Maybe.

Maybe not?

I need to get a grip either way and respond with something. Anything. I'm not so young that I haven't thought about wanting to have kids in the next few years, but I'm not going to walk through my ideal timeline as we're getting ready to hang out with his family and friends. And my friends. I think.

Focus, Samantha. You're not going to tell him you'd like to be on your way to starting a family before you're thirty...he doesn't need to know that your brain has an arbitrary three-year timeline ticking down. Just keep it light and fun.

"I think we'd be able to handle sunscreen," I say, feeling pretty proud that I didn't say something ridiculous about us being parents.

But he would make a pretty spectacular parent, that's for sure... Oh boy, I need to not picture Tommy Landen holding a baby or I'm going to have a new obsession.

He lets out a shaky chuckle, like he was the one who was nervous. "If anyone on this ranch could remember, I think we'd be the ones."

His eyes go wide once more, like he said something he didn't mean to. And then I realize he mentioned people on the ranch. Does he picture us here? Am I crazy for thinking that? I suppose we haven't talked about where each of us hopes to live, but I'm guessing he'd like to stay on the family ranch. Maybe it's because he asks me not to hide, or maybe I've unlocked some new version of myself who has an extra boost of confidence, but I actually ask the question on my mind.

"Truth or dare."

Okay, maybe I don't come right out and ask it.

Tommy's cheek twitches and there's a moment's pause before he replies. "Truth."

I chose my wording carefully, so he's not boxed into a corner with having to be too specific, but giving enough leeway where he can. "When you picture your future children, where are you living?"

His Adam's apple bobs as he swallows and adjusts his towel that's sitting low on his hips before making eye contact with me.

"I think I automatically picture those scenes playing out here on the ranch," he pauses, resting one hand on the vanity. "But I know that living at Landen Acres isn't for everyone, and I'd rather live in town with the right person rather than finding out they don't like life on a ranch like my mom. And I know that the main house comes with a few of my brothers and that won't likely change much…they'll have families here, too, or somewhere else on the property. But I hope to stay near the ranch so I can continue to be hands-on."

It seems like I'm not the only one choosing their words carefully.

"Did you grow up with any aunts or uncles living in the main house?" I ask, keeping the conversation semi-neutral because I'm not sure how things work with that many adults in a house, even one this big.

Tommy shakes his head. "Our grandfather died before our mom left and I was still pretty young when that happened. But our uncle Kent, Jesse's dad, moved out when we left for college and wasn't interested in ranching."

"Oh, I guess I hadn't thought about what would happen if one of you didn't want to live and work here. I suppose that's something you've all figured out over the years?" I decide against putting on makeup and walk out of the bathroom with Tommy right behind me.

"Yeah, especially after our dad passed, we started having more conversations that were concrete about what we wanted and what we didn't want. All five of us have said we'd like to stay and as people have retired, we've officially started taking over those positions ourselves."

"That makes sense," I say, wondering where someone like me could fit in. I suppose I have the work I do for the co-op, but Avery is the mastermind behind that and Tommy has the contacts. I just help organize things and fill in some of the details.

"Do you think you could see yourself," Tommy clears his throat while he digs through his drawer, "not living in a big city?"

"Well, I did move to Greenstone," I point out, my heart racing at his question. Is he asking me if I could see myself living *here*? With him?

By the time I'm tugging my underwear on, he's already wearing a pair of black sweatpants and I can see the band of his boxer briefs peeking out of the waistband which is sitting low on his hips. I don't think I've ever seen him in these before and, as Tommy says, I think I could get used to seeing him in these more often. Especially without a shirt on.

"Yeah, but going from a big city to Greenstone is one thing. Living on a ranch is entirely different."

He's right. And I don't know what living in this house would feel like…especially since three of his brothers live here, too. There truly is so much space in this house, but could it one day feel like a home where I can pop downstairs in my pajamas for a late night snack?

"That's true, it would be very different living on a ranch. But different isn't necessarily a bad thing, especially when you're with your person."

To that, he nods. "I definitely agree with you. I just know that some people aren't fond of this lifestyle so it's always good to talk about concerns as they arise if anyone were open to the idea of living here."

Pulling a shirt over my head hides my smile at hearing him say: living here. "It's good to know that any concerns, or questions, can be addressed."

"Always," he says, now with a t-shirt on to my dismay. Although, it's probably good he has one on so I'm not just rubbing his bare chest in front of everyone downstairs.

I go back to the bathroom for my brush, freeing my hair from my quick-dry hair towel and then making quick work of detangling a couple of snarls. "I'll be ready to go down in a minute, don't feel like you have to wait for me."

Why on earth did I say that? Wouldn't it be weird if we went down at different times? Oh no, it would look like we showered together if we went down at the same time. Right?

My brain is practically tripping over itself trying to analyze the different ways for us to go downstairs and I find myself cringing over the ridiculousness of these thoughts. Thankfully, Tommy walks in, effectively derailing that train of thought because he steps up behind me with his arms around my stomach and kisses my cheek.

Watching our reflection, this looks like home.

Chapter 52
Tommy

Four bowls of popcorn, two plates of cookies, and a variety of veggies are on the coffee table. All nine of us watch some competition show that didn't seem to garner any boos when we were voting.

Sam is tucked into my side with our shared bowl of snacks on my lap and my arm around her. Courtney's in the middle of the couch next to Sam with Avery and Jackson on her other side. Actually, Avery is on Jackson's lap. He saw that there wasn't space for him to fit next to her, so he simply picked her up and sat down with her on top.

I steal a glance over Sam's head at my oldest brother with one of my best friends curled up on him. They finally figured things out after all these years of silently pining for each other. About damn time. I think about how long I was with the wrong person and how long it took me to really heal from that relationship. Getting over Maisy was the easiest part. It just took me a lot longer to trust someone enough to not fuck me over again. I suppose it was good I thought Sam and Jax dated…it gave me time to get to know her a little while I figured myself out.

Everything feels good right now. No one is out of place and nothing is awkward with this many people gathered. Taking in the full scene around me, my eyes catch on what appears to be fairly fresh ink sticking out of Bryant's tank top.

"You got another one?" I ask, drawing everyone's attention first to me and then to Bryant who just looks back at me with one eyebrow raised.

"What'd you get this time?" Caleb calls out from his spot on a cushion in front of Matt's chair, even though there are two other recliners available and a smaller couch.

Bryant's gaze drifts to Caleb and instead of a grunt or a monosyllabic response, he leans forward, pulls off his shirt.

Courtney is the first to speak, squealing out, "No shit!"

She's already walking up to him to examine the designs up close. I swear she doesn't have boundaries when it comes to looking at tattoos or piercings. The rest of us just take in the swirling lines across his chest.

"None of you knew he got that huge tattoo?" Sam whispers to me while everyone else weighs in.

I shake my head. "He got his first not long after our dad died and every now and then, we notice a new one, but it's always a mystery."

"Oh," she says just as Courtney plunks back down.

Oh, is about right. Our big, burly brother continues to be a mystery at times.

"How many hours did this one take?" Caleb asks.

"Six." Bryant's voice is matter of fact.

"When were you gone for six hours?" Chuck asks, his beer halfway to his mouth.

Bryant only shrugs his shirt over his head and turns the volume up on the show, effectively ending the Q and A session.

"He really is this quiet most of the time, isn't he?" Sam asks, still whispering.

"He definitely is." I give her a quick kiss since her lips are so close to mine. "He's very capable of having conversations, but he typically chooses to be as succinct as possible with his words."

"Court, put the phone away." Avery tiredly swats at Courtney's device. "You don't need to look up tattoo designs right now, we can talk to your artist soon."

"Fine," she replies, glaring a little at Avery without any heat behind it.

"Sam, you should come, too," Avery says.

"Oh please come with, I'm always indecisive and Avery just pulls out more designs to add to the pile." Courtney's genuine enthusiasm makes me smile.

"Is it okay that I don't have any tattoos?" Sam asks.

"There are no qualifications needed besides being a friend," Avery says, reaching across Court to touch Sam's arm. "And also making sure Courtney doesn't get something she's going to regret right after it heals."

A little pink appears on Samantha's cheeks. "I think I can do that."

"Good, I'll see when he has time for a consult." Courtney types furiously on her phone before tucking it back into her pocket.

It shouldn't be that big of a deal to me. I know my two best friends are amazing. But they seem to be trying to naturally bring Sam into our little world. It was something that I know they didn't like doing with Maisy, and they tried for my sake to be friendly with her, but they rarely asked her to hang out with just the two of them. Another sign I should have noticed so much sooner...neither of them could bear being around the person I was dating for any length of time without getting frustrated.

But here they are, inviting Sam to go to Courtney's next tattoo consultation. They would never invite her if they didn't want her there.

My eyes close and I just let myself feel everything this moment has to give. My brothers in one place, my two best friends right here, Caleb, who has basically become an honorary Landen, and the girl of my dreams.

All here.

All happy.

Two hours later, it's time to get a few things done around the ranch. Caleb volunteers to help Matt make dinner for everyone, Chuck takes the four-wheeler out to check on a pregnant cow who has been showing signs of possible early labor.

"Do you want to come see the new horse Jackson's working with?" Avery asks both Courtney and Sam. "He has to head back for an afternoon training session."

"Sure," Courtney says, looping her arm through Sam's. "Let's go."

Sam looks back at me, likely wondering if I had anything planned. "I have a few orders to finalize, so I won't be exciting company."

"Let's go," she echoes, her eyes bright with her infectious smile as they pull on their boots and pile into Jax's SUV.

After a few hours of hearing Bryant intermittently chopping wood, everyone is back together around our family dinner table with one of the extenders in place. We laugh and talk, the food getting passed around and everyone just being themselves. Sam's leg pressed against mine during the whole meal.

This right here is the dream.

And I'm ready to make it happen.

Chapter 53
Sam

Two weeks later

Final decision time, Sam. What will it be: the brown skirt with the salmon top, or the navy sailor pants with the beige top? I resist the urge to chew my thumbnail, something I never thought I'd stop doing.

I hold each up in front of me as I look in the mirror, smiling when I see Tommy's flannel shirt in my chair from the other night. It's Maybel's, so it's not a dressy place.

But it's our first time eating out.

Our first public date.

Tommy doesn't seem to have favorites for what I wear...everything I put on seems to make him do that slow smile of approval. I settle on the pants deciding they're cute with a casual feel that will work at Maybel's without standing out too much.

Once I'm dressed, I take out each of my curlers, thinking of how Tommy so gently did the same thing not too long ago. I'm still baffled how I landed someone as amazing as him. He's sweet, thoughtful, funny, and so sexy. He brings out a confidence in me that I didn't know existed.

It's no wonder I'm head over heels in love with him.

Not that I've told him. I don't want to pressure him into saying anything he's not ready for. But Courtney and Avery have hinted he loves me, too. So maybe it wouldn't be so scary to tell him...

My stomach gives a flip at the nerves that even make my fingers tremble a little at the thought of giving voice to what simply happened. It's like loving him was inevitable.

Ding. I look down at my phone to find a message from him.

Tommy: I'm earlier than usual, Chuck was belting out nineties love ballads...

I can picture it. Chuck is probably stealing spoons from Matt to use as a microphone while Matt tries to cook.

Sam: Oh poor you! Was anyone else home? I'll be down in one minute.

Making sure nothing is out of place, I grab my purse from the bed and shut off the lights except the one right inside my door.

Tommy: Bryant left after the first song and is chopping wood, but Matt and Caleb are making a big batch of stock, so they're trapped. Also, Chuck changed my alert sound to Gertrude eating something, so feel free to take your time, I'm going to check all my sounds.

I snort out a laugh reading about a new cow sound. Maybe one day we'll figure out how Chuck keeps accessing Tommy's phone. But until then, it's harmless and pretty darn funny.

Right as I leave the building, Tommy's head pops up from his phone and his eyes take me in.

"Stunning as always," he says, taking my hand and bringing me in for a kiss, his cowboy hat tipping back. He tastes like his toothpaste this evening and I'm tempted to pull him into the building and into my apartment, missing yet another dinner reservation.

"You look as handsome as ever," I say, looking down at his blue button down shirt and perfectly fitting brown dress pants. There's no doubt in my mind that his butt looks fantastic in these. As he opens the door for me, I give him a little more room that's necessary, but I get a good look at his backside.

Oh I totally called it. These might tie for first with how good his butt looks in his jeans. And that's saying something.

As we're buckling our seatbelts, our phones chime in unison.

Courtney: I found Avery at the store and persuaded her to come over for a spa night. No phones, no devices. Only chick flicks, nail polish, and facials. You both in?

"Wasn't she going on a date tonight?" I ask Tommy.

He makes a face. "I'm guessing something came up... again."

"That can't be good."

He shakes his head.

Avery: OMG you two have your first date! You're officially uninvited because it's high time you go on a real date.

Courtney: Dates are overrated.

Courtney: This is Avery, I took her phone. Dates are not overrated and she knows it. Go on your date and we'll get all the juicy details tomorrow.

"Are we supposed to be part of this conversation?" I ask, laughing while typing as Tommy runs his hand over his face, groaning. "We can stop by to make sure they're okay, maybe."

Sam: Are you sure? We can reschedule...it sounds like distractions might be in order for tonight.

Tommy: Did you get the name? If he canceled twice on her, I need to know who I should hate.

Avery: She still won't say who it is or why he canceled.

Avery: But really, go have your date and I'll add extra chocolate to the cookies.

"What are you thinking?" I ask Tommy as he reads Avery's reply with a frown.

"It's not like Courtney to keep things from us, so this has just been strange. But..." He trails off.

"But what?"

"But I also know if we show up, Avery will turn us right around and march us to Maybel's if she has to." Another pause. "And I'd really like to take you out to dinner."

Courtney: HA! You can't take my watch! But yes, you two go on your date. We'll toast you two with our cookies and milk.

Tommy looks over at me, eyebrows raised. "Shall we keep our reservation for once?"

Avery seems to have things under control but it was nice to be included. I really haven't had friends like these before. It's more spontaneous and more...passionate. They're fiercely protective of each other and they seem to have folded me into their dynamic. "Maybe we can drop off dessert on our way back to my place?"

"I love that." His smile is so warm it melts my heart.

Avery: Honk when you pass Court's house, we're turning off our phones!

"Perfect. Should we ask what they want?"

Tommy shakes his head. "I've got their favorites down, so we'll get a slice of chocolate cake and a slice of apple pie with caramel drizzle."

I just smile and hold his hand as he pulls out of the lot. Of course he knows their favorite desserts. He's the kind of guy that remembers the little things that can make a big difference in someone's day.

Right now, I don't know how I could love him more.

Chapter 54
Tommy

Maybel's is more of a bar than a restaurant, but walking in while holding Sam's hand feels like we're at a five-star place with a private chef. There's one table in the far corner with a white tablecloth, a single rose, and a little sign that says "reserved" just like Keith said.

"Is this for us?" Sam asks.

"I might know a few people who work here," I reply, pulling out a chair for her so she can see the rest of the bar if she'd like. I'll only be looking at her so it doesn't matter which one I take.

"Thank you," she says, looking around for a moment before leaning her purse against the wall next to her chair so no one can trip on it.

"If you'll give me a minute, I have something to get at the bar."

"Okay, I'll go check my lipstick to make sure I'm still wearing some after greeting you."

I flash her a full smile, kiss her cheek, and walk over to the bar where Elliot is working tonight. There are a handful of people ordering so I wait as patiently as possible to catch his attention. I just want tonight to be perfect for Sam.

It's not like this is the first time she's been out to eat in town, let alone here at Maybel's. We've already been here the night of

Sharon's presentation. But I want her to see how much she means to me and what this town has to offer someone who is used to a big city. I don't want her to feel stuck or trapped here like our mom. I don't want her to think there aren't hidden perks to everyone knowing each other, even if most of what's here is casual. She didn't actually grow up with cotillions, but she's used to having plenty of restaurants to choose from, versus two main ones that are bars plus one cafe.

A hand removes my Stetson and I hold still for a moment. Is Samantha wearing my hat in front of everyone here? Does she remember what it means? I catch Elliot's confused look at Sam right before I turn around, which doesn't make much sense.

Except, when I turn, it's not Samantha Davies wearing my hat...

It's Maisy Jones.

Sam

Oh seriously, my heart is so fluttery that my brain has apparently stopped working because I get to the bathroom only to realize I didn't bring my purse which has my lipstick in it. And I could use a touch up because half of it seems to be missing from my lips. Rolling my eyes at my forgetfulness, I push the door open and cross over to our adorable little table.

It's really the sweetest thing. Whenever it was set up, they pushed the closest tables a little farther away. They must host fancier events than I was led to believe because the cloth is commercial grade and silky and while the rose in the mini vase is real, there are fabric rose petals carefully dropped around it. From what their website and Hank have said, they do great wings and pizza for large crowds.

Once I grab my purse, I push in my chair and look for Tommy's white hat at the bar. His back should be to me so if I'm lucky, I'll get another peek at his butt in these pants.

Huh, I don't see it.

I take my first step back to the bathrooms when something white catches my eye. Smiling, I turn to see him for a second.

But it doesn't make sense.

Tommy's at the far end of the bar, so I can't see his butt because he's leaning against the bar itself. And he's facing a gorgeous, short, curvy woman wearing his hat.

What on earth?

He said that wearing a cowboy's hat was a signal to everyone that you're riding the cowboy and that it's a big deal to do that. Is this a cousin I haven't heard about? I know I haven't met everyone in this town enough times to memorize their names and faces, but I can't place her at any events or even the grocery store. But she looks a little familiar.

And then my eyes are drawn to something shiny as she swings her purse. It's completely bedazzled. It's the woman from the office who acted oddly while asking for a printout of the upcoming events.

Oh my God. Her name was Maisy.

I'm looking at Tommy's Maisy.

No, I'm looking at Tommy's Maisy wearing his hat in the middle of a bar.

Wear the hat, ride the cowboy.

My stomach clenches in knots and I'm about to go hide in the bathroom for a few minutes when one other motion catches my attention…

Maisy reaches out and takes Tommy's hand in hers and leads him off towards the back door.

I think I'm going to throw up.

I can't stay here. His ex who broke his heart wants him back. And he went with her.

How do I leave?

I have to leave a note so my absence is explained. My instinct to do things properly gives me some semblance of order in the well of emotions that's threatening to erupt right here in front of all these people. I'm trembling as I open my purse, grab a pen and my little notebook scrawling "I'm so sorry, I got sick. - Sam" as fast as I can. I tear it out, fold it in half, and tuck it under the vase so it won't somehow get blown away.

One final deep breath to gather my courage, I stand up tall, resolving to not sprint out of here, and walk out the front door with my head held high. Not one tear on my face.

Tommy

I storm past the bar, needing to see Samantha. Just being near her will calm me after that fucking bogus attempt at manipulating me again. Because Maisy Jones misses me.

Yeah right.

Her rodeo guy stopped bringing her on the circuit, she realized he was seeing other people, and now she wants another chance with the person she could walk all over.

She got exactly one minute. I'm sure I looked like the biggest dick ever pulling out my phone to set the timer. But I agreed to give her one minute of my time so she'd give me back my hat and leave for the evening. Well, I didn't specify the hat, I just hoped she wasn't that much of an asshole to keep the one my dad gave me. I couldn't handle the thought of her doing something to make Sam feel uncomfortable and she proved herself to be in an especially confident mood by starting things off by taking it and putting it on like she had any right to do so.

I sit down in my chair, my hands shaking. The table is empty and I can't sit here just getting more and more worked up over this, so I stand up and walk briskly to the men's room. No one seems to be in here so I let out a frustrated groan and splash water on my face.

The cool water gives me a little shock and resets my lungs so I can finally take a deep breath.

Dabbing the water from my face with a paper towel, I close my eyes and picture Sam. Sam on a horse, Sam at a meeting, Sam tucked against me, Sam in the shower, Sam asleep next to me.

Just Sam.

Confident that I won't be shaking now from how upset I am, I go back to our table, which is still empty. My mind runs through a worst-case scenario where Maisy approached Sam in the bathroom and said something to her that made her leave.

Except that would have happened in the last thirty seconds at the most because I spent that amount of time in the bathroom.

It's fine. Everything's fine.

Sam could be changing all of her makeup, painting her thumbnail if she bit it, or, you know, using the bathroom. I just need to sit down and chill out.

Easier said than done.

Chapter 55
Sam

Breathe.

Samantha Davies, you are going to breathe evenly, get those tears in check, and keep walking until you're at Courtney's door. Then, you're going to knock and say you're here to join girl's night. You're going to stay as long as Avery and get a ride home with her. It doesn't matter if it's in twenty minutes, or tomorrow morning.

You can cry your heart out when you're back at the apartment. Right now, that's too far to walk to in the off chance Tommy sees the note anytime soon because even if Maisy's in the truck, he's too much of a gentleman to let me walk home.

Oh the nausea's back. I pause and press my hand against a tree in someone's yard, steadying myself. My eyes squeeze shut, trying to stop the onslaught of tears threatening to come out at any moment.

What if he's on his way to the truck right now, with *her*, and he hasn't even noticed I'm gone?

I mentally chide myself because that's unfair. Tommy wouldn't leave me to fend for myself. Even if I was just a placeholder.

My feet continue forward and soon I'm on Courtney's block. Oh my goodness, how did I misread everything so poorly? I try to think back to any conversation regarding past relationships. Did we explicitly talk about Maisy? Or has he been avoiding anything specific to her because he's been in love with her but couldn't have her? Or did he think he was over her and was trying to move on?

What if he tries to call me? The thought leaps out of the jumbled mess in my brain.

I almost drop my purse in my rush to pull out my cell. No missed calls or messages. Good. I proceed to fully shut my phone down, squashing the little voice that's telling me it's rude to shut your phone off when you're expecting some sort of communication.

But right now, I'm not worried about being proper. My focus is on ringing the doorbell, plastering a smile on my face, and hoping a decent excuse comes to mind before Courtney opens the door for why I'm here, alone, and not on my date with Tommy.

It's Avery who opens the door and her face lights up with excitement when she sees it's me.

"Oh my God, hi!" She pulls me into the house with a hug and a squeal and looks along the road. "Wait, it's your date night, why did you guys come here? Did Tommy park around the corner or something?"

"Something came up and I walked, it's lovely out right now," I say, feeling terrible about not just saying what happened. But these are Tommy's best friends who have been in his life for twenty years. They're not going to want to believe me, and even if they do, they'll need to distance themselves from me to make room for Maisy again even though they didn't really like her all that much.

All I need right now is to not spiral. They'll find out when they turn their phones on and I'll leave them. Just one evening of having girlfriends in this little town before everything falls apart seems like something that's acceptable.

"What came up?" Avery asks, sounding surprised. I don't blame her...the Tommy I've known, my Tommy, would have never done this.

But he's not mine anymore. He's Maisy's.

"Something confusing, I'm not sure what the details are." Again, that's sort of true.

Thankfully, Courtney yells from downstairs to come down and Avery motions for me to go down.

"I came up for milk with the cookies, I'll get a glass for you, too."

"Water is good for me," I say, not wanting to get sick on top of everything else from dairy, which most people don't know I have restrictions on.

Tommy knows.

Avery shrugs with a smile, "Fine by me."

When I'm down the stairs, I see Courtney pulling a fourth chair over to the table filled with home spa night items and a plate of Avery's oatmeal chocolate chunk cookies in the middle. They're pretty darn tasty, but my favorite cookie is peanut butter, and she makes amazing ones. But Tommy was the one who asked her to make them for me once. And they won't need to know that I love peanut butter cookies more than oatmeal chocolate chunk cookies because...

Stop it, Samantha. No more of that tonight.

Courtney is already telling me about the different masks we can try as she hands me the polish remover and some cotton balls. "Avery and I just finished taking off our old polish. The nail polish options are in the cupboard over there if you want to pick one out now. But we should put on our masks before starting our nails, I think."

She pauses and blinks a few times, so I reach out to grab her hand. I can be brave tonight and not overthink everything.

"I'm sorry he canceled." It's so much easier to focus on someone else. Not that I want Courtney to have gone through this again.

She gives a quick smile. "Thanks, guys just suck some days, even if they have a good reason."

Her watch lights up.

"Wait a minute. I thought we were unplugging?"

Courtney gives me a sheepish look, "Avery hadn't noticed…"

I realize mine is still on, too. "Okay, we'll take them off together and we'll put them under a stack of pillows so we can't hear them vibrate. Deal?"

"Deal," she replies.

We both remove our watches and, while Courtney looks like she might regret removing it, I feel a huge sense of relief because I hadn't thought about my notifications. Shutting off my phone doesn't mean messages won't come through to my watch one bit.

"How about in the recliner? We'll be piled on the couch like teenagers after our nails are done."

"That makes sense, let's put them there."

Courtney lifts the cushion and places our watches side by side. I catch her tapping hers one last time before putting the cushion back.

"What is taking them so long? Avery was just getting milk and, even if Tommy wants some, they can both carry two glasses each." Courtney turns on some music as she comes back to the table.

Oh, Courtney didn't hear the conversation. I begin removing the polish on my nails, starting with the thumb that so often has chips from chewing it.

"Tommy isn't here, something came up," I say, trying to make sure the story is the same. "I chose to walk here."

"Is he picking you up later to have your date?"

"Nope, I'll hitch a ride with Avery."

She frowns. "What came up? Are his brothers okay?"

How the heck am I supposed to keep evading the truth?

"The brothers are fine," I say, grabbing a handful of pretzels to buy me time to think.

And then I realize that I don't want to evade the truth with these two. I want to trust that they're the kind of people I believe them to be: loyal, yes, but also mature enough to figure out how to stay friends with me.

"When Avery gets down, I'll fill you both in," I say, my voice getting a little wobbly.

"Are *you* okay?" she asks, reaching across just like I did moments ago.

Footsteps descend the stairs and Avery appears with her attention in the three cups in her hands. "Sorry, I put a half batch of peanut butter cookies into the oven. Those are your favorites, right Sam?"

Those *are* my favorite. And Tommy didn't have to ask her. She just remembered because that's what friends do.

Instead of explaining first and crying later, my heart decides that sobbing now is necessary.

So that's exactly what I do.

Chapter 56
Tommy

A few minutes of sitting and my knee is bouncing up and down, but my hands aren't shaking so I'll call that a win.

God, I wish she'd come out of the bathroom. I'd go in there myself if I didn't think it might freak her out with my desperation to be near her.

It's not about Maisy being back.

Well, I suppose it is a little. But only in the sense that I don't want anything to do with Maisy and I *really* don't want Maisy to have a chance to pull any shit with Sam. Fuck, Maisy can be so manipulative without the other person figuring it out until it's too late and Sam is so trusting and kind because she wants people to feel at ease. She wants to see the best in them.

And without having a heads up, Maisy could walk all over her.

My jaw is sore from clenching since I turned to see Maisy wearing my hat and not Samantha so I rub it remembering the drinks that I hadn't ordered. Maybe Elliot saw me and started making hers though. It would be nice to have hers here when she's back.

Keith walks by and I wave him over. "Hey, could you see if Elliot made the drink I requested when I called earlier? He knew I was going to get it tonight and I dropped off the oat milk yesterday. I didn't actually order it tonight, but there's a chance he started it," I say like it was one continuous sentence.

"Is this for you?" he asks, a little confused.

"No, it's for Sam when she's back from the restroom."

Keith's face shifts into pain and then pity. "I'm sorry, man, but she left a few minutes ago."

"That wouldn't make sense, we're on our date."

He shrugs. "I don't know what else to tell you, Tommy. She wrote something down and walked right out the door without looking back."

My eyes search the table for something with my name on it until it lands on a piece of notebook paper folded in half under the vase.

Fuck.

I think Keith is still talking but every sound is drowned out by the ringing in my ears. My hands shake as I open the letter. It's written by Sam, but not with the usual neatness.

I'm sorry. I got sick.

-Sam

What? What happened to her? And why didn't she wait for ninety seconds for me to come back? I wasn't gone longer than that. But how did she leave without her car if she wasn't feeling okay?

"Did she get in a car or anything?" I ask, cutting off Keith.

"I didn't see," he says, looking sorry for me.

"Um, can we do a raincheck?" I ask, pulling out some cash from my wallet and handing him a few bills.

"You didn't order anything, there's no charge, Tommy." The pity in his voice is going to rub away my resolve.

She didn't walk out on me.

No, I'm going to find her and help her feel better.

I focus on Keith again and gesture to the table. "Consider it a tip for everything you put into this. I have to go, sorry."

As I walk, I send Sam a text to find out where she is. By the time I'm in the truck, there's no reply.

That's because you sent it thirty seconds ago, Tommy. Calm down.

When I'm pulling out of the parking lot, though, I call her and hang up when the automated message comes on. She'll see a text before she listens to a message.

But what if the message didn't get sent for some reason?

I pull over and look at my messages, I see it was delivered, but not seen. Tapping my screen a few times, I call her back and this time, I leave a message.

"Hey Sam, what happened? Are you okay? I'm going to go to your apartment. If you need privacy for whatever you're sick with, I'll respect that. I just need to know you're okay."

Resisting the urge to say "I love you" at the end of the message, I hang up. I drive past Courtney's house and think to call her or Avery, just in case they knew she wasn't feeling well or had ideas about what might have just happened, but remember their phones are off.

Everything is familiar on these streets. I remember playing in many of these houses when I was a kid. When I pass Jesse's house, I'm reminded that Uncle Kent is retiring and has been out of town for well over a month to tie up his leads and transition over his clients to his replacement. Sort of his last hurrah. We should do something to celebrate. Dad would have.

Automatically, I want to call Sam and ask her what she thinks we should do. At the stop light a few blocks from her apartment building, I peek at my phone.

Still nothing.

What if she's throwing up? Who's going to hold her hair back? What if her cramps came back and she forgot to get her meds? Why did she just leave?

My head is a complete mess of worry and confusion when I park and hop out of my truck like I was stung by something. I jog to the front door and take the step in one stride, hitting her button as fast as I can.

Forcing myself to take a step back from the call buttons, I breathe slowly six times. Then I hit the buzzer again, this time holding it down longer.

I repeat the process and breathing to give her time to be sick but know I'm here. After several rounds of that, I try to remember who lives in each apartment number. For privacy, the names aren't written, just the suite numbers.

My nerves ratchet up each time I step back to breathe, realizing that she's not there. And she's not reading my messages, all five at this point, and every call has gone to voicemail. Why the hell is her phone off?

I pace and try to quell the rising panic that something happened to *us*. What did I miss this time?

Chapter 57
Sam

Two sets of arms wrap around me as I cry. Tears fall out of confusion, hurt, and heartbreak and they hold me through them, which makes me cry harder. At some point Courtney steps away and comes back with a box of tissues so I can blow my nose and sop up my tears.

Finally, I'm only sniffling, so I give their hands a little squeeze. They sit in the chairs next to mine and both wait patiently. It's time to rip the band-aid off as efficiently as possible.

"Maisy came back for him," I whisper.

"Maisy what?" Courtney asks, her eyes huge.

"She came back."

Avery looks from Courtney to me and back again. "Maybe it's best to walk us through what happened."

My stomach knots in dread. This is when they pick Tommy over me. Their history is too strong to balance out a friendship with me if we're not dating.

I think of their arms holding me. About our plans to go to Courtney's tattoo consultation coming up and Avery putting in a batch of my favorite cookies when I show up unexpectedly.

Give them a chance.

So, I walk them through what I saw. Both looking confused and ready to interject, likely on Tommy's behalf which I understand, until I tell them he held her hand.

"He did what now?" Courtney asks.

"She took his hand and they went to the back door." My voice sounds small, even to myself.

"And she was wearing his Stetson? And you're sure it was him?" Avery asks as if she's trying to find an explanation to rationalize this whole situation in a way that makes sense.

"If it wasn't him, then it was someone wearing the same outfit as him with his haircut, too. I mean, I wasn't close, but his hat wasn't on his head and she had a white one on that looked just like his."

"It was definitely Maisy since you mentioned her purse," Courtney mumbles. "What the fuck was he thinking?"

"It doesn't add up," Avery says. "He's been over her for a long time."

"And he's crazy about you," Courtney points out, looking at me.

I'm sure I look pathetic right now. "I thought so, too. But we were wrong."

Tears well up in my eyes and I don't try to hold them back. Courtney rubs my back and Avery holds one hand while keeping me stocked with fresh tissues and leaving only to get the cookies from the oven and bringing them down piping hot.

I cry for my naiveness.

I cry for everything I felt for him.

I cry for the future I saw with him.

Through all my sobbing and sniffling, Courtney and Avery stay with me.

And when my tears have dried up, we paint our nails, prep our face mask scrubs, and instead of watching a chick flick or a rom-com, we settle on an action/adventure movie with dinosaurs and no romance.

"Oh my goodness these are incredible, Avery," I say around a mouthful of peanut butter cookie.

"Thank you. With Jackson around, I make huge batches now, especially my chocolate ones, but I love making peanut butter dough. I'll whip up a mega batch so you can freeze the dough and bake fresh ones whenever you have a craving."

Thankfully, the lights are low, so the little wince I made at the mention of Tommy's oldest brother was hidden. "That sounds perfect, thank you."

"What happens if you add chocolate chunks to the peanut butter cookies?" Courtney asks from the other side of me.

"You'd have chocolate chunk peanut butter cookies?" Avery replies as if she's trying to figure out if Courtney was setting her up for a joke.

"Excellent. I request those for our next girls' night." Courtney puts her hand on my leg, giving me a soft smile.

My heart warms at the thought of more nights like this.

"Deal," Avery says, doing the same.

Against every proper etiquette that has been ingrained in me, I shove the rest of the cookie in my mouth so both hands are free, catching theirs.

"Yes, please." Except, it sounds nothing like that, but the girls seem to know what I mean before we all burst out laughing. Somehow, I manage to keep every morsel of that cookie in my mouth.

Halfway through the movie, the doorbell rings.

"That should be the wings we ordered," Courtney shrieks, leaping over the back of the sofa with her long legs. Avery pauses the movie and offers to refill my water.

"Thanks, I'm just going to use the bathroom real quick." I haven't had a moment to myself since I got here, which is exactly what I needed, but this intermission has my eyes watering again.

I close the door and look at my reflection. My makeup is nonexistent and my eyes are a little puffy and pink, but not as terrible as I expected. I run the cold water and splash some on my face, grabbing one of Courtney's rolled up wash clothes to dab it dry. I look around trying to see where she moved her hamper to since I came over with Tommy last week but can't find it.

Nope, not thinking about him right now. I'm going to have to drink a ton of water just to rehydrate from all my tears so far.

As I reach for the doorknob, I hear Courtney whisper-yelling something that I can't quite make out. I frown and pause, taking a breath as I clearly hear Courtney whisper, "Don't you dare."

But the door is already opening without my help, revealing a very frazzled looking Thomas Landen.

Chapter 58
Tommy

She's here.

I have no idea what Courtney has been saying to me, but I know she tried to tug me back from opening the bathroom door. Sam locks the door, so the worst that's going to happen is I'll jiggle the handle. Thankfully, it's unlocked and I can check on her. God, my heart is still pounding a full hour since Maisy pulled me aside at Maybel's.

"What's wrong?" I ask, not bothering to hide the desperation in my voice. My hands reach for her but don't make contact in case I touch something sensitive. The thought of her being sick or in pain is still driving me crazy. I just need to know how to help her and I can calm down.

But she's not answering me.

"Sam, I need to know how to help you, please."

Her eyes look past me and Courtney pulls on my arm. "Let her breathe, Tommy, she's in one piece."

I realize that I just barged into the bathroom on someone who might be very ill.

"Oh my God, I'm so sorry," I begin. "I've been losing my mind with worry and the moment Courtney said you were here I couldn't even think about anything besides getting to you."

"I'm okay now, there's nothing you need to worry about. I'm in good hands." She has a washcloth in her hands that she's twisting up as tight as possible. That's the only sign she's upset if it wasn't for the tight set of her jaw. It looks like she's barely holding it together.

What the fuck happened?

"Did Maisy say something to you?" I ask, trying to keep the frustration out of my voice at how I somehow missed Maisy crossing paths with Sam. Sam's eyes are pleading with Courtney.

"Dude," Courtney says, her hand still holding my arm.

Why does Courtney sound so frustrated? And with me?

"What?" I turn and ask her, trying with every fiber of my being to not snap at one of my best friends as Avery comes down, her eyes wide.

"I asked you to explain upstairs and you barge in like a fucking bull, ignore the fact that Sam was in the bathroom—"

"I apologized for that," I mumble.

Courtney makes a frustrated sound. "You ignored that and now you're asking her to tell you about Maisy? I love you, Tommy, but it sounds like you made your decision and I can't, for the life of me, figure out why you're rubbing it in."

"What?" I ask again. I notice that Avery is now at Sam's side, rubbing her back. "What decision did I make?"

Sam's voice is so fucking small, it shreds my heart. "You left with Maisy."

"I *what*?"

Tears fall down her face. "I saw it and I'm not standing in the way. She's the one who got away and I get that. But please, just give me space."

Everything plays back in my head in triple time.

"Oh fuck," I say, sounding, and feeling, like I got punched in the gut. "It's not what it looked like."

I look at all three women. One looks like her heart has been ripped apart and the other two look confused but ready to ask me to leave.

Shit, I really fucked this up.

"Please let me tell you what happened, all three of you because I think my two best friends are close to castrating me, but mostly you, Samantha." I take a deep breath, thinking of the order of events so I can fill in anything that she might not have seen. "I was waiting to get Elliot's attention at the bar to make an oat milk coffee drink. They usually only have rice milk but Sam likes oat and he said I could drop some off and he'd make it for her during our date. While I was there, someone took my Stetson. Honestly, I thought it was you so I was surprised because, well, you know what it means and I didn't know that you were comfortable with that...public statement."

"But it wasn't Sam," Avery fills in for me.

I shake my head, letting out a rueful laugh. "Not even close. I stopped opening her messages months ago, stopped replying long before that, and finally blocked her, so I had no idea she was moving back before the fall. She caught me completely off guard and asked for five minutes. I told her no and she was persistent, even going as far as threatening to go talk to you and I freaked out. This was our first date in public and here was Maisy Jones pulling some childish shit. She said if I gave her one minute she'd stay away from both of us if that's what I wanted. So, I told her she had one minute, no more.

"Maisy complained that it was too loud, grabbed my hand, and drug me to the back door. I was in complete shock at her assumption that it was okay to make any sort of physical contact with me and it wasn't until we were almost to the door that I yanked my hand free. I grabbed my phone, set a one-minute timer, placed it on the table between us, and hit start."

My eyes don't leave Sam's and all I want is to hold her in my arms and tell her everything she means to me. That I would *never* put her through what she thinks happened. But she deserves to understand what she saw, whatever pieces of that nightmare conversation.

"Maisy used her minute to tell me the reasons we should be together again. And I listened. For the full minute. I let the timer go off, took my hat off of her head, reminded her that she agreed to leave us alone, and walked away for the last time."

"Oh Tommy," Courtney murmurs.

"We can unpack that shitshow later," I say, waving off her concern for me. "But after I said all that I'll ever need to Maisy, I went back to the table. I thought you were still refreshing your lipstick, and I went into the bathroom to try to get my shit together. I was shaking with the audacity of Maisy and didn't want to bring all of that negative energy into our date. It wasn't until a few minutes later that Keith came by and I found your note. I drove right to your apartment and couldn't get a hold of you, any of you, and eventually decided to take my chances here."

Sam's knuckles are white as she grips the washcloth, sadness mixed with hope in her eyes now. I keep my feet right where they are, respecting that she asked for space, but dying to go to her.

"I thought you left me to be with her."

"Never."

Chapter 59
Sam

Yes, he left. But he didn't leave.

And he didn't leave me.

"Never," he says again.

The rollercoaster of emotions I've already been through feels like a kiddie train ride compared to what I just learned.

Avery's hand at my back is still now, offering silent support. Courtney is holding Tommy's arm, I think. But as hard as it has been, I've been unable to look away from Tommy. I thought he was going to confirm what I told the girls, but the truth is so vastly different than what it looked like. The scenes play again through my mind, but this time, I let Tommy's words narrate.

Everything falls into place. I think about any time Tommy's ex was mentioned, someone noted that he was over her.

"So, you're not getting back together with Maisy?"

"Absolutely not," Tommy says resolutely.

"Should we..." Courtney begins, pointing between herself and Avery and the stairs.

"I'm okay," I tell them. "Thank you."

And I mean it from the bottom of my heart.

Tommy watches me carefully while fidgeting as they leave.

"There's nothing I want more than you. I'm so sorry that you saw that. I should have come back to the table right away, damn Maisy if she followed. But I let her lead me away. I should have never let her manipulation take a single moment from our date. All I could think of was keeping her out of our lives. Not because she holds any part of my heart, she doesn't. But because she is a master of manipulation and I couldn't stand the thought of her pulling any crap with you."

He takes one step towards me as my chest expands with emotion.

"The only thing that's going to take me away from you is you telling me you're done. I'll respect that, but no one, ex or not, is getting any of my heart." One more step. "You hold my entire heart Samantha Davies and I'm completely in love with you. If you're okay with it, I'm not going anywhere, not without you at my side."

"Truth or truth?" I ask, leaving a little space between us even though my body is screaming to close it.

Tommy looks a little confused. "Aren't you supposed to ask me 'truth or dare?'"

"Not this time."

"Okay, truth."

I take a breath to steel my nerves and ask what I need to know. "How much did I mess up?"

He opens his mouth and closes it. "How much did *you* mess up?"

I nod. "Yes, how much did I mess up?"

"You—" He lets out a sharp breath and starts again, putting his hands on my shoulders and sending shivers down my spine. I didn't think I was going to feel his touch again, other than a pity hug during the official break up. Tears threaten to spill out again. "You did *nothing* wrong, Sam. Nothing."

"I made you worry."

"I made you think I was capable of leaving you." Okay, he does have a point, there.

"Can I kiss you now?" Tommy's eyes search my entire face as I nod because at this moment, nothing else matters. "Thank fucking God."

We both close the remaining space between us as we collide. My hands find purchase on the back of his neck while his kiss is almost burning with its intensity. Fisting my hair to keep me in place, his tongue dives into my mouth. The way he plunges in again and again has me wanting to have him inside of me. I'm craving that connection right now and I can feel that he's interested, too.

When his hand scoops my butt, my legs clamp around his waist like a vise and I'm so grateful I picked the outfit with pants so I didn't rip my skirt trying to do this. My back is pressed against either a wall or a door. I'm not even sure and right now, I don't care. I'm just soaking in every touch from a man I'm in love with who I thought…God, I'm not even going to let that cross my mind again tonight. I'm sure I'll replay the horror I felt later, but not now that he's here, and he's choosing me.

And Maisy Jones won't take another moment from us.

He even said that he's staying with me until I ask him to leave. Was that just about tonight and us not being apart, or was it about something more permanent? A new tingle runs down my spine from both the thought of Tommy wanting to stay with me for a while and those three words coming from his lips.

Those very lips that I pull back from for a moment, cradling his face in my hands.

"What? Is something wrong?" His voice is a little breathless.

Placing one soft kiss on his lips I take a second to soothe the worry that I can see building in his eyes. Then I speak the words I've wanted to say.

"I love you, too."

He groans and kisses me with renewed enthusiasm, peppering my neck with kisses while repeating that he loves me.

"Please don't have sex on my couch," Courtney calls from the top of the stairs, effectively cooling us down.

We hear a muffled "ouch" and then, "What? It's still new."

Tommy gives me a wicked smile and calls back, "Don't worry, we're against the bathroom door."

"But we're not doing anything!" I add, mortified at the thought of having sex in my friend's basement. "You should come down, actually."

"We're counting to ten to give you time to put your clothes back on. One," Courtney begins.

"Oh my God, I can't take you anywhere." I can almost hear Avery's eyes roll as she says that. "We're coming down the stairs. If you're naked this fast, then that's on you two."

"Psht, you and Jax should talk."

"Jackson and I are not in your basement when our clothes are shed, we're in our own house."

By the time those two come around the corner, Tommy has set me down and spun me to face Avery and Courtney while he's pressed against me with his hands clasped in front of my belly.

Avery lets out a content sigh. "I'm so happy for you two. We're going to put on face masks and then finish the movie, and I'm guessing you two need to head out."

"We'll get the details from each of you tomorrow." Courtney gives us a wink.

Tommy looks down at me, giving me one hell of a sexy smile and tells them, "Yeah, we might need some time alone and we'll join you two next time."

I smile because I love his plan. I can already picture more nights like this to come. Hopefully with less drama and fewer tears. Or maybe just tears of joy…

We say goodbye as Tommy scoops up my purse and guides me up the stairs and to this truck. His arm tightens around me and he whispers into my ear, "Your place or mine?"

I'm about to say 'mine' simply because it's closer, but I pause and think about how it would feel to stay at Landen Acres. To wake up in his arms on the ranch. To figure out how to navigate life around his brothers. Or with his brothers.

And I want that.

"Yours."

Chapter 60
Tommy

I throw my truck in park once we're in the garage and practically jump out of the cab. With Sam's hand in mine we make a beeline to the house, passing Matt and Caleb playing video games. We don't stop to answer whatever questions they ask because I'm not focused on anything other than the woman who hasn't stopped touching me since Courtney's house.

Once the door to my room is closed, we're tearing at each other's clothes while our kisses get more and more frantic. We leave a trail of shirts and pants leading right to our bed.

"Do you have protection?" she asks, out of breath.

"I do."

"Good." Sam, only in a matching blue bra and underwear combo, drops to her knees in front of me. She tugs my boxer briefs off, freeing my dick that has been hard since Courtney's house. Without preamble, she holds my shaft and licks the precum leaking from my tip.

"Fuck, Samantha." My hands lock into her hair so I have something to hold onto as she keeps licking her way around the tip and all the way to the base, leaving a wet sheen as she goes. The cool air hits it right after her warm tongue, driving me up a wall.

Then she wraps her lips around me, her hands grab my ass, and she starts bobbing her head. Her hot mouth fucking me beautifully.

"Jesus Christ, just like that," I tell her, my eyes wanting to roll back from the pleasure. But I keep them glued on her, not wanting to miss the sight of her taking more of me while her tongue flutters against my head whenever she pulls back.

Her fingers dig into me and she hollows out her cheeks, creating a suction that has me gasping.

"I'm not going to be able to fuck you properly if you do that again."

She releases me with a popping sound and gives me a sly smile. "We should definitely make sure we're doing things properly."

The next thing I know, she's in my arms and I'm claiming her mouth with mine. Fuck, I almost lost her and I won't ever let her have any reason to doubt how I feel about her. Reaching behind her, I undo the clasp of her bra, needing to feel more of her skin against mine. She drops her arms from around my neck to let the fabric fall with a sigh as she presses against my chest. Her nipples are hard and my hand goes to one of her breasts automatically, barely running my finger over and around her nipple. I give it a soft tug and it's her turn to gasp.

Walking her backwards a few steps until the back of her knees hit the edge of the bed, I pull the quilt back and lay her onto the sheets. Her hair fans out when her head hits the mattress and I pause for a moment to just drink in the sight before me. The flush on her cheeks, the rise and fall of her chest, the way her knees part so there's space for me. Before touching her panties, I can see how ready she is to be here and to be with me. She makes a sound of surprise as one arm scoops her waist in the air and I tug her underwear off her ass with my free hand then toss it towards the door.

She won't be needing it for a while, anyways.

Sam takes that moment to move to the center of the bed and I crawl over her. Those gorgeous legs wrap around my waist, pulling me on top of her.

"Are you hiding a condom somewhere I can't see?"

"Oh we don't need one yet, cowgirl," I say, dropping my head and flicking my tongue over her nipple. My fingers mirror everything my mouth is doing so both breasts are receiving equal attention. She makes a choked sound of pleasure and grabs hold of my hair, causing me to smirk against her skin.

"I suppose I can wait a little longer," she sighs.

"You're going to be nice and ready each and every time I'm going to be inside you." I capture her nipple between my teeth and give a gentle tug and she arches into me making little noises as I continue to work her incredible breasts. Even these smell faintly of lilacs.

My knee slides up and she starts grinding down on my upper thigh. Fuck she's wet. But I'm not slipping inside of her without her coming at least once. Her fingers tug my head up and I look at her heaving chest, pink cheeks, and dilated pupils.

"I need you."

"And you have me," I reply, pushing myself up her body until her tongue is in my mouth. She still tastes faintly of Avery's peanut butter cookies. "All of me."

Her hands hold my face, softly kissing my lips. "And you have all of me," she whispers.

"I love you so much, Sam," I tell her.

She smiles. "I love that you call me Sam and Samantha."

"Is that your official answer then?" I ask.

"Wait, you remember asking me my preference?" Her eyes widen with surprise.

"Of course I remember. That was the first day I laid eyes on you."

"It was." Her thumb strokes my cheek. "I knew you were someone special."

"The feeling was mutual. And now I'm all yours," I say, tipping my head to kiss her.

"And now I'm all yours," she echoes against my lips and she deepens our kiss before she pulls back. "And I love you, too, so much."

I give her a confused look.

"I didn't say it back this last time and didn't want you to worry. Because I do."

Slowly, we pick up where we left off moments ago, but we take our time. The frantic nature of when we came into the room gives way to us drawing out each touch, each kiss. Her hips drop fully down to the bed as my hand slips between us. I dip one finger deep inside to gather her wetness, feeling her squirm a little.

"Is everything okay?" I ask.

"I want that to feel better?" she says like it's a question.

"It will, I have a plan."

"Really?"

"Oh yeah." My fingers start rubbing next to her clit and she twitches. "I promise it's a good one, too."

Chapter 61
Sam

My mind is right back to wanting *everything* with Tommy. Did I have a moment of doubt for what we're about to do feeling good? Yes.

But I'm not hiding anymore so, for once, I said something. And Tommy has a plan. Apparently a good one. Is my brain capable of trying to guess what that plan might entail? Absolutely not.

Not when his body is on top of mine like this with his hand doing something he is *fantastic* at, and I'm lying on his bed which smells like cedar and a little hint of garlic. A bed that I plan on waking up in tomorrow morning. In Tommy Landen's arms.

I chose this and I love it.

He braces his free hand up by my head and kisses down my neck and along my collarbone with his tongue darting out every so often. Goosebumps follow each path he chooses. My hips tilt to give him even better access to my most sensitive area. The combination of all his touches cause my eyes to close and at least one moan to escape my lips. Instead of feeling embarrassed, I simply feel emboldened to stop hiding my natural responses. Tommy seems to soak up any hint, big or small, that my body gives him and works his way up my neck.

A little nibble on my ear timed with an increase in pressure from Tommy's fingers has me gasping. I think I'm more sensitive than usual because I'm close to coming already and I swear he's only been touching my clit for a minute. But when you spent what felt like a long truck ride to get here and have been touching each other in different ways, it's not such a surprise. There's a coil of pleasure building deep inside me, tightening, getting ready to spring at any moment.

My hands grip Tommy's back while my back arches, pressing my chest into his. He flicks his tongue against the sensitive spot behind my ear and I give a little cry as my toes curl.

"Here we go, Samantha," he says against my ear, moving his finger a little faster. "Come for me, cowgirl."

A few seconds later my body shudders as my orgasm takes over. The crest of each wave washes over every single inch of me. Tommy curses between the kisses he places up and down my neck and rolls his hips, but his fingers keep going until my twitches stop. Those beautiful lips caress my own and he makes a humming sound while I melt onto the bed, my body going blissfully limp.

"I'm going to stay here for a minute, and then I'm grabbing two things from my nightstand if you're interested," Tommy says while bracing himself on his elbows so he can look at me better.

"I think I know what one item is," I say, feeling so content.

"Would you like to guess what the other item is?" he asks.

"I think my brain needs more than twenty seconds after something like," I pause and gesture to the minimal space between our bodies, "*this*, so you might want to just show it to me."

A chuckle rumbles in his chest right as he rolls onto his back and tucks me into him, kissing my temple. My body feels so at home with him in ways I didn't think could be possible. I don't even care that I'm sweaty like I used to.

Tommy reaches for the drawer at the top of his bedside table, tosses a little foil package next to him on the bed and a little pink box. I look at it, confused.

"There's truly no pressure for this, but I got it in case you wanted to try it as we learn what feels the best for you." He opens the box to reveal a small container, equally pink in color.

"Is this one of those gifts where the containers get smaller and smaller?" I ask.

"No, this is as small as it gets," he says, holding it out for me.

I sit up so I can properly see and hold this mystery item. The moment I open it though, I snap it shut feeling embarrassed automatically. I've never been around another person with one of these.

"As I said, there's no pressure. At all."

Taking a breath, I open it again and look down at a small vibrator which, of course, is pink. This one isn't designed to go *inside* but has a small curve in its shape so it could likely hit someone's clit while they're having sex in a variety of positions.

"How did you..." I begin before pausing.

"Pick that out?"

"Yes, how did you pick this out?" I ask.

"Well, I know what *does* feel good for you and may have looked up a few designs for people who liked clit stimulation." It's his turn to pause. "Is it okay that I went ahead with that? It's brand new, but I may have washed and charged it just in case."

Here I am, sitting naked on Tommy's bed holding a vibrator while he tells me he spent time learning what would likely give me the best experience. I shouldn't be surprised by this, not with Tommy. But I'm stunned into silence. Incredibly turned on silence.

"We can just put it away, that's completely fine," he says, reaching for it.

Moving it so it's out of his reach, I frown at him. "I never said I didn't want to use it."

A little smirk appears on his lips. "So, what are you saying?"

I look down at the little device and decide it's time to take the bull by the horns. "We're using it."

He sits up next to me and kisses me until his smile is too wide to continue. "Alright, let's do it."

A few moments later, I've checked the settings and Tommy has the condom on. As he leans forward to lay me on my back, I put a hand on his chest. "What if I'd like to try something?"

"Anything."

"Can you lay back for me?"

He gives me one long kiss with his tongue finding mine and he picks me up so I'm straddling his lap before he lies down. His eyes trail from my face and over every inch of my body that's in sight as his hands squeeze my hips. "I'm here for everything you want, and if you change your mind at any point, just tell me and it's okay."

Nodding, I start the vibrator and get it up to a medium intensity. Then, I raise up to my knees and start lowering myself over him, taking him inch by inch. This is usually the start of my discomfort, but between having just come and how I'm now holding this vibrator next to my clit, I feel like I'm being filled completely and I already have pleasure building.

"Is this okay?" I ask Tommy.

Groaning, he replies, "Oh fuck it's so much better than okay, Samantha."

Once I'm fully seated on him, I lift and rock my hips, noticing the changing pressure based on how I move. His hips shift with me just a little.

"Ride me just how you like, cowgirl," he says.

And I do just that, knowing that he's here with me, taking pleasure from making sure I find plenty of my own first.

Chapter 62
Tommy

The way Sam is riding me is fucking unbelievable. She fits me like a glove, a tight glove, actually, and I can feel the vibrations faintly deep inside of her. It's amazing.

"Tell me what you'd like from me."

She looks down at me, one hand on my chest, the other holding the little pink vibrator in place, as she says, "This is good."

"Just let me know if I should shift, move, or stay still and enjoy the view."

Biting her lip, she thinks for a moment. "Can you move with me?"

"Fuck yes, I can." I try to not be too enthusiastic with my thrusts because, my God, she feels amazing. Right now, I'm enjoying every damn moment being inside of her. It's like she was made for me with how we fit.

"Oh, just like that," she says, her head tipping back, shifting her hair over her shoulders.

"Anything for you, Samantha."

Her tits look spectacular bouncing to the rhythm she's picked. My eyes travel down her belly and just past the vibrator to watch her meet my thrusts with a soft slap. If I keep watching the way she's taking me again and again, I'm going to come right now.

Sweat beads on my forehead. Both of our bodies are glistening from it, making my grip on her hips tenuous. Each time she raises back up, I help pull her down, adding to the intensity as her mouth opens and she gasps, then whimpers.

"What do you need?" I ask.

"I'm not sure, I'm getting close though."

"Why don't you turn up the intensity?" I suggest, looking pointedly at the vibrator.

Her fingers shift while she keeps it in place, and I both hear and feel the vibrations increase in intensity.

"Oh my stars," she exclaims, a little surprised. "I forgot this wasn't all the way up."

I groan at the barrage of sensations hitting me, including her propensity to use phrases only older generations still say. Everything about this woman is so damn attractive.

"You're the sexiest fucking person I've ever met, you know that?" I ask, my voice uneven while she quickens her cadence. In response, I hear a cross between a squeak and a whimper from her closed mouth. Her lips are rolled in between her teeth as she drives herself closer to an orgasm. I desperately want to kiss her right now but she looks so damn close to coming I don't dare shift my position under her.

"I love you so much," I say instead, my breathing labored.

Her eyes focus on mine again. "I love you, too."

The hand on my chest curls a little, digging her fingers into my skin, as her motions become more erratic, her hips taking on a rhythm of their own. I do my best to match each one, giving her everything, our bodies smacking together now. She slams down one more time and cries out, holding herself so I'm buried to the hilt as she comes. Each wave of her orgasm tightens the grip around my dick and I'm seeing stars as I come with her. Her muscles contract again and again, milking every last drop from me until I'm completely spent.

Sam turns off the vibrator, tosses it next to us in the bed, and collapses over me, sighing in contentment. We're a sweaty tangle of limbs, her hair is already stuck to my chest, and I'm still buried inside of her.

It's fucking perfect.

"For the record, that wasn't a fake orgasm," I say, holding her close.

Sam bursts out laughing and it's one of the most beautiful sounds I'll ever hear.

"No, it was absolutely the real deal," she replies, kissing my chest. "Also, you were right."

"I definitely was." I place a kiss in her lilac-scented hair. God, I'm going to buy a ton of this for when she showers here. "About what?"

"You said I'd be riding like a pro in no time." Her voice says she's completely joking.

"There was never any doubt in my mind, cowgirl," I tell her, tipping her chin up so I can kiss her properly. "You're fucking perfect."

She rolls her eyes.

"I'm right, and it might take some time for you to see it, but I'll show you what you mean to me." I shift her to my pillow and hop out of bed. "I'll be right back, don't you dare move this time."

"I'm not having ridiculous cramps," she calls to me while I'm taking care of the condom in the bathroom.

"I know, but we're cuddling for a while."

Sam is in the bed where I left her, except she's under the covers. As I leave the bathroom, she lifts the edge of the sheet up for me to slip under. "I suppose I can stay put for cuddles with Tommy Landen."

I tuck her against me, her head rests on my shoulder, arm drapes over my stomach, and her legs twist up with mine. As early as this may be in a relationship, I can see how this can feel and how this can be. I'll fight to keep it, and everything just feels right.

"Will you stay tonight?" I ask,

"I would love to, Tommy," she says through a yawn. "It's a good thing my boyfriend wrote me a list of things to keep here so I'm ready at any time."

"Good, then we can have breakfast together in the morning."

She goes still against me.

"What?" I ask, trying to figure out how breakfast might have made her nervous.

"What do you all wear in the mornings?" she asks.

"Pants or shorts, sometimes shirts."

She groans against my chest. "I didn't pack a robe."

"You don't need to wear one," I say, kissing the top of her head.

"I'm not going down in just my pajamas."

"Then you can wear one of my shirts over your pajamas." The image of her walking around in *just* my shirt has me getting hard again. Well, that, and the fact that Sam is naked and pressed against me in my bed.

"I suppose I could do that. And maybe I'll wear your hat down to breakfast, too, just to avoid any questions your brothers might ask," she says, tipping her face up at me with a sly look.

"That would explain everything that we just did without needing to say a thing." Now I'm picturing Sam walking around in this house only in my shirt and hat.

"Perfect, then we have a plan for the morning."

"And tonight, hang on." I reach over to my bedside table and open the top drawer and pull out a handful of bars and snacks.

"You are an incredibly smart guy," she says, shifting so we can kiss.

"More like a guy who's in love with his girlfriend and wants to be able to keep her in his bed as long as possible."

"That, too," she says before her lips find mine.

Chapter 63
Sam

Months later - at the second annual dating auction fundraiser

I swear Chuck is up to something. There's only one more person to announce for the auction, so things should be calm backstage.

They're not.

Someone swears, it sounded like Bryant oddly enough, and there are muffled clanging sounds every now and then and a draft about every ten seconds. Jacksy likes to take breaks outside, but this is just getting silly. Tommy assured me that Chuck wasn't up to any shenanigans, but I swear something is going on.

The applause dies down and I announce the final bachelorette of the evening for the group date, which includes a dinner of Jesse's barbecue and desserts from Sarah, much to everyone's delight.

"Our final lady likely needs no introduction, but just in case you haven't met Mrs. Helena Fields, let me share a little about her." Mrs. Fields, technically Ms. Fields, steps out from between the curtains with the grace of a dancer, even though she's more than eighty years old. "Helena has been a citizen of Greenstone for her whole life and, she'd like me to point out, she has been single for more than two years, a new record."

The crowd hoots and hollers as she walks along the stage and I read off a few of her accomplishments over the years. There are three more breezes coming right from where I know the back door to be but I keep my focus on the notes in front of me. When the bidding starts, just like I hoped, it's boisterous, the young single guys really getting into it. She soaks everything up and blows kisses to keep things going. In the end, she brings in almost as much as Caleb Harlow did last year, which is astonishing.

She saunters off stage and waves at the crowd one last time. There are only a few more things to cover and I can get out of the spotlight. My eyes catch on Susan, the Fire Chief, standing near the main door.

Huh, I thought work was keeping her from attending this year. She holds the door open and it looks like the newest recruit for the fire department enters. My pulse picks up. Shifting my papers around for a second, I try to remember if I missed anything. I know I quadruple-checked the permits, so if she's working, then I must have missed something.

One thing at a time, Sam. Finish this first, get off of this stage, and then I can make things right with the permits. Only, I can't imagine what the oversight could have been.

"Before we open up the silent auction, there are a few people and businesses we wanted to thank because, without their generosity, tonight would not have been possible." Another light gust of air shifts the curtains behind me. Why is that door being opened so often?

Stealing my growing nerves and trying to block out intrusive thoughts of what could possibly be happening backstage, I force my attention to the list in front of me. These people donated their time and talents so I'd like to genuinely thank them and allow others to as well. Even with whispered voices that seem to be directly on the other side of the curtain from me.

The mic can't pick that up. Right?

No, absolutely not. But, just to be safe, I lean in a little closer in case I can physically block the sounds from carrying. Who the heck is moving around so much back there? At this point, I really don't think it's Chuck pulling a prank. He might be a jokester, but whatever is happening seems to have started fifteen minutes ago.

I hope everyone is okay back there.

Oh no, maybe Susan is here because someone is hurt? Marking my place in the list with my finger, I glance up, trying to find her, but she's not by the door anymore. My mind is too scattered to risk reciting everyone from memory, so I refocus on the names printed before me.

Thankfully, time seems to be on my side and the silent auction officially starts and I can turn off my microphone, standing awkwardly while the crowd claps for the event. They're all watching me while they should be turning around to look at everything on the tables to start placing their bids. Did I forget something? An instruction? Glancing down at the sheet still on the podium, I'm reassured I hit every point.

Before I break out in a sweat from a combination of the spotlight and nerves, I give everyone a wave. Instead of walking down the steps to mingle, curiosity gets the better of me as the curtain flutters again from a breeze. Practically running right into Avery and Courtney the moment I'm backstage, my body stiffens.

I smell smoke.

"What's—"

"Take a breath," Avery cuts me off, putting her hand on my arm.

"Everything is fine, we promise." Courtney's words are confident, even as she takes in my expression. I can only imagine the fear they both see written all over my face.

"Pardon?" I ask, sure I misheard them. How can everything be fine if there's smoke backstage?

Then I see candles and my confusion only grows when the girls each take one of my hands, pulling me toward them. There are two rows of candles leading to the door, which is propped open. And each pillar is lit.

"Is this—" I begin.

"Everything is fine, truly," Avery says again.

"Okay, this is where we get to send you off on your own, but we'll be right here the whole time," Courtney says as she and Avery release my hands and gesture toward the open door.

The candles create a path for me to walk within, so I follow the winding trail out the door.

Oh my.

Before me stands all five Landen brothers wearing suits: Matt and Jackson on the left, and Bryant and Chuck on the right, and Tommy is in the middle under a structure I've never seen before. My brain tries desperately to put the whole scene together properly, but I can't take my eyes off of Tommy. It's hard to see his face because there's a small fire in a raised stand behind him and the outside lights are off.

The lines of candles. The mini bonfire. This is why Susan is here while she's working, and why the new guy is with her.

"Sam, would you join me?" he asks, holding a hand out for me.

Apparently, I stopped in my tracks two steps from the door. Of all the times for my mind to go blank versus walking through rational explanations, this wasn't an ideal one. My heart flutters in my chest as my feet take me to him, my eyes never leaving his shadowed face.

When I'm standing in front of him, he simply smiles at me for a moment and takes my hand. I look around, trying to find a real clue for what's happening. We're standing under some sort of...small pergola maybe? It looks hand-crafted with long, skinny tree trunks that have been stripped with branches loosely woven across the top. There are a handful or more glowing glass orbs hanging from thick twine. My eyes are already adjusting to the light out here after the brightness from the spotlight.

Tommy is looking right at me, those blue eyes full of sincerity and longing, and I swear my heart stops beating.

"Samantha Davies, I have one question for you, but first, I'd like to go over some numbers."

Oh my goodness, could this be...

Chapter 64
Tommy

Oh my God, I'm such a mess right now. Sam is so fucking beautiful in her sequin dress for tonight that everything I had planned has effectively left my brain momentarily. The damn wind keeps picking up, threatening to push smoke in our direction and extinguish the candles. We barely got everything set up before she was done because they kept going out.

But I remind myself that, even with the wind, we have everything here and even if not everything stays lit, the symbolism is there. This went so much faster than our test run yesterday, actually. Courtney and Avery were going to have to stall Sam for a while if Bryant hadn't decided to have the top of the arch woven together and stored under the stage inside. Last night, Sarah and Jesse asked her to meet them at the picnic site so we'd have the time and space to try setting up the arch Bryant and I have been building out back as well as lighting hundreds of pillar candles, the small candles in the globes hanging from the arch, and getting the flowers set. But we did it. She didn't see any of the components before the auction started tonight because we got it all under the stage until twenty minutes ago when the auction began. Still, I've been a nervous wreck the past week.

My nerves from the preparation are nothing compared to how hard my heart is pounding seeing her here. Focusing on Sam's hand in mine and wanting to show her she's worth everything and more to me, I start.

"You might have noticed that there are a few candles. Well, there are three-hundred sixty-five. One for each day that I've hoped we would be, and stay, together." Her eyes begin to water, so I pull out the handkerchief Matt told me to have on me and give it to her.

"And, before you worry too much, yes, Susan got all the correct permits and documentation for this to happen, especially the line of candles inside, and no, the sprinklers will not start soaking everyone here tonight. But back to why there are three-hundred sixty-five burning candles right now... Last year, at this very event, actually, was when that hope took root inside of me." I don't mention what gave me hope was Jax telling me he and Sam never actually dated when she first moved to Greenstone. "So I wanted you to be able to see that hope and the light you've brought into my life."

I lean forward and say quietly, "I know that was cheesy, but Chuck insisted I keep that line in."

Sam dabs at her eyes and gives a little laugh and glances at my brothers. Then those beautiful, shimmering blue eyes are locked back on mine.

"There are seventy-eight flowers, one for every time you've been on a horse. I've ridden next to you for seventy-five of those times, but the first three, I had the privilege of watching. At our feet, there are fifty-six rose petals, one for each time we've been out to eat together."

I don't mention the thirty-two times we've made reservations but stayed in.

"And, if you look up, you'll see seven glass globes, one for each month we've been together." Bending carefully, so I don't fall into the dirt like I did last night, I get down on one knee before Sam and release her hand. She blinks back more tears but clasps her hands in front of her, like she's unsure what to do.

"Now, for the final number," I say, pulling out a little box from my jacket pocket and popping it open so she can see. "I have one ring that I would like to give to you tonight. This ring doesn't signify what has gone before, but what's to come. It represents the years we'll spend together officially as a family, of being true partners in life. Of facing the obstacles that will surely come our way. It represents a lifetime of you and me and all the ways our love will grow.

"I want to watch all the rom-coms snuggled up with you. I want to always carry a notebook in my pocket just so you can write in it. I want to raise a family with you. I want to grow old and wrinkled with you and hold your hand as we watch the sun set in the evenings. I want everything and every day with you."

One deep breath later, I say, "Samantha Davies, I love you more than anything. Will you marry me?"

She lets out a choked sob, covering her face with the hankie for a second as she takes a few shallow breaths. Then she nods and everyone gathered explodes into applause with Chuck letting out a loud *whoop*.

"Yes, of course, yes," she says in a jumble, letting me take her hand and put the ring on her finger. She looks down at it in surprise. "It fits!"

"I should hope so, isn't knowing your fiancée's ring size pretty elementary?" I tell her as I stand up, thinking of the night I spent with little pieces of string to measure her finger while she slept.

"You just called me your fiancée," she says, her cheeks wet with fresh tears and a smile filled with joy.

"I most certainly did," I say, wrapping her in my arms. "Can I kiss you now?"

"Yes please," she replies, draping her arms around my neck as I lean down to give her a slow kiss, my body relaxing with the contact. We'll have plenty of time to truly savor our engagement tonight when we don't have an audience, even if everyone here has already seen us kiss a few times.

"I love you so much," I say.

"I love you so much." She gives me one more kiss. Avery and Courtney squeal, hugging Sam the moment we break apart while my brothers pat me on the back, shake my hand, and even hug me before they congratulate my fiancé. My heart couldn't be more full watching everyone here together.

Sam turns to look at me again. "You had this whole thing planned for a while," she states.

"Down to the very last details," I say, "with the exception of wind, that was a last-minute stressor."

"There's a…" she waves at the arch, "small pergola?"

"Yes and it's a good thing Bryant designed it to be put together in just a few minutes, don't you think?" I reply. Bryant blushes.

"How?"

Bryant shifts uncomfortably with everyone watching him, so I pull the group's attention back to the two of us. "Some things are meant to be mysterious. You don't want to hear about the frantic scramble that was going on backstage during the auction. It doesn't matter how things happened, just that the end result was this."

I grab her left hand and Sam looks down at her ring. It's a simple gold band with a square cut diamond.

"It's perfect. The ring, the pergola, the petals, the flowers, the candles…you. Just perfect."

"Thank God," I say, the relief evident in my voice. "Because I wanted to give you a glimpse of everything you are to me and how much I want to spend the rest of my life with you."

"You did that and more, Tommy Landen," she says.

I get to spend the rest of that evening, with the woman of my dreams next to me, knowing that she'll be there with me for everything to come.

I'm not sure I'll ever stop smiling.

Acknowledgements

There are so many incredible people who have supported me so far and I am so grateful for each and every one of you! I'm especially thankful for:

The family who supports this dream of mine in so many ways.

The alpha and beta readers who provide amazing feedback: Andra, Ashley, Evy, and Jeanne.

The Kickstarter backers who helped fund another book box and let me put together such a fun combination of goodies.

The editors and formatters who help make the story more beautiful.

The authors who provide guidance, encouragement, and more.

The early readers who leave honest reviews and help spread the word.

The readers picking up this book right now.

Thank you all!

-Natalie

About the Author

Portrait by Three Ravens Art

Natalie Jess is a Midwest author who loves living in a place with snowy winters. She grew up reading way past her bedtime and never broke that habit - except now the books she reads, and writes, are definitely for adults.

Don't miss Matt's story: https://books2read.com/for-caleb

Milton Keynes UK
Ingram Content Group UK Ltd.
UKHW031040230724
445880UK00011B/83/J